THE PITS OF OPAR!

Through the main corridor the ape-man made his way, noting again the tablets of gold with their ancient and long undeciphered hieroglyphics.

Through the chamber of the seven golden pillars he passed and across the golden floor of an adjoining room. Still there were only silence and emptiness, yet with vague suggestions of figures moving in the galleries that overlooked the apartment through which he was passing.

Then at last he came to a heavy door beyond which would be either priests or priestesses of the Flaming God. Fearlessly he pushed it open and stepped across the threshold, and in the same instant a knotted club descended heavily upon his head, felling him senseless to the floor!

The *Authorized Editions* of
Edgar Rice Burroughs'
TARZAN NOVELS
available in Ballantine Books Editions
at your local bookstore:

COMPLETE AND UNABRIDGED!

TARZAN
THE INVINCIBLE

Edgar Rice Burroughs

BALLANTINE BOOKS • NEW YORK

Tarzan the Invincible was first published serially in *The Blue Book Magazine,* October, 1930, to April, 1931, under the title, "Tarzan, Guard of the Jungle."

Copyright © 1930, 1931 Edgar Rice Burroughs, Inc.

ISBN 0-345-28989-7

This authorized edition published by arrangement with Edgar Rice Burroughs, Inc.

Manufactured in the United States of America

First Edition: March 1964
Seventh Printing: April 1981

Cover painting by Neal Adams

CONTENTS

I

Little Nkíma

I AM no historian, no chronicler of facts, and, furthermore, I hold a very definite conviction that there are certain subjects which fiction writers should leave alone, foremost among which are politics and religion. However, it seems to me not unethical to pirate an idea occasionally from one or the other, provided that the subject be handled in such a way as to impart a definite impression of fictionizing.

Had the story that I am about to tell you broken in the newspapers of two certain European powers, it might have precipitated another and a more terrible world war. But with that I am not particularly concerned. What interests me is that it is a good story that is particularly well adapted to my requirements through the fact that Tarzan of the Apes was intimately connected with many of its most thrilling episodes.

I am not going to bore you with dry political history, so do not tax your intellect needlessly by attempting to decode such fictitious names as I may use in describing certain people and places, which, it seems to me, to the best interest of peace and disarmament, should remain incognito.

Take the story simply as another Tarzan story, in which, it is hoped, you will find entertainment and relaxation. If you find food for thought in it, so much the better.

Doubtless, very few of you saw, and still fewer will remember having seen, a news dispatch that appeared inconspicuously in the papers some time since, reporting a rumor that French Colonial Troops stationed in Somaliland, on the northeast coast of Africa, had invaded an Italian African colony. Back of that news item is a story of conspiracy, intrigue, adventure and love—a story of scoundrels and of fools, of brave men, of beautiful women, a story of the beasts of the forest and the jungle.

If there were few who saw the newspaper account of the invasion of Italian Somaliland upon the northeast coast of Africa, it is equally a fact that none of you saw a harrowing incident that occurred in the interior some time previous to this affair. That it could possibly have any connection whatsoever with European international intrigue, or with the fate of nations, seems not even remotely possible, for it was only a very little monkey fleeing through the tree tops and screaming in terror. It was little Nkima, and pursuing him was a large, rude monkey—a much larger monkey than little Nkima.

Fortunately for the peace of Europe and the world, the speed of the pursuer was in no sense proportionate to his unpleasant disposition, and so Nkima escaped him; but for long after the larger monkey had given up the chase, the smaller one continued to flee through the tree tops, screeching at the top of his shrill little voice, for terror and flight were the two major activities of little Nkima.

Perhaps it was fatigue, but more likely it was a caterpillar or a bird's nest that eventually terminated Nkima's flight and left him scolding and chattering upon a swaying bough, far above the floor of the jungle.

The world into which little Nkima had been born seemed a very terrible world, indeed, and he spent most of his waking hours scolding about it, in which respect he was quite as human as he was simian. It seemed to little Nkima that the world was populated with large, fierce creatures that liked monkey meat. There were Numa, the lion, and Sheeta, the panther, and Histah, the snake—a triumvirate that rendered unsafe his entire world from the loftiest tree top to the ground. And then there were the great apes, and the lesser apes, and the baboons, and countless species of monkeys, all of which God had made larger than He had made little Nkima, and all of which seemed to harbor a grudge against him.

Take, for example, the rude creature which had just been pursuing him. Little Nkima had done nothing more than throw a stick at him while he was asleep in the crotch of a tree, and just for that he had pursued little Nkima with unquestionable homicidal intent—I use the word without purposing any reflection upon Nkima. It had never occurred to Nkima, as it never seems to occur to some people, that, like beauty, a sense of humor may sometimes be fatal.

Brooding upon the injustices of life, little Nkima was very sad. But there was another and more poignant cause of sadness that depressed his little heart. Many, many moons ago his master had gone away and left him. True, he had left him in a nice, comfortable home with kind people who fed him, but little Nkima missed the great Tarmangani, whose naked shoulder was the one harbor of refuge from which he could with perfect impunity hurl insults at the world. For a long time now little Nkima had braved the dangers of the forest and the jungle in search of his beloved Tarzan.

Because hearts are measured by content of love and loyalty, rather than by diameters in inches, the heart of little Nkima was very large—so large that the average human being could hide his own heart and himself, as well, behind it—and for a long time it had been just one great ache in his diminutive breast. But fortunately for the little Manu his mind was so ordered that it might easily be distracted even from a great sorrow. A butterfly or a luscious grub might suddenly claim his attention from the depths of brooding, which was well, since otherwise he might have grieved himself to death.

And now, therefore, as his melancholy thoughts returned to contemplation of his loss, their trend was suddenly altered by the shifting of a jungle breeze that brought to his keen ears a sound that was not primarily of the jungle sounds that were a part of his hereditary instincts. It was a discord. And what is it that brings discord into the jungle as well as into every elsewhere that it enters? Man. It was the voices of men that Nkima heard.

Silently the little monkey glided through the trees into the direction from which the sounds had come; and presently, as the sounds grew louder, there came also that which was the definite, final proof of the identity of the noise makers, as far as Nkima, or, for that matter, any other of the jungle folk, might be concerned—the scent spoor.

You have seen a dog, perhaps your own dog, half recognize you by sight; but was he ever entirely satisfied until the evidence of his eyes had been tested and approved by his sensitive nostrils?

And so it was with Nkima. His ears had suggested the presence of men, and now his nostrils definitely assured him that men were near. He did not think of them as men, but as great apes. There were Gomangani, Great Black Apes, Negroes, among them. This his nose told him. And there were

Tarmangani, also. These, which to Nkima would be Great White Apes, were white men.

Eagerly his nostrils sought for the familiar scent spoor of his beloved Tarzan, but it was not there—that he knew even before he came within sight of the strangers.

The camp upon which Nkima presently looked down from a nearby tree was well established. It had evidently been there for a matter of days and might be expected to remain still longer. It was no overnight affair. There were the tents of the white men and the beyts of Arabs neatly arranged with almost military precision and behind these the shelters of the Negroes, lightly constructed of such materials as Nature had provided upon the spot.

Within the open front of an Arab beyt sat several white bournoosed Beduins drinking their inevitable coffee; in the shade of a great tree before another tent four white men were engrossed in a game of cards; among the native shelters a group of stalwart Galla warriors were playing at minkala. There were blacks of other tribes too—men of East Africa and of Central Africa, with a sprinkling of West Coast Negroes.

It might have puzzled an experienced African traveller or hunter to catalog this motley aggregation of races and colors. There were far too many blacks to justify a belief that all were porters, for with all the impedimenta of the camp ready for transportation there would have been but a small fraction of a load for each of them, even after more than enough had been included among the askari, who do not carry any loads beside their rifles and ammunition.

Then, too, there were more rifles than would have been needed to protect even a larger party. There seemed, indeed, to be a rifle for every man. But these were minor details which made no impression upon Nkima. All that impressed him was the fact that here were many strange Tarmangani and Gomangani in the country of his master; and as all strangers were, to Nkima, enemies, he was perturbed. Now more than ever he wished that he might find Tarzan.

A swarthy, turbaned East Indian sat cross-legged upon the ground before a tent, apparently sunk in meditation; but could one have seen his dark, sensuous eyes, he would have discovered that their gaze was far from introspective—they were bent constantly upon another tent that stood a little apart from its fellows—and when a girl emerged from this tent, Raghunath Jafar arose and approached her. He smiled an oily smile as he spoke to her, but the girl did not smile as she replied. She spoke civilly, but she did not pause, continuing her way toward the four men at cards.

As she approached their table they looked up; and upon the face of each was reflected some pleasurable emotion, but whether it was the same in each, the masks that we call faces, and which are trained to conceal our true thoughts, did not divulge. Evident it was, however, that the girl was popular.

"Hello, Zora!" cried a large, smooth-faced fellow. "Have a good nap?"

"Yes, Comrade," replied the girl; "but I am tired of napping. This inactivity is getting on my nerves."

"Mine, too," agreed the man.

"How much longer will you wait for the American, Comrade Zveri?" asked Raghunath Jafar.

The big man shrugged. "I need him," he replied. "We might easily carry on without him, but for the moral effect upon the world of having a rich and high-born American identified actively with the affair it is worth waiting."

"Are you quite sure of this gringo, Zveri?" asked a swarthy young Mexican sitting next to the big, smooth-faced man, who was evidently the leader of the expedition.

"I met him in New York and again in San Francisco," replied Zveri. "He has been very carefully checked and favorably recommended."

"I am always suspicious of these fellows who owe everything they have to capitalism," declared Romero. "It is in their blood—at heart they hate the proletariat, just as we hate them."

"This fellow is different, Miguel," insisted Zveri. "He has been won over so completely that he would betray his own father for the good of the cause—and already he is betraying his country."

A slight, involuntary sneer, that passed unnoticed by the others, curled the lip of Zora Drinov as she heard this description of the remaining member of the party, who had not yet reached the rendezvous.

Miguel Romero, the Mexican, was still unconvinced. "I have no use for gringos of any sort," he said.

Zveri shrugged his heavy shoulders. "Our personal animosities are of no importance," he said, "as against the interests of the workers of the world. When Colt arrives we must accept him as one of us; nor must we forget that however much we may detest America and Americans nothing of any moment may be accomplished in the world of today without them and their filthy wealth."

"Wealth ground out of the blood and sweat of the working class," growled Romero.

"Exactly," agreed Raghunath Jafar, "but how appropriate that this same wealth should be used to undermine and overthrow capitalistic America and bring the workers eventually into their own."

"That is precisely the way I feel about it," said Zveri. "I would rather use American gold in furthering the cause than any other—and after that British."

"But what do the puny resources of this single American mean to us?" demanded Zora. "A mere nothing compared to what America is already pouring into Soviet Russia. What is his treason compared with the treason of those others who are already doing more to hasten the day of world communism than the Third Internationale itself—it is nothing, not a drop in the bucket."

"What do you mean, Zora?" asked Miguel.

"I mean the bankers, and manufacturers, and engineers of America, who are selling their own country and the world to us in the hope of adding more gold to their already bursting coffers. One of their most pious and lauded citizens is building great factories for us in Russia, where we may turn out tractors and tanks; their manufacturers are vying with one another to furnish us with engines for countless thousands of airplanes; their engineers are selling us their brains and their skill to build a great modern manufacturing city, in which ammunitions and engines of war may be produced. These are the traitors, these are the men who are hastening the day when Moscow shall dictate the policies of a world."

"You speak as though you regretted it," said a dry voice at her shoulder.

The girl turned quickly. "Oh, it is you, Sheykh Abu Batn?" she said, as she recognized the swart Arab who had strolled over from his coffee. "Our own good fortune does not blind me to the perfidiousness of the enemy, nor cause me to admire treason in anyone, even though I profit by it."

"Does that include me?" demanded Romero, suspiciously.

Zora laughed. "You know better than that, Miguel," she said. "You are of the working class—you are loyal to the workers of your own country—but these others are of the capitalistic class; their government is a capitalistic government that is so opposed to our beliefs that it has never recognized our government; yet, in their greed, these swine are selling out their own kind and their own country for a few more rotten dollars. I loathe them."

Zveri laughed. "You are a good Red, Zora," he cried; "you hate the enemy as much when he helps us as when he hinders."

"But hating and talking accomplish so little," said the girl. "I wish we might do something. Sitting here in idleness seems so futile."

"And what would you have us do?" demanded Zveri, good naturedly.

"We might at least make a try for the gold of Opar," she said. "If Kitembo is right, there should be enough there to finance a dozen expeditions such as you are planning, and we do not need this American—what do they call them, cake eaters?—to assist us in that venture."

"I have been thinking along similar lines," said Raghunath Jafar.

Zveri scowled. "Perhaps some of the rest of you would like to run this expedition," he said, crustily. "I know what I am doing and I don't have to discuss all my plans with anyone. When I have orders to give, I'll give them. Kitembo has already received his, and preparations have been under way for several days for the expedition to Opar."

"The rest of us are as much interested and are risking as much as you, Zveri," snapped Romero. "We were to work together—not as master and slaves."

"You'll soon learn that I am master," snarled Zveri in an ugly tone.

"Yes," sneered Romero, "the czar was master, too, and Obregon. You know what happened to them?"

Zveri leaped to his feet and whipped out a revolver, but as he levelled it at Romero the girl struck his arm up and stepped between them. "Are you mad, Zveri?" she cried.

"Do not interfere, Zora; this is my affair and it might as well be settled now as later. I am chief here and I am not going to have any traitors in my camp. Stand aside."

"No!" said the girl with finality. "Miguel was wrong and so were you, but to shed blood—our own blood—now would utterly ruin any chance we have of success. It would sow the seed of fear and suspicion and cost us the respect of the blacks, for they would know that there was dissension among us. Furthermore, Miguel is not armed; to shoot him would be cowardly murder that would lose you the respect of every decent man in the expedition." She had spoken rapidly in Russian, a language that was understood by only Zveri and herself, of those who were present; then she turned again to Miguel and addressed him in English. "You were wrong, Miguel," she said gently. "There must be one responsible head, and Comrade Zveri was chosen for the responsibility. He regrets that he acted hastily. Tell him that you are sorry for what you said, and then the two of you shake hands and let us all forget the matter."

For an instant Romero hesitated; then he extended his hand toward Zveri. "I am sorry," he said.

The Russian took the proffered hand in his and bowed stiffly. "Let us forget it, Comrade," he said; but the scowl was still upon his face, though no darker than that which clouded the Mexican's.

Little Nkima yawned and swung by his tail from a branch far overhead. His curiosity concerning these enemies was sated. They no longer afforded him entertainment, but he knew that his master should know about their presence; and that thought, entering his little head, recalled his sorrow and his great yearning for Tarzan, to the end that he was again imbued with a grim determination to continue his search for the ape-man. Perhaps in half an hour some trivial occurrence might again distract his attention, but for the moment it was his life work. Swinging through the forest, little Nkima held the fate of Europe in his pink palm, but he did not know it.

The afternoon was waning. In the distance a lion roared. An instinctive shiver ran up Nkima's spine. In reality, however, he was not much afraid, knowing, as he did, that no lion could reach him in the tree tops.

A young man marching near the head of a safari cocked his head and listened. "Not so very far away, Tony," he said.

"No, sir; much too close," replied the Filipino.

"You'll have to learn to cut out that 'sir' stuff, Tony, before we join the others," admonished the young man.

The Filipino grinned. "All right, Comrade," he assented. "I got so used calling everybody 'sir' it hard for me to change."

"I'm afraid you're not a very good Red then, Tony."

"Oh, yes I am," insisted the Filipino emphatically. "Why else am I here? You think I like come this God forsaken country full of lion, ant, snake, fly, mosquito just for the walk? No, I come lay down my life for Philippine independence."

"That's noble of you all right, Tony," said the other gravely;

"but just how is it going to make the Philippines free?"

Antonio Mori scratched his head. "I don't know," he admitted; "but it make trouble for America."

High among the tree tops a little monkey crossed their path. For a moment he paused and watched them; then he resumed his journey in the opposite direction.

A half hour later the lion roared again, and so disconcertingly close and unexpected rose the voice of thunder from the jungle beneath him that little Nkima nearly fell out of the tree through which he was passing. With a scream of terror he scampered as high aloft as he could go and there he sat, scolding angrily.

The lion, a magnificent full-maned male, stepped into the open beneath the tree in which the trembling Nkima clung. Once again he raised his mighty voice until the ground itself trembled to the great, rolling volume of his challenge. Nkima looked down upon him and suddenly ceased to scold. Instead he leaped about excitedly, chattering and grimacing. Numa, the lion, looked up; and then a strange thing occurred. The monkey ceased its chattering and voiced a low, peculiar sound. The eyes of the lion, that had been glaring balefully upward, took on a new and almost gentle expression. He arched his back and rubbed his side luxuriously against the bole of the tree, and from those savage jaws came a soft, purring sound. Then little Nkima dropped quickly downward through the foliage of the tree, gave a final nimble leap, and alighted upon the thick mane of the king of beasts.

2

The Hindu

WITH the coming of a new day came a new activity to the camp of the conspirators. Now were the Bedaùwy drinking no coffee in the múk'aad; the cards of the whites were put away and the Galla warriors played no longer at minkala.

Zveri sat behind his folding camp table directing his aides and with the assistance of Zora and Raghunath Jafar issued ammunition to the file of armed men marching past them. Miguel Romero and the two remaining whites were supervising the distribution of loads among the porters. Savage black Kitembo moved constantly among his men, hastening laggards from belated breakfast fires and forming those who had received their ammunition into companies. Abu Batn, the sheykh, squatted aloof with his sun-bitten warriors. They, always ready, watched with contempt the disorderly preparations of their companions.

"How many are you leaving to guard the camp?" asked Zora.

"You and Comrade Jafar will remain in charge here," replied Zveri. "Your boys and ten askaris also will remain as camp guard."

"That will be plenty," replied the girl. "There is no danger."

"No," agreed Zveri, "not now, but if that Tarzan were here it would be different. I took pains to assure myself as to that before I chose this region for our base camp, and I have learned that he has been absent for a great while—went on some fool dirigible expedition that has never been heard from. It is almost certain that he is dead."

16

When the last of the blacks had received his issue of ammunition, Kitembo assembled his tribesmen at a little distance from the rest of the expedition and harangued them in a low voice. They were Basembos, and Kitembo, their chief, spoke to them in the dialect of their people.

Kitembo hated all whites. The British had occupied the land that had been the home of his people since before the memory of man; and because Kitembo, hereditary chief, had been irreconcilable to the domination of the invaders they had deposed him, elevating a puppet to the chieftaincy.

To Kitembo, the chief—savage, cruel and treacherous—all whites were anathema, but he saw in his connection with Zveri an opportunity to be avenged upon the British; and so he had gathered about him many of his tribesmen and enlisted in the expedition that Zveri promised him would rid the land forever of the British and restore Kitembo to even greater power and glory than had formerly been the lot of Basembo chiefs.

It was not, however, always easy for Kitembo to hold the interest of his people in this undertaking. The British had greatly undermined his power and influence, so that warriors, who formerly might have been as subservient to his will as slaves, now dared openly to question his authority. There had been no demur so long as the expedition entailed no greater hardships than short marches, pleasant camps, and plenty of food, with West Coast blacks, and members of other tribes less warlike than the Basembos, to act as porters, carry the loads, and do all of the heavy work; but now, with fighting looming ahead, some of his people had desired to know just what they were going to get out of it, having, apparently, little stomach for risking their hides for the gratification of the ambitions or hatreds of either the white Zveri or the black Kitembo.

It was for the purpose of mollifying these malcontents that Kitembo was now haranguing his warriors, promising them loot on the one hand and ruthless punishment on the other as a choice between obedience and mutiny. Some of the rewards he dangled before their imaginations might have caused Zveri and the other white members of the expedition considerable perturbation could they have understood the Basembo dialect; but perhaps a greater argument for obedience to his commands was the genuine fear that most of his followers still entertained for their pitiless chieftain.

Among the other blacks of the expedition were outlaw

members of several tribes and a considerable number of porters hired in the ordinary manner to accompany what was officially described as a scientific expedition.

Abu Batn and his warriors were animated to temporary loyalty to Zveri by two motives—a lust for loot and hatred for all Nasrâny as represented by the British influence in Egypt and out into the desert, which they considered their hereditary domain.

The members of other races accompanying Zveri were assumed to be motivated by noble, humanitarian aspirations; but it was, nevertheless, true that their leader spoke to them more often of the acquisition of personal riches and power than of the advancement of the brotherhood of man or the rights of the proletariat.

It was, then, such a loosely knit, but none the less formidable expedition, that set forth this lovely morning upon the sack of the treasure vaults of mysterious Opar.

As Zora Drinov watched them depart, her beautiful, inscrutable eyes remained fixed steadfastly upon the person of Peter Zveri until he had disappeared from view along the river trail that led into the dark forest.

Was it a maid watching in trepidation the departure of her lover upon a mission fraught with danger, or——

"Perhaps he will not return," said an oily voice at her shoulder.

The girl turned her head to look into the half-closed eyes of Raghunath Jafar. "He will return, Comrade," she said. "Peter Zveri always returns to me."

"You are very sure of him," said the man, with a leer.

"It is written," replied the girl as she started to move toward her tent.

"Wait," said Jafar.

She stopped and turned toward him. "What do you want?" she asked.

"You," he replied. "What do you see in that uncouth swine, Zora? What does he know of love or beauty? I can appreciate you, beautiful flower of the morning. With me you may attain the transcendent bliss of perfect love, for I am an adept in the cult of love. A beast like Zveri would only degrade you."

The sickening disgust that the girl felt she hid from the eyes of the man, for she realized that the expedition might be gone for days and that during that time she and Jafar would be practically alone together, except for a handful of savage black warriors whose attitude toward a matter of this nature between an alien woman and an alien man she could not anticipate; but she was none the less determined to put a definite end to his advances.

"You are playing with death, Jafar," she said quietly. "I am here upon no mission of love, and if Zveri should learn of what you have said to me he would kill you. Do not speak to me again on this subject."

"It will not be necessary," replied the Hindu, enigmatically. His half-closed eyes were fixed steadily upon those of the girl. For perhaps less than half a minute the two stood thus, while there crept through Zora Drinov a sense of growing weakness, a realization of approaching capitulation. She fought against it, pitting her will against that of the man. Suddenly she tore her eyes from his. She had won, but victory left her weak and trembling as might be one who had but just experienced a stubbornly contested physical encounter. Turning quickly away, she moved swiftly toward her tent, not daring to look back for fear that she might again encounter those twin pools of vicious and malignant power that were the eyes of Raghunath Jafar; and so she did not see the oily smile of satisfaction that twisted the sensuous lips of the Hindu, nor did she hear his whispered repetition—"It will not be necessary."

*   *   *

As the expedition wound along the trail that leads to the foot of the barrier cliffs that hem the lower frontier of the arid plateau beyond which stand the ancient ruins that are Opar, Wayne Colt, far to the west, pushed on toward the base camp of the conspirators. To the south, a little monkey rode upon the back of a great lion, shrilling insults now with perfect impunity at every jungle creature that crossed their path; while, with equal contempt for all lesser creatures, the mighty carnivore strode haughtily down wind, secure in the knowledge of his unquestioned might. A herd of antelope, grazing in his path, caught the acrid scent of the cat and moved nervously about; but when he came within sight of them they trotted only a short distance to one side, making a path for him; and, while he was still in sight, they resumed their feeding, for Numa, the lion, had fed well and the herbivores knew, as creatures of the wild know many things that are beyond the dull sensibilities of man, and felt no fear of Numa with a full belly.

To others, yet far off, came the scent of the lion; and they, too, moved nervously, though their fear was less than had been the first fear of the antelopes. These others were the great apes of the tribe of To-yat, whose mighty bulls had little cause to fear even Numa himself, though their shes and their balus might well tremble.

As the cat approached, the Mangani became more restless and more irritable. To-yat, the king ape, beat his breast and bared his great fighting fangs. Ga-yat, his powerful shoulders hunched, moved to the edge of the herd nearest the approaching danger. Zu-tho thumped a warning menace with his calloused feet. The shes called their balus to them, and many took to the lower branches of the larger trees or sought positions close to an arborial avenue of escape.

It was at this moment that an almost naked white man dropped from the dense foliage of a tree and alighted in their midst. Taut nerves and short tempers snapped. Roaring and snarling, the herd rushed upon the rash and hated manthing. The king ape was in the lead.

"To-yat has a short memory," said the man in the tongue of the Mangani.

For an instant the ape paused, surprised perhaps to hear the language of his kind issuing from the lips of a man-thing. "I am To-yat!" he growled. "I kill."

"I am Tarzan," replied the man, "mighty hunter, mighty fighter. I come in peace."

"Kill! Kill!" roared To-yat, and the other great bulls advanced, bare-fanged, menacingly.

"Zu-tho! Ga-yat!" snapped the man, "it is I, Tarzan of the Apes"; but the bulls were nervous and frightened now, for the scent of Numa was strong in their nostrils, and the shock of Tarzan's sudden appearance had plunged them into a panic.

"Kill! Kill!" they bellowed, though as yet they did not charge, but advanced slowly, working themselves into the necessary frenzy of rage that would terminate in a sudden, blood-mad rush that no living creature might withstand and which would leave naught but torn and bloody fragments of the object of their wrath.

And then a shrill scream broke from the lips of a great, hairy mother with a tiny balu on her back. "Numa!" she shrieked, and, turning, fled into the safety of the foliage of a nearby tree.

Instantly the shes and balus remaining upon the ground took to the trees. The bulls turned their attention for a moment from the man to the new menace. What they saw

upset what little equanimity remained to them. Advancing
straight toward them, his round, yellow-green eyes blazing in
ferocity, was a mighty, yellow lion; and upon his back perched
a little monkey, screaming insults at them. The sight was too
much for the apes of To-yat, and the king was the first to
break before it. With a roar, the ferocity of which may have
salved his self esteem, he leaped for the nearest tree; and
instantly the others broke and fled, leaving the white giant to
face the angry lion alone.

With blazing eyes the king of beasts advanced upon the
man, his head lowered and flattened, his tail extended, the
brush flicking. The man spoke a single word in a low tone
that might have carried but a few yards. Instantly the head
of the lion came up, the horrid glare died in his eyes; and at
the same instant the little monkey, voicing a shrill scream of
recognition and delight, leaped over Numa's head and in three
prodigious bounds was upon the shoulder of the man, his
little arms encircling the bronzed neck.

"Little Nkima!" whispered Tarzan, the soft cheek of the
monkey pressed against his own.

The lion strode majestically forward. He sniffed the bare
legs of the man, rubbed his head against his side and lay
down at his feet.

"Jad-bal-ja!" greeted the ape man.

The great apes of the tribe of To-yat watched from the
safety of the trees. Their panic and their anger had subsided.
"It is Tarzan," said Zu-tho.

"Yes, it is Tarzan," echoed Ga-yat.

To-yat grumbled. He did not like Tarzan, but he feared
him; and now, with this new evidence of the power of the
great Tarmangani, he feared him even more.

For a time Tarzan listened to the glib chattering of little
Nkima. He learned of the strange Tarmangani and the many
Gomangani warriors who had invaded the domain of the
Lord of the Jungle.

The great apes moved restlessly in the trees, wishing to
descend; but they feared Numa, and the great bulls were too
heavy to travel in safety upon the high flung leafy trails
along which the lesser apes might pass with safety, and so
could not depart until Numa had gone.

"Go away!" cried To-yat, the King. "Go away, and leave
the Mangani in peace."

"We are going," replied the ape-man, "but you need not
fear either Tarzan or the Golden Lion. We are your friends.

I have told Jad-bal-ja that he is never to harm you. You may descend."

"We shall stay in the trees until he has gone," said To-yat; "he might forget."

"You are afraid," said Tarzan contemptuously. "Zu-tho or Ga-yat would not be afraid."

"Zu-tho is afraid of nothing," boasted that great bull.

Without a word Ga-yat climbed ponderously from the tree in which he had taken refuge and, if not with marked enthusiasm, at least with slight hesitation, advanced toward Tarzan and Jad-bal-ja, the Golden Lion. His fellows eyed him intently, momentarily expecting to see him charged and mauled by the yellow-eyed destroyer that lay at Tarzan's feet watching every move of the shaggy bull. The Lord of the Jungle also watched great Numa, for none knew better than he, that a lion, however accustomed to obey his master, is still a lion. The years of their companionship, since Jad-bal-ja had been a little, spotted, fluffy ball, had never given him reason to doubt the loyalty of the carnivore, though there had been times when he had found it both difficult and dangerous to thwart some of the beast's more ferocious hereditary instincts.

Ga-yat approached, while little Nkima scolded and chattered from the safety of his master's shoulder; and the lion, blinking lazily, finally looked away. The danger, if there had been any, was over—it is the fixed, intent gaze of the lion that bodes ill.

Tarzan advanced and laid a friendly hand upon the shoulder of the ape. "This is Ga-yat," he said addressing Jad-bal-ja, "friend of Tarzan; do not harm him." He did not speak in any language of man. Perhaps the medium of communication that he used might not properly be called a language at all, but the lion and the great ape and the little Manu understood him.

"Tell the Mangani that Tarzan is the friend of little Nkima," shrilled the monkey. "He must not harm little Nkima."

"It is as Nkima has said," the ape-man assured Ga-yat.

"The friends of Tarzan are the friends of Ga-yat," replied the great ape.

"It is well," said Tarzan, "and now I go. Tell To-yat and the others what we have said and tell them also that there are strange men in this country which is Tarzan's. Let them watch them, but do not let the men see them, for these are bad men, perhaps, who carry the thunder sticks that hurl death with smoke and fire and a great noise. Tarzan goes now to see why these men are in his country."

*   *   *

Zora Drinov had avoided Jafar since the departure of the expedition to Opar. Scarcely had she left her tent, feigning a headache as an excuse, nor had the Hindu made any attempt to invade her privacy. Thus passed the first day. Upon the morning of the second Jafar summoned the head man of the askaris that had been left to guard them and to procure meat.

"Today," said Raghunath Jafar, "would be a good day to hunt. The signs are propitious. Go, therefore, into the forest, taking all your men, and do not return until the sun is low in the west. If you do this there will be presents for you, besides all the meat you can eat from the carcasses of your kills. Do you understand?"

"Yes, Bwana," replied the black.

"Take with you the boy of the woman. He will not be needed here. My boy will remain to cook for us."

"Perhaps he will not come," suggested the Negro.

"You are many, he is only one; but do not let the woman know that you are taking him."

"What are the presents?" demanded the head man.

"A piece of cloth and cartridges," replied Jafar.

"And the curved sword that you carry when we are on the march."

"No," said Jafar.

"This is not a good day to hunt," replied the black, turning away.

"Two pieces of cloth and fifty cartridges," suggested Jafar.

"And the curved sword," and thus, after much haggling, the bargain was made.

The head man gathered his askaris and bade them prepare for the hunt, saying that the brown bwana had so ordered, but he said nothing about any presents. When they were ready, he dispatched one to summon the white woman's servant.

"You are to accompany us on the hunt," he said to the boy.

"Who said so?" demanded Wamala.

"The brown bwana," replied Kahiya, the head man.

Wamala laughed. "I take my orders from my mistress—not from the brown bwana."

Kahiya leaped upon him and clapped a rough palm across his mouth as two of his men seized Wamala upon either side. "You take your orders from Kahiya," he said. Hunting spears were pressed against the boy's trembling body. "Will you go upon the hunt with us?" demanded Kahiya.

"I go," replied Wamala. "I did but joke."

As Zveri led his expedition toward Opar, Wayne Colt, impatient to join the main body of the conspirators, urged his men to greater speed in their search for the camp. The principal conspirators had entered Africa at different points that they might not arouse too much attention by their numbers. Pursuant to this plan Colt had landed on the west coast and had travelled inland a short distance by train to railhead, from which point he had had a long and arduous journey on foot; so that now, with his destination almost in sight, he was anxious to put a period to this part of his adventure. Then, too, he was curious to meet the other principals in this hazardous undertaking, Peter Zveri being the only one with whom he was acquainted.

The young American was not unmindful of the great risks he was inviting in affiliating himself with an expedition which aimed at the peace of Europe and at the ultimate control of a large section of Northeastern Africa through the disaffection by propaganda of large and warlike native tribes, especially in view of the fact that much of their operation must be carried on within British territory, where British power was considerably more than a mere gesture. But, being young and enthusiastic, however misguided, these contingencies did not weigh heavily upon his spirits, which, far from being depressed, were upon the contrary eager and restless for action.

The tedium of the journey from the coast had been unrelieved by pleasurable or adequate companionship, since the childish mentality of Tony could not rise above a muddy conception of Philippine independence and a consideration of the fine clothes he was going to buy when, by some vaguely visualized economic process, he was to obtain his share of the Ford and Rockefeller fortunes.

However, notwithstanding Tony's mental shortcomings, Colt was genuinely fond of the youth and as between the companionship of the Filipino or Zveri, he would have chosen the former, his brief acquaintance with the Russian in New York and San Francisco having convinced him that as a playfellow he left everything to be desired; nor had he any reason to anticipate that he would find any more congenial associates among the conspirators.

Plodding doggedly onward, Colt was only vaguely aware of the now familiar sights and sounds of the jungle, both of which by this time, it must be admitted, had considerably palled upon him. Even had he taken particular note of the latter, it is to be doubted that his untrained ear would have caught the persistent chatter of a little monkey that followed in the trees behind him; nor would this have particularly impressed him, unless he had been able to know that this particular little monkey rode upon the shoulder of a bronzed Apollo of the forest, who moved silently in his wake along a leafy highway of the lower terraces.

Tarzan had guessed that perhaps this white man, upon whose trail he had come unexpectedly, was making his way toward the main camp of the party of strangers for which the Lord of the Jungle was searching; and so, with the persistence and patience of the savage stalker of the jungle, he followed Wayne Colt; while little Nkima, riding upon his shoulder, berated his master for not immediately destroying the Tarmangani and all his party, for little Nkima was a bloodthirsty soul when the spilling of blood was to be accomplished by someone else.

And while Colt impatiently urged his men to greater speed and Tarzan followed and Nkima scolded, Raghunath Jafar approached the tent of Zora Drinov. As his figure darkened the entrance, casting a shadow across the book she was reading, the girl looked up from the cot upon which she was lying.

The Hindu smiled his oily, ingratiating smile. "I came to see if your headache was better," he said.

"Thank you, no," said the girl coldly; "but perhaps with undisturbed rest I may be better soon."

Ignoring the suggestion, Jafar entered the tent and seated himself in a camp chair. "I find it lonely," he said, "since the others have gone. Do you not also?"

"No," replied Zora. "I am quite content to be alone and resting."

"Your headache developed very suddenly," said Jafar. "A short time ago you seemed quite well and animated."

The girl made no reply. She was wondering what had become of her boy, Wamala, and why he had disregarded her explicit instructions to permit no one to disturb her.

Perhaps Raghunath Jafar read her thoughts, for to East Indians are often attributed uncanny powers, however little warranted such a belief may be. However that may be, his next words suggested the possibility.

"Wamala has gone hunting with the askaris," he said.

"I gave him no such permission," said Zora.

"I took the liberty of doing so," said Jafar.

"You had no right," said the girl angrily, sitting up upon the edge of her cot. "You have presumed altogether too far, Comrade Jafar."

"Wait a moment, my dear," said the Hindu soothingly. "Let us not quarrel. As you know, I love you and love does not find confirmation in crowds. Perhaps I have presumed, but it was only for the purpose of giving me an opportunity to plead my cause without interruption; and then, too, as you know, all is fair in love and war."

"Then we may consider this as war," said the girl, "for it certainly is not love, either upon your side or upon mine. There is another word to describe what animates you, Comrade Jafar, and that which animates me now is loathing. I could not abide you if you were the last man on earth, and when Zveri returns, I promise you that there shall be an accounting."

"Long before Zveri returns I shall have taught you to love me," said the Hindu, passionately. He arose and came toward her. The girl leaped to her feet, looking about quickly for a weapon of defense. Her cartridge belt and revolver hung over the chair in which Jafar had been sitting, and her rifle was upon the opposite side of the tent.

"You are quite unarmed," said the Hindu; "I took particular note of that when I entered the tent. Nor will it do you any good to call for help; for there is no one in camp but you, and me, and my boy and he knows that, if he values his life, he is not to come here unless I call him."

"You are a beast," said the girl.

"Why not be reasonable, Zora?" demanded Jafar. "It would not harm you any to be kind to me, and it will make it very much easier for you. Zveri need know nothing of it, and once we are back in civilization again, if you still feel that you do not wish to remain with me I shall not try to hold you; but I am sure that I can teach you to love me and that we shall be very happy together."

"Get out!" ordered the girl. There was neither fear nor hysteria in her voice. It was very calm and level and controlled.

To a man not entirely blinded by passion, that might have meant something—it might have meant a grim determination to carry self-defense to the very length of death—but Raghunath Jafar saw only the woman of his desire, and stepping quickly forward he seized her.

Zora Drinov was young and lithe and strong, yet she was no match for the burly Hindu, whose layers of greasy fat belied the great physical strength beneath them. She tried to wrench herself free and escape from the tent, but he held her and dragged her back. Then she turned upon him in a fury and struck him repeatedly in the face, but he only enveloped her more closely in his embrace and bore her backward upon the cot.

3

Out of the Grave

W AYNE COLT's guide, who had been slightly in advance of the American, stopped suddenly and looked back with a broad smile. Then he pointed ahead. "The camp, Bwana!" he exclaimed triumphantly.

"Thank the Lord!" exclaimed Colt with a sigh of relief.

"It is deserted," said the guide.

"It does look that way, doesn't it?" agreed Colt. "Let's have a look around," and, followed by his men, he moved in among the tents. His tired porters threw down their loads and, with the askaris, sprawled at full length beneath the shade of the trees, while Colt, followed by Tony, commenced an investigation of the camp.

Almost immediately the young American's attention was attracted by the violent shaking of one of the tents. "There is someone or something in there," he said to Tony, as he walked briskly toward the entrance.

The sight within that met his eyes brought a sharp ejaculation to his lips—a man and woman struggling upon the ground, the former choking the bare throat of his victim while the girl struck feebly at his face with clenched fists.

So engrossed was Jafar in his unsuccessful attempt to subdue the girl that he was unaware of Colt's presence until a heavy hand fell upon his shoulder and he was jerked violently aside.

Consumed by maniacal fury, he leaped to his feet and struck at the American only to be met with a blow that sent him reeling backward. Again he charged and again he was struck heavily upon the face. This time he went to the ground, and as he staggered to his feet, Colt seized him, wheeled him around and hurtled him through the entrance of the tent, accelerating his departure with a well-timed kick. "If he tries to come back, Tony, shoot him," he snapped at the Filipino, and then turned to assist the girl to her feet. Half carrying her, he laid her on the cot and then, finding water in a bucket, bathed her forehead, her throat and her wrists.

Outside the tent Raghunath Jafar saw the porters and the askaris lying in the shade of a tree. He also saw Antonio Mori with a determined scowl upon his face and a revolver in his hand, and with an angry imprecation he turned and made his way toward his own tent, his face livid with anger and murder in his heart.

Presently Zora Drinov opened her eyes and looked up into the solicitous face of Wayne Colt, bending over her.

From the leafy seclusion of a tree above the camp, Tarzan of the Apes overlooked the scene below. A single, whispered syllable had silenced Nkima's scolding. Tarzan had noted the violent shaking of the tent that had attracted Colt's attention, and he had seen the precipitate ejection of the Hindu from its interior and the menacing attitude of the Filipino preventing Jafar's return to the conflict. These matters were of little interest to the ape-man. The quarrelings and defections of these people did not even arouse his curiosity. What he wished to learn was the reason for their presence here, and for the purpose of obtaining this information he had two plans. One was to keep them under constant surveillance until their acts divulged that which he wished to know. The other was to determine definitely the head of the expedition and then to enter the camp and demand the information he desired. But this he would not do until he had obtained sufficient information to give him an advantage. What was going on within the tent he did not know, nor did he care.

For several seconds after she opened her eyes Zora Drinov gazed intently into those of the man bent upon her. "You must be the American," she said finally.

"I am Wayne Colt," he replied, "and I take it from the fact that you guessed my identity that this is Comrade Zveri's camp."

She nodded. "You came just in time, Comrade Colt," she said.

"Thank God for that," he said.

"There is no God," she reminded him.

Colt flushed. "We are creatures of heredity and habit," he explained.

Zora Drinov smiled. "That is true," she said, "but it is our business to break a great many bad habits not only for ourselves, but for the entire world."

Since he had laid her upon the cot, Colt had been quietly appraising the girl. He had not known that there was a white woman in Zveri's camp, but had he it is certain that he would not have anticipated one at all like this girl. He would rather have visualized a female agitator capable of accompanying a band of men to the heart of Africa as a coarse and unkempt peasant woman of middle age; but this girl, from her head of glorious, wavy hair to her small well-shaped foot, suggested the antithesis of a peasant origin and, far from being unkempt, was as trig and smart as it were possible for a woman to be under such circumstances and, in addition, she was young and beautiful.

"Comrade Zveri is absent from camp?" he asked.

"Yes, he is away on a short expedition."

"And there is no one to introduce us to one another?" he asked, with a smile.

"Oh, pardon me," she said. "I am Zora Drinov."

"I had not anticipated such a pleasant surprise," said Colt. "I expected to find nothing but uninteresting men like myself. And who was the fellow I interrupted?"

"That was Raghunath Jafar, a Hindu."

"He is one of us?" asked Colt.

"Yes," replied the girl, "but not for long—not after Peter Zveri returns."

"You mean———?"

"I mean that Peter will kill him."

Colt shrugged. "It is what he deserves," he said. "Perhaps I should have done it."

"No," said the girl, "leave that for Peter."

"Were you left alone here in this camp without any protection?" demanded Colt.

"No. Peter left my boy and ten askaris, but in some way Jafar got them all out of camp."

"You will be safe now," he said. "I shall see to that until Comrade Zveri returns. I am going now to make my camp, and I shall send two of my askaris to stand guard before your tent."

"That is good of you," she said, "but I think now that you are here it will not be necessary."

"I shall do it anyway," he said. "I shall feel safer."

"And when you have made camp, will you come and have supper with me?" she asked, and then, "Oh, I forgot, Jafar has sent my boy away, too. There is no one to cook for me."

"Then, perhaps, you will dine with me," he said. "My boy is a fairly good cook."

"I shall be delighted, Comrade Colt," she replied.

As the American left the tent, Zora Drinov lay back upon the cot with half-closed eyes. How different the man had been from what she had expected. Recalling his features, and especially his eyes, she found it difficult to believe that such a man could be a traitor to his father or to his country, but then, she realized, many a man has turned against his own for a principle. With her own people it was different. They had never had a chance. They had always been ground beneath the heel of one tyrant or another. What they were doing they believed implicitly to be for their own and for their country's good. Among those of them who were motivated by honest conviction there could not fairly be brought any charge of treason, and yet, Russian though she was to the core, she could not help but look with contempt upon the citizens of other countries who turned against their governments to aid the ambitions of a foreign power. We may be willing to profit by the act of foreign mercenaries and traitors, but we cannot admire them.

As Colt crossed from Zora's tent to where his men lay to give the necessary instructions for the making of his camp, Raghunath Jafar watched him from the interior of his own tent. A malignant scowl clouded the countenance of the Hindu, and hatred smoldered in his eyes.

Tarzan, watching from above, saw the young American issuing instructions to his men. The personality of this young stranger had impressed Tarzan favorably. He liked him as well as he could like any stranger, for deeply ingrained in the fiber of the ape-man was the wild beast suspicion of all strangers and especially of all white strangers. As he watched him now nothing else within the range of his vision escaped him. It was thus that he saw Raghunath Jafar emerge from his tent, carrying a rifle. Only Tarzan and little Nkima saw this, and only Tarzan placed any sinister interpretation upon it.

Raghunath Jafar walked directly away from camp and entered the jungle. Swinging silently through the trees, Tarzan of the Apes followed him. Jafar made a half circle of the camp just within the concealing verdure of the jungle, and then he halted. From where he stood the entire camp was visible to him, but his own position was concealed by foliage.

Colt was watching the disposition of his loads and the pitching of his tent. His men were busy with the various duties assigned to them by their headman. They were tired and there was little talking. For the most part they worked in silence, and an unusual quiet pervaded the scene—a quiet that was suddenly and unexpectedly shattered by an anguished scream and the report of a rifle, blending so closely that it was impossible to say which had preceded the other. A bullet whizzed by Colt's head and nipped the lobe off the ear of one of his men standing behind him. Instantly the peaceful activities of the camp were supplanted by pandemonium. For a moment there was a difference of opinion as to the direction from which the shot and the scream had come, and then Colt saw a wisp of smoke rising from the jungle just beyond the edge of camp.

"There it is," he said, and started toward the point.

The headman of the askaris stopped him. "Do not go, Bwana," he said. "Perhaps it is an enemy. Let us fire into the jungle first."

"No," said Colt, "we will investigate first. Take some of your men in from the right, and I'll take the rest in from the left. We'll work around slowly through the jungle until we meet."

"Yes, Bwana," said the headman, and calling his men he gave the necessary instructions.

No sound of flight or any suggestion of a living presence greeted the two parties as they entered the jungle; nor had they discovered any signs of a marauder when, a few moments later, they made contact with one another. They were now formed in a half circle that bent back into the jungle and, at a word from Colt, they advanced toward the camp.

It was Colt who found Raghunath Jafar lying dead just at the edge of camp. His right hand grasped his rifle. Protruding from his heart was the shaft of a sturdy arrow.

The Negroes gathering around the corpse looked at one another questioningly and then back into the jungle and up into the trees. One of them examined the arrow. "It is not like any arrow I have ever seen," he said. "It was not made by the hand of man."

Immediately the blacks were filled with superstitious fears.

"The shot was meant for the bwana," said one; "therefore the demon who shot the arrow is a friend of our bwana. We need not be afraid."

This explanation satisfied the blacks, but it did not satisfy Wayne Colt. He was puzzling over it as he walked back into camp, after giving orders that the Hindu be buried.

Zora Drinov was standing in the entrance to her tent, and as she saw him she came to meet him. "What was it?" she asked. "What happened?"

"Comrade Zveri will not kill Raghunath Jafar," he said.

"Why?" she asked.

"Because Raghunath Jafar is already dead."

"Who could have shot the arrow?" she asked, after he had told her of the manner of the Hindu's death.

"I haven't the remotest idea," he admitted. "It is an absolute mystery, but it means that the camp is being watched and that we must be very careful not to go into the jungle alone. The men believe that the arrow was fired to save me from an assassin's bullet; and while it is entirely possible that Jafar may have been intending to kill me, I believe that if I had gone into the jungle alone instead of him it would have been I that would be lying out there dead now. Have you been bothered at all by natives since you made camp here, or have you had any unpleasant experiences with them at all?"

"We have not seen a native since we entered this camp. We have often commented upon the fact that the country seems to be entirely deserted and uninhabited, notwithstanding the fact that it is filled with game."

"This thing may help to account for the fact that it is uninhabited," suggested Colt, "or rather apparently uninhabited. We may have unintentionally invaded the country of some unusually ferocious tribe that takes this means of acquainting newcomers with the fact that they are persona non grata."

"You say one of our men was wounded?" asked Zora.

"Nothing serious. He just had his ear nicked a little."

"Was he near you?"

"He was standing right behind me," replied Colt.

"I think there is no doubt that Jafar meant to kill you," said Zora.

"Perhaps," said Colt, "but he did not succeed. He did not even kill my appetite; and if I can succeed in calming the excitement of my boy, we shall have supper presently."

From a distance Tarzan and Nkima watched the burial of

Raghunath Jafar and a little later saw the return of Kahiya and his askaris with Zora's boy Wamala, who had been sent out of camp by Jafar.

"Where," said Tarzan to Nkima, "are all the many Tarmangani and Gomangani that you told me were in this camp?"

"They have taken their thundersticks and gone away," replied the little Manu. "They are hunting for Nkima."

Tarzan of the Apes smiled one of his rare smiles. "We shall have to hunt them down and find out what they are about, Nkima," he said.

"But it grows dark in the jungle soon," pleaded Nkima, "and then will Sabor, and Sheeta, and Numa, and Histah be abroad, and they, too, search for little Nkima."

Darkness had fallen before Colt's boy announced supper, and in the meantime Tarzan, changing his plans, had returned to the trees above the camp. He was convinced that there was something irregular in the aims of the expedition whose base he had discovered. He knew from the size of the camp that it had contained many men. Where they had gone and for what purpose were matters that he must ascertain. Feeling that this expedition, whatever its purpose, might naturally be a principal topic of conversation in the camp, he sought a point of vantage wherefrom he might overhear the conversations that passed between the two white members of the party beneath him; and so it was that as Zora Drinov and Wayne Colt seated themselves at the supper table, Tarzan of the Apes crouched amid the foliage of a great tree just above them.

"You have passed through a rather trying ordeal today," said Colt, "but you do not appear to be any the worse for it. I should think that your nerves would be shaken."

"I have passed through too much already in my life, Comrade Colt, to have any nerves left at all," replied the girl.

"I suppose so," said Colt. "You must have passed through the revolution in Russia."

"I was only a little girl at the time," she explained, "but I remember it quite distinctly."

Colt was gazing at her intently. "From your appearance," he ventured, "I imagine that you were not by birth of the proletariat."

"My father was a laborer. He died in exile under the Tzarist regime. That was how I learned to hate everything monarchistic and capitalistic. And when I was offered this opportunity to join Comrade Zveri, I saw another field in which to encompass my revenge, while at the same time advancing the interests of my class throughout the world."

"When I last saw Zveri in the United States," said Colt, "he evidently had not formulated the plans he is now carrying out, as he never mentioned any expedition of this sort. When I received orders to join him here, none of the details was imparted to me; and so I am rather in the dark as to what his purpose is."

"It is only for good soldiers to obey," the girl reminded him.

"Yes, I know that," agreed Colt, "but at the same time even a poor soldier may act more intelligently sometimes if he knows the objective."

"The general plan, of course, is no secret to any of us here," said Zora, "and I shall betray no confidence in explaining it to you. It is a part of a larger plan to embroil the capitalistic powers in wars and revolutions to such an extent that they will be helpless to unite against us.

"Our emissaries have been laboring for a long time toward the culmination of the revolution in India that will distract the attention and the armed forces of Great Britain. We are not succeeding so well in Mexico as we had planned, but there is still hope, while our prospects in the Philippines are very bright. The conditions in China you well know. She is absolutely helpless, and we have hope that with our assistance she will eventually constitute a real menace to Japan. Italy is a very dangerous enemy, and it is largely for the purpose of embroiling her in war with France that we are here."

"But just how can that be accomplished in Africa?" asked Colt.

"Comrade Zveri believes that it will be simple," said the girl. "The suspicion and jealousy that exist between France and Italy are well known; their race for naval supremacy amounts almost to a scandal. At the first overt act of either against the other, war might easily result, and a war between Italy and France would embroil all of Europe."

"But just how can Zveri, operating in the wilds of Africa, embroil Italy and France in war?" demanded the American.

"There is now in Rome a delegation of French and Italian Reds engaged in this very business. The poor men know only a part of the plan and, unfortunately for them, it will be necessary to martyr them in the cause for the advancement of our world plan. They have been furnished with papers outlining a plan for the invasion of Italian Somaliland by

French troops. At the proper time one of Comrade Zveri's secret agents in Rome will reveal the plot to the Fascist Government; and almost simultaneously a considerable number of our own blacks, disguised in the uniforms of French native troops, led by the white men of our expedition, uniformed as French officers, will invade Italian Somaliland.

"In the meantime our agents are carrying on in Egypt and Abyssinia and among the native tribes of North Africa, and already we have definite assurance that with the attention of France and Italy distracted by war and Great Britain embarrassed by a revolution in India the natives of North Africa will arise in what will amount almost to a holy war for the purpose of throwing off the yoke of foreign domination and the establishment of autonomous soviet states throughout the entire area."

"A daring and stupendous undertaking," exclaimed Colt, "but one that will require enormous resources in money as well as men."

"It is Comrade Zveri's pet scheme," said the girl. "I do not know, of course, all the details of his organization and backing; but I do know that while he is already well financed for the initial operations, he is depending to a considerable extent upon this district for furnishing most of the necessary gold to carry on the tremendous operations that will be necessary to insure final success."

"Then I am afraid he is foredoomed to failure," said Colt, "for he surely cannot find enough wealth in this savage country to carry on any such stupendous program."

"Comrade Zveri believes to the contrary," said Zora; "in fact, the expedition that he is now engaged upon is for the purpose of obtaining the treasure he seeks."

Above them, in the darkness, the silent figure of the apeman lay stretched at ease upon a great branch, his keen ears absorbing all that passed between them, while curled in sleep upon his bronzed back lay little Nkima, entirely oblivious of the fact that he might have listened to words well calculated to shake the foundations of organized government throughout the world.

"And where," demanded Colt, "if it is no secret, does Comrade Zveri expect to find such a great store of gold?"

"In the famous treasure vaults of Opar," replied the girl. "You certainly must have heard of them."

"Yes," answered Colt, "but I never considered them other

than purely legendary. The folk lore of the entire world is filled with these mythical treasure vaults."

"But Opar is no myth," replied Zora.

If the startling information divulged to him affected Tarzan, it induced no outward manifestation. Listening in silence imperturbably, trained to the utmost refinement of self control, he might have been part and parcel of the great branch upon which he lay, or of the shadowy foliage which hid him from view.

For a time Colt sat in silence, contemplating the stupendous possibilities of the plan that he had just heard unfolded. It seemed to him little short of the dream of a mad man, and he did not believe that it had the slightest chance for success. What he did realize was the jeopardy in which it placed the members of the expedition, for he believed that there would be no escape for any of them once Great Britain, France, and Italy were apprised of their activities; and, without conscious volition, his fears seemed centered upon the safety of the girl. He knew the type of people with whom he was working and so he knew that it would be dangerous to voice a doubt as to the practicability of the plan, for scarcely without exception the agitators whom he had met had fallen naturally into two separate categories, the impractical visionary, who believed everything that he wanted to believe, and the shrewd knave, actuated by motives of avarice, who hoped to profit either in power or riches by any change that he might be instrumental in bringing about in the established order of things. It seemed horrible that a young and beautiful girl should have been enticed into such a desperate situation. She seemed far too intelligent to be merely a brainless tool, and even his brief association with her made it most difficult for him to believe that she was a knave.

"The undertaking is certainly fraught with grave dangers," he said, "and as it is primarily a job for men I cannot understand why you were permitted to face the dangers and hardships that must of necessity be entailed by the carrying out of such a perilous campaign."

"The life of a woman is of no more value than that of a man," she declared, "and I was needed. There is always a great deal of important and confidential clerical work to be done which Comrade Zveri can entrust only to one in whom he has implicit confidence. He reposes such trust in me and, in addition, I am a trained typist and stenographer. Those reasons in themselves are sufficient to explain why I am here, but another very important one is that I desire to be with Comrade Zveri."

In the girl's words Colt saw the admission of a romance; but to his American mind this was all the greater reason why the girl should not have been brought along, for he could not conceive of a man exposing the girl he loved to such dangers.

Above them Tarzan of the Apes moved silently. First he reached over his shoulder and lifted little Nkima from his back. Nkima would have objected, but the veriest shadow of a whisper silenced him. The ape-man had various methods of dealing with enemies—methods that he had learned and practiced long before he had been cognizant of the fact that he was not an ape. Long before he had ever seen another white man he had terrorized the Gomangani, the black men of the forest and the jungle, and had learned that a long step toward defeating an enemy may be taken by first demoralizing its morale. He knew now that these people were not only the invaders of his own domain and, therefore, his own personal enemies, but that they threatened the peace of Great Britain, which was dear to him, and of the rest of the civilized world, with which, at least, Tarzan had no quarrels. It is true that he held civilization in general in considerable contempt, but in even greater contempt he held those who interfered with the rights of others or with the established order of jungle or city.

As Tarzan left the tree in which he had been hiding, the two below him were no more aware of his departure than they had been of his presence. Colt found himself attempting to fathom the mystery of love. He knew Zveri, and it appeared inconceivable to him that a girl of Zora Drinov's type could be attracted by a man of Zveri's stamp. Of course, it was none of his affair, but it bothered him nevertheless because it seemed to constitute a reflection upon the girl and to lower her in his estimation. He was disappointed in her, and Colt did not like to be disappointed in people to whom he had been attracted.

"You knew Comrade Zveri in America, did you not?" asked Zora.

"Yes," replied Colt.

"What do you think of him?" she demanded.

"I found him a very forceful character," replied Colt. "I believe him to be a man who would carry on to a conclusion anything that he attempted. No better man could have been chosen for this mission."

If the girl had hoped to surprise Colt into an expression of personal regard or dislike for Zveri, she had failed, but if such was the fact she was too wise to pursue the subject further. She realized that she was dealing with a man from whom she would get little information that he did not wish her to have; but on the other hand a man who might easily wrest information from others, for he was that type which seemed to invite confidences, suggesting as he did, in his attitude, his speech and his manner a sterling uprightness of character that could not conceivably abuse a trust. She rather liked this upstanding young American, and the more she saw of him the more difficult she found it to believe that he had turned traitor to his family, his friends and his country. However, she knew that many honorable men had sacrificed everything to a conviction and, perhaps, he was one of these. She hoped that this was the explanation.

Their conversation drifted to various subjects—to their lives and experiences in their native lands—to the happenings that had befallen them since they had entered Africa, and, finally, to the experiences of the day. And while they talked, Tarzan of the Apes returned to the tree above them, but this time he did not come alone.

"I wonder if we shall ever know," she said, "who killed Jafar."

"It is a mystery that is not lessened by the fact that none of the askaris could recognize the type of arrow with which he was slain, though that, of course, might be accounted for by the fact that none of them are of this district."

"It has considerably shaken the nerves of the men," said Zora, "and I sincerely hope that nothing similar occurs again. I have found that it does not take much to upset these natives, and while most of them are brave in the face of known dangers, they are apt to be entirely demoralized by anything bordering on the supernatural."

"I think they felt better when they got the Hindu planted under ground," said Colt, "though some of them were not at all sure that he might not return anyway."

"There is not much chance of that," rejoined the girl, laughing.

She had scarcely ceased speaking when the branches above them rustled, and a heavy body plunged downward to the table top between them, crushing the flimsy piece of furniture to earth.

The two sprang to their feet, Colt whipping out his revolver and the girl stifling a cry as she stepped back. Colt felt the hairs rise upon his head and goose flesh form upon his arms and back, for there between them lay the dead body of Raghunath Jafar upon its back, the dead eyes rolled backward staring up into the night.

4

Into the Lion's Den

NKIMA was angry. He had been awakened from the depth of a sound sleep, which was bad enough, but now his master had set out upon such foolish errands through the darkness of the night that, mingled with Nkima's scoldings were the whimperings of fear, for in every shadow he saw Sheeta, the panther, lurking and in each gnarled limb of the forest the likeness of Histah, the snake. While Tarzan had remained in the vicinity of the camp, Nkima had not been particularly perturbed, and when he had returned to the tree with his burden the little Manu was sure that he was going to remain there for the rest of the night; but instead he had departed immediately and now was swinging through the black forest with an evident fixity of purpose that boded ill for either rest or safety for little Nkima during the remainder of the night.

Whereas Zveri and his party had started slowly along winding jungle trails, Tarzan moved almost in an air line through the jungle toward his destination, which was the same as that of Zveri. The result was that before Zveri reached the almost perpendicular crag which formed the last and greatest natural barrier to the forbidden valley of Opar, Tarzan and Nkima had disappeared beyond the summit and were crossing the desolate valley, upon the far side of which loomed the great walls and lofty spires and turrets of ancient Opar. In the bright light of the African sun, domes and minarets shone red and gold above the city; and once again the ape-man experienced the same feeling that had impressed him upon the occasion, now years gone, when his eyes had first alighted upon the splendid panorama of mystery that had unfolded before them.

No evidence of ruin was apparent at this great distance. Once again, in imagination, he beheld a city of magnificent beauty, its streets and temples thronged with people; and once again his mind toyed with the mystery of the city's origin, when back somewhere in the dim vista of antiquity a race of rich and powerful people had conceived and built this enduring monument to a vanished civilization. It was possible to conceive that Opar might have existed when a glorious civilization flourished upon the great continent of Atlantis, which, sinking beneath the waves of the ocean, left this lost colony to death and decay.

That its few inhabitants were direct descendants of its once powerful builders seemed not unlikely in view of the rites and ceremonies of the ancient religion which they practiced, as well as by the fact that by scarcely any other hypothesis could the presence of a white-skinned people be accounted for in this remote inaccessible African vastness.

The peculiar laws of heredity, which seemed operative in Opar as in no other portion of the world, suggested an origin differing materially from that of other men; for it is a peculiar fact that the men of Opar bear little or no resemblance to the females of their kind. The former are short, heavy set, hairy, almost ape-like in their conformation and appearance, while the women are slender, smooth skinned and often beautiful. There were certain physical and mental attributes of the men that had suggested to Tarzan the possibility that at some time in the past the colonists had, either by choice or necessity, interbred with the great apes of the district; and he also was aware that owing to the scarcity of victims for the human sacrifice, which their rigid worship demanded it was common practice among them to use for this purpose either males or females who deviated considerably from the standard time had established for each sex, with the result that through the laws of natural selection an overwhelming majority of the males would be grotesque and the females normal and beautiful.

It was with such reveries that the mind of the ape-man was occupied as he crossed the desolate valley of Opar, which lay shimmering in the bright sunlight that was relieved only by the shade of an occasional gnarled and stunted tree. Ahead of him and to his right was the small rocky hillock, upon the summit of which was located the outer entrance to the treasure vaults of Opar. But with this he was not now interested, his sole object being to forewarn La of the approach of the invaders that she might prepare her defense.

It had been long since Tarzan had visited Opar; but upon that last occasion, when he had restored La to her loyal people and re-established her supremacy following the defeat of the forces of Cadj, the high priest, and the death of the latter beneath the fangs and talons of Jad-bal-ja, he had carried away with him for the first time a conviction of the friendliness of all of the people of Opar. He had for years known that La was secretly his friend, but her savage, grotesque retainers always heretofore had feared and hated him; and so it was now that he approached Opar as one might approach any citadel of one's friends, without stealth and without any doubt but that he would be received in friendship.

Nkima, however, was not so sure. The gloomy ruins terrified him. He scolded and pleaded, but all to no avail; and at last terror overcame his love and loyalty so that, as they were approaching the outer wall, which loomed high above them, he leaped from his master's shoulder and scampered away from the ruins that confronted him, for deep in his little heart was an abiding fear of strange and unfamiliar places, that not even his confidence in Tarzan could overcome.

Nkima's keen eyes had noted the rocky hillock which they had passed a short time before, and to the summit of this he scampered as a comparatively safe haven from which to await the return of his master from Opar.

As Tarzan approached the narrow fissure which alone gave entrance through the massive outer walls of Opar, he was conscious, as he had been years before on the occasion of his first approach to the city, of unseen eyes upon him, and at any moment he expected to hear a greeting when the watchers recognized him.

Without hesitation, however, and with no apprehensiveness, Tarzan entered the narrow cleft and descended a flight of concrete steps that led to the winding passage through the thick outer wall. The narrow court, beyond which loomed the inner wall, was silent and deserted; nor was the silence broken as he crossed it to another narrow passage which led through it; at the end of this he came to a broad avenue, upon the opposite side of which stood the crumbling ruins of the great temple of Opar.

In silence and solitude he entered the frowning portal,

flanked by its rows of stately pillars, from the capitals of
which grotesque birds glared down upon him as they had
stared through all the countless ages since forgotten hands
had carved them from the solid rock of the monoliths. On
through the temple toward the inner courtyard, where he
knew the activities of the city were carried on, Tarzan made
his way in silence. Perhaps another man would have given
notice of his coming, voicing a greeting to apprise them of
his approach; but Tarzan of the Apes in many respects is
less man than beast. He goes the silent way of most beasts,
wasting no breath in useless mouthing. He had not sought to
approach Opar stealthily, and he knew that he had not arrived unseen. Why a greeting was delayed he did not know,
unless it was that, after carrying word of his coming to
La, they were waiting for her instructions.

Through the main corridor Tarzan made his way, noting
again the tablets of gold with their ancient and long undeciphered hieroglyphics. Through the chamber of the seven
golden pillars he passed and across the golden floor of an
adjoining room, and still only silence and emptiness, yet with
vague suggestions of figures moving in the galleries that overlooked the apartment through which he was passing; and then
at last he came to a heavy door beyond which he was sure
he would find either priests or priestesses of this great temple
of the Flaming God. Fearlessly he pushed it open and stepped
across the threshold, and in the same instant a knotted club
descended heavily upon his head, felling him senseless to the
floor.

Instantly he was surrounded by a score of gnarled and
knotted men; their matted beards fell low upon their hairy
chests as they rolled forward upon their short, crooked legs.
They chattered in low, growling gutturals as they bound
their victim's wrists and ankles with stout thongs, and then
they lifted him and carried him along other corridors and
through the crumbling glories of magnificent apartments to
a great tiled room, at one end of which a young woman sat
upon a massive throne, resting upon a dais a few feet above
the level of the floor.

Standing beside the girl upon the throne was another of
the gnarled and knotted men. Upon his arms and legs were
bands of gold and about his throat many necklaces. Upon
the floor beneath these two was a gathering of men and
women—the priests and priestesses of the Flaming God of
Opar.

Tarzan's captors carried their victim to the foot of the throne and tossed his body upon the tile floor. Almost simultaneously the ape-man regained consciousness and, opening his eyes, looked about him.

"Is it he?" demanded the girl upon the throne.

One of Tarzan's captors saw that he had regained consciousness and with the help of others dragged him roughly to his feet.

"It is he, Oah," exclaimed the man at her side.

An expression of venomous hatred convulsed the face of the woman. "God has been good to His high priestess," she said. "I have prayed for this day to come as I prayed for the other, and as the other came so has this."

Tarzan looked quickly from the woman to the man at her side. "What is the meaning of this, Dooth?" he demanded. "Where is La? Where is your high priestess?"

The girl rose angrily from her throne. "Know, man of the outer world, that I am high priestess. I, Oah, am high priestess of the Flaming God."

Tarzan ignored her. "Where is La?" he demanded again of Dooth.

Oah flew into a frenzy of rage. "She is dead!" she screamed, advancing to the edge of the dais as though to leap upon Tarzan, the jeweled handle of her sacrificial knife gleaming in the sunlight, which poured through a great aperture where a portion of the ancient roof of the throne room had fallen in. "She is dead!" she repeated. "Dead as you will be when next we honor the Flaming God with the life blood of a man. La was weak. She loved you, and thus she betrayed her God, who had chosen you for sacrifice. But Oah is strong—strong with the hate she has nursed in her breast since Tarzan and La stole the throne of Opar from her. Take him away!" she screamed to his captors, "and let me not see him again until I behold him bound to the altar in the court of sacrifice."

They cut the bonds now that secured Tarzan's ankles so that he might walk; but even though his wrists were tied behind him it was evident that they still held him in great fear, for they put ropes about his neck and his arms and led him as man might lead a lion. Down into the familiar darkness of the pits of Opar they led him, lighting the way with torches; and when finally they had brought him to the dungeon in which he was to be confined it was some time before they could muster sufficient courage to cut the bonds that held his wrists, and even then they did not do so until they had again bound his ankles securely so that they might escape from the chamber and bolt the door before he could release his feet and pursue them. Thus greatly had the prowess of Tarzan impressed itself upon the brains of the crooked priests of Opar.

Tarzan had been in the dungeons of Opar before and, before, he had escaped; and so he set to work immediately seeking for a means of escape from his present predicament, for he knew that the chances were that Oah would not long delay the moment for which she had prayed—the instant when she should plunge the gleaming sacrificial knife into his breast. Quickly removing the thongs from his ankles, Tarzan groped his way carefully along the walls of his cell until he had made a complete circuit of it; then, similarly, he examined the floor. He discovered that he was in a rectangular chamber about ten feet long and eight wide and that by standing upon his tiptoes he could just reach the ceiling. The only opening was the door through which he had entered, in which an aperture, protected by iron bars, gave the cell its only ventilation but, as it opened upon a dark corridor, admitted no light. Tarzan examined the bolts and the hinges of the door, but they were, as he had conjectured, too substantial to be forced; and then, for the first time, he saw that a priest sat on guard in the corridor without, thus putting a definite end to any thoughts of surreptitious escape.

For three days and nights priests relieved each other at intervals; but upon the morning of the fourth day Tarzan discovered that the corridor was empty, and once again he turned his attention actively to thoughts of escape.

It had so happened that at the time of Tarzan's capture his hunting knife had been hidden by the tail of the leopard skin that formed his loin cloth; and, in their excitement, the ignorant, half-human priests of Opar had overlooked it when they took his other weapons away from him. Doubly thankful was Tarzan for this good fortune, since, for sentimental reasons, he cherished the hunting knife of his long dead sire— the knife that had started him upon the upward path to ascendancy over the beasts of the jungle that day, long gone, when, more by accident than intent, he had plunged it into the heart of Bolgani, the gorilla. But for more practical reasons it was, indeed, a gift from the gods, since it afforded him not only a weapon of defense, but an instrument wherewith he might seek to make good his escape.

Years before had Tarzan of the Apes escaped from the pits of Opar, and so he well knew the construction of their massive walls. Granite blocks of various sizes, hand hewn to fit with perfection, were laid in courses without mortar, the one wall that he had passed through having been fifteen feet in thickness. Fortune had favored him upon that occasion in that he had been placed in a cell which, unknown to the present inhabitants of Opar, had a secret entrance, the opening of which was closed by a single layer of loosely laid courses that the ape-man had been able to remove without great effort.

Naturally he sought for a similar condition in the cell in which he now found himself, but his search was not crowned with success. No single stone could be budged from its place, anchored as each was by the tremendous weight of the temple walls they supported; and so, perforce, he turned his attention toward the door.

He knew that there were few locks in Opar since the present degraded inhabitants of the city had not developed sufficient ingenuity either to repair old ones or construct new. Those locks that he had seen were ponderous affairs opened by huge keys and were, he guessed, of an antiquity that reached back to the days of Atlantis; but, for the most part, heavy bolts and bars secured such doors as might be fastened at all, and he guessed that it was such a crude contrivance that barred his way to freedom.

Groping his way to the door, he examined the small opening that let in air. It was about shoulder high and perhaps ten inches square and was equipped with four vertical iron bars half an inch square, set an inch and a half apart—too close to permit him to insert his hands between them, but this fact did not entirely discourage the ape-man. Perhaps there was another way.

His steel thewed fingers closed upon the center of one of the bars. With his left hand he clung to another, and bracing one knee high against the door he slowly flexed his right elbow. Rolling like plastic steel, the muscles of his forearm and his biceps swelled, until gradually the bar bent inward toward him. The ape-man smiled as he took a new grip upon the iron bar. Then he surged backward with all his weight and all the strength of that mighty arm, and the bar bent to a wide U as he wrenched it from its sockets. He tried to insert his arm through the new opening, but it still was too small. A moment later another bar was torn away, and now, his

arm through the aperture to its full length, he groped for the
bar or bolts that held him prisoner.

At the fullest extent to which he could reach his fingertips
downward against the door, he just touched the top of the
bar, which was a timber about three inches in thickness. Its
other dimensions, however, he was unable to ascertain, or
whether it would release by raising one end or must be drawn
back through keepers. It was most tantalizing! To have freedom almost within one's grasp and yet to be denied it was
maddening.

Withdrawing his arm from the aperture, he removed his
hunting knife from his scabbard and, again reaching outward,
pressed the point of the blade into the wood of the bar. At
first he tried lifting the bar by this means, but his knife point
only pulled out of the wood. Next, he attempted to move the
bar backward in a horizontal plane, and in this he was successful. Though the distance that he moved it in one effort
was small, he was satisfied, for he knew that patience would
win its reward. Never more than a quarter of an inch, sometimes only a sixteenth of an inch at a time, Tarzan slowly
worked the bar backward. He worked methodically and carefully, never hurrying, never affected by nervous anxiety,
although he never knew at what moment a savage warrior
priest of Opar might make his rounds; and at last his efforts
were rewarded, and the door swung upon its hinges.

Stepping quickly out, Tarzan shot the bar behind him and,
knowing no other avenue of escape, turned back up the corridor along which his captors had conducted him to his prison
cell. Faintly in the distance he discerned a lessening darkness,
and toward this he moved upon silent feet. As the light increased slightly, he saw that the corridor was about ten feet
wide and that at irregular intervals it was pierced by doors,
all of which were closed and secured by bolts or bars.

A hundred yards from the cell in which he had been incarcerated he crossed a transversed corridor, and here he
paused an instant to investigate with palpitating nostrils and
keen eyes and ears. In neither direction could he discern any
light, but faint sounds came to his ears indicating that life
existed somewhere behind the doors along this corridor, and
his nostrils were assailed by a medley of scents—the sweet
aroma of incense, the odor of human bodies and the acrid
scent of carnivores; but there was nothing there to attract his
further investigation, so he continued on his way along the
corridor toward the rapidly increasing light ahead.

He had advanced but a short distance when his keen ears detected the sound of approaching footsteps. Here was no place to risk discovery. Slowly he fell back toward the transverse corridor, seeking to take concealment there until the danger had passed; but it was already closer than he had imagined, and an instant later half a dozen priests of Opar turned into the corridor from one just ahead of him. They saw him instantly and halted, peering through the gloom.

"It is the ape-man," said one. "He has escaped," and with their knotted cudgels and their wicked knives they advanced upon him.

That they came slowly evidenced the respect in which they held his prowess, but still they came; and Tarzan fell back, for even he, armed only with a knife, was no match for six of these savage half-men with their heavy cudgels. As he retreated, a plan formed quickly in his alert mind, and when he reached the transverse corridor he backed slowly into it. Knowing that now that he was hidden from them they would come very slowly, fearing that he might be lying in wait for them, he turned and ran swiftly along the corridor. He passed several doors, not because he was looking for any door in particular, but because he knew that the more difficult it was for them to find him the greater his chances of eluding them; but at last he paused before one secured by a huge wooden bar. Quickly he raised it, opened the door and stepped within just as the leader of the priests came into view at the intersection of the corridor.

The instant that Tarzan stepped into the dark and gloomy chamber beyond he knew that he had made a fatal blunder. Strong in his nostrils was the acrid scent of Numa, the lion; the silence of the pit was shattered by a savage roar; in the dark background he saw two yellow-green eyes flaming with hate, and then the lion charged.

5

Before the Walls of Opar

PETER ZVERI established his camp on the edge of the forest at the foot of the barrier cliff that guards the desolate valley of Opar. Here he left his porters and a few askaris as guards and then, with his fighting men, guided by Kitembo, commenced the arduous climb to the summit.

None of them had ever come this way before, not even Kitembo, though he had known the exact location of Opar from one who had seen it; and so when the first view of the distant city broke upon them they were filled with awe, and vague questionings arose in the primitive minds of the black men.

It was a silent party that filed across the dusty plain toward Opar; nor were the blacks the only members of the expedition to be assailed with doubt, for in their black tents on distant deserts the Arabs had imbibed with the milk of their mothers the fear of jân and ghrôl and had heard, too, of the fabled city of Nimmr, which it was not well for men to approach. With such thoughts and forebodings were the minds of the men filled as they approached the towering ruins of the ancient Atlantian city.

From the top of the great boulder that guards the outer entrance to the treasure vaults of Opar a little monkey watched the progress of the expedition across the valley. He was a very much distraught little monkey, for in his heart he knew that his master should be warned of the coming of these many Gomangani and Tarmangani with their thundersticks; but fear of the forbidding ruins gave him pause, and so he danced about upon the top of the rock, chattering and scolding. The warriors of Peter Zveri marched right past and never paid any attention to him; and as they marched, other eyes were upon them, peering from out of the foliage of the trees that grew rank among the ruins.

If any member of the party saw a little monkey scampering quickly past upon their right, or saw him clamber up the ruined outer wall of Opar, he doubtless gave the matter no thought; for his mind, like the minds of all his fellows, was occupied by speculation as to what lay within that gloomy pile.

Kitembo did not know the location of the treasure vaults of Opar. He had but agreed to guide Zveri to the city, but, like Zveri, he entertained no doubt but that it would be easy to discover the vaults if they were unable to wring its location from any of the inhabitants of the city. Surprised, indeed, would they have been had they known that no living Oparian knew either of the location of the treasure vaults or of their existence and that, among all living men, only Tarzan and some of his Waziri warriors knew their location or how to reach them.

"The place is nothing but a deserted ruin," said Zveri to one of his white companions.

"It is an ominous looking place though," replied the other, "and it has already had its effect upon the men."

Zveri shrugged. "This might frighten them at night, but not in broad daylight; they are certainly not that yellow."

They were close to the ruined outer wall now, which frowned down upon them menacingly, and here they halted while several searched for an opening. Abu Batn was the first to find it—the narrow crevice with the flight of concrete steps leading upward. "Here is a way through, Comrade," he called to Zveri.

"Take some of your men with you and reconnoiter," ordered Zveri.

Abu Batn summoned a half dozen of his black men, who advanced with evident reluctance.

Gathering the skirt of his thôb about him, the sheykh entered the crevice, and at the same instant a piercing screech broke from the interior of the ruined city—a long drawn, high pitched shriek that ended in a series of low moans. The Bedaùwy halted. The blacks froze in terrified rigidity.

"Go on!" yelled Zveri. "A scream can't kill you!"

"Wullah!" exclaimed one of the Arabs; "but jân can."

"Get out of there, then!" cried Zveri angrily. "If you damned cowards are afraid to go, I'll go in myself."

There was no argument. The Arabs stepped aside. And then a little monkey, screaming with terror, appeared upon the top of the wall from the inside of the city. His sudden and noisy appearance brought every eye to bear upon him. They saw him turn an affrighted glance backward over his shoulder and then, with a loud scream, leap far out to the ground below. It scarcely seemed that he could survive the jump, yet it barely sufficed to interrupt his flight, for he was on his way again in an instant as, with prodigious leaps and bounds, he fled screaming out across the barren plains.

It was the last straw. The shaken nerves of the superstitious blacks gave way to the sudden strain; and almost with one accord they turned and fled the dismal city, while close upon their heels were Abu Batn and his desert warriors in swift and undignified retreat.

Peter Zveri and his three white companions, finding themselves suddenly deserted, looked at one another questioningly. "The dirty cowards!" exclaimed Zveri angrily. "You go back, Mike, and see if you can rally them. We are going on in, now that we are here."

Michael Dorsky, only too glad of any assignment that took him farther away from Opar, started at a brisk run after the fleeing warriors, while Zveri turned once more into the fissure with Miguel Romero and Paul Ivitch at his heels.

The three men passed through the outer wall and entered the court yard, across which they saw the lofty inner wall rising before them. Romero was the first to find the opening that led to the city proper and, calling to his fellows, he stepped boldly into the narrow passage. Then once again the hideous scream shattered the brooding silence of the ancient temple.

The three men halted. Zveri wiped the perspiration from his brow. "I think we have gone as far as we can alone," he said. "Perhaps we had all better go back and rally the men. There is no sense in doing anything foolhardy." Miguel Romero threw him a contemptuous sneer, but Ivitch assured Zveri that the suggestion met with his entire approval.

The two men crossed the court quickly without waiting to see whether the Mexican followed them or not and were soon once again outside the city.

"Where is Miguel?" asked Ivitch.

Zveri looked around. "Romero!" he shouted in a loud voice, but there was no reply.

"It must have got him," said Ivitch with a shudder.

"Small loss," grumbled Zveri.

But whatever the thing was that Ivitch feared, it had not, as yet, gotten the young Mexican, who, after watching his companions' precipitate flight, had continued on through the opening in the inner wall determined to have at least one look at the interior of the ancient city of Opar that he had travelled so far to see and of the fabulous wealth of which he had been dreaming for weeks.

Before his eyes spread a magnificent panorama of stately ruins, before which the young and impressionable Latin-American stood spellbound; and then once again the eerie wail rose from the interior of a great building before him, but if he was frightened Romero gave no evidence of it. Perhaps he grasped his rifle a little more tightly; perhaps he loosened his revolver in his holster, but he did not retreat. He was awed by the stately grandeur of the scene before him, where age and ruin seemed only to enhance its pristine magnificence.

A movement within the temple caught his attention. He saw a figure emerge from somewhere, the figure of a gnarled and knotted man that rolled on short crooked legs; and then another and another came until there were fully a hundred of the savage creatures approaching slowly toward him. He saw their knotted bludgeons and their knives, and he realized that here was a menace more effective than an unearthly scream.

With a shrug he backed into the passageway. "I cannot fight an army single-handed," he muttered. Slowly he crossed the outer court, passed through the first great wall and stood again upon the plain outside the city. In the distance he saw the dust of the fleeing expedition and, with a grin, he started in pursuit, swinging along at an easy walk as he puffed upon a cigarette. From the top of the rocky hill at his left a little monkey saw him pass—a little monkey, which still trembled from fright, but whose terrified screams had become only low, pitiful moans. It had been a hard day for little Nkima.

So rapid had been the retreat of the expedition that Zveri, with Dorsky and Ivitch, did not overtake the main party until the greater part of it was already descending the barrier cliffs; nor could any threats or promises stay the retreat, which ended only when camp was reached.

Immediately Zveri called Abu Batn, together with Dorsky and Ivitch, into council. The affair had been Zveri's first reverse, and it was a serious one inasmuch as he had relied heavily upon the inexhaustible store of gold to be found in the treasure vaults of Opar. First, he berated Abu Batn, Kitembo, their ancestors and all their followers for cowardice; but all that he accomplished was to arouse the anger and resentment of these two.

"We came with you to fight the white men, not demons and ghosts," said Kitembo. "I am not afraid. I would go into the city, but my men will not accompany me and I cannot fight the enemy alone."

"Nor I," said Abu Batn, a sullen scowl still further darkening his swart countenance.

"I know," sneered Zveri, "you are both brave men, but you are much better runners than you are fighters. Look at us. We were not afraid. We went in and we were not harmed."

"Where is Comrade Romero?" demanded Abu Batn.

"Well, perhaps, he is lost," admitted Zveri. "What do you expect? To win a battle without losing a man?"

"There was no battle," said Kitembo, "and the man who went farthest into the accursed city did not return."

Dorsky looked up suddenly. "There he is now!" he exclaimed, and as all eyes turned up the trail toward Opar, they saw Miguel Romero strolling jauntily into camp.

"Greeting, my brave comrades!" he cried to them. "I am glad to find you alive. I feared that you might all succumb to heart failure."

Sullen silence greeted his raillery, and no one spoke until he had approached and seated himself near them.

"What detained you?" demanded Zveri presently.

"I wanted to see what was beyond the inner wall," replied the Mexican.

"And you saw?" asked Abu Batn.

"I saw magnificent buildings in splendid ruin," replied Romero; "a dead and moldering city of the dead past."

"And what else?" asked Kitembo.

"I saw a company of strange warriors, short heavy men on crooked legs, with long powerful arms and hairy bodies. They came out of a great building that might have been a temple. There were too many of them for me. I could not fight them alone, so I came away."

"Did they have weapons?" asked Zveri.

"Clubs and knives," replied Romero.

"You see," exclaimed Zveri, "just a band of savages armed with clubs. We could take the city without the loss of a man."

"What did they look like?" demanded Kitembo. "Describe them to me," and when Romero had done so, with careful attention to details, Kitembo shook his head. "It is as I thought," he said. "They are not men; they are demons."

"Men or demons, we are going back there and take their city," said Zveri angrily. "We must have the gold of Opar."

"You may go, white man," returned Kitembo, "but you will go alone. I know my men, and I tell you that they will not follow you there. Lead us against white men, or brown men, or black men, and we will follow you. But we will not follow you against demons and ghosts."

"And you, Abu Batn?" demanded Zveri.

"I have talked with my men on the return from the city, and they tell me that they will not go back there. They will not fight the jân and ghrôl. They heard the voice of the jin warning them away, and they are afraid."

Zveri stormed and threatened and cajoled, but all to no effect. Neither the Aarab sheykh nor the African chief could be moved.

"There is still a way," said Romero.

"And what is that?" asked Zveri.

"When the gringo comes and the Philippine, there will be six of us who are neither Aarabs nor Africans. We six can take Opar." Paul Ivitch made a wry face, and Zveri cleared his throat.

"If we are killed," said the latter, "our whole plan is wrecked. There will be no one left to carry on."

Romero shrugged. "It was only a suggestion," he said, "but, of course, if you are afraid——"

"I am not afraid," stormed Zveri, "but neither am I a fool."

An ill-concealed sneer curved Romero's lips. "I am going to eat," he said, and, rising, he left them.

*　*　*

The day following his advent into the camp of his fellow conspirators, Wayne Colt wrote a long message in cipher and dispatched it to the Coast by one of his boys. From her tent Zora Drinov had seen the message given to the boy. She had seen him place it in the end of a forked stick and start off upon his long journey. Shortly after, Colt joined her in the shade of a great tree beside her tent.

"You sent a message this morning, Comrade Colt," she said.

He looked up at her quickly. "Yes," he replied.

"Perhaps you should know that only Comrade Zveri is permitted to send messages from the expedition," she told him.

"I did not know," he said. "It was merely in relation to some funds that were to have been awaiting me when I reached the Coast. They were not there. I sent the boy back after them."

"Oh," she said, and then their conversation drifted to other topics.

That afternoon he took his rifle and went out to look for game and Zora went with him, and that evening they had supper together again, but this time she was the hostess. And so the days passed until an excited native aroused the camp one day with an announcement that the expedition was returning. No words were necessary to apprise those who had been left behind that victory had not perched upon the banner of their little army. Failure was clearly written upon the faces of the leaders. Zveri greeted Zora and Colt, introducing the latter to his companions, and when Tony had been similarly presented the returning warriors threw themselves down upon cots or upon the ground to rest.

That night, as they gathered around the supper table, each party narrated the adventures that had befallen them since the expedition had left camp. Colt and Zora were thrilled by the stories of weird Opar, but no less mysterious was their tale of the death of Raghunath Jafar and his burial and uncanny resurrection.

"Not one of the boys would touch the body after that," said Zora. "Tony and Comrade Colt had to bury him themselves."

"I hope you made a good job of it this time," said Miguel.

"He hasn't come back again," rejoined Colt with a grin.

"Who could have dug him up in the first place?" demanded Zveri.

"None of the boys certainly," said Zora. "They were all too much frightened by the peculiar circumstances surrounding his death."

"It must have been the same creature that killed him," suggested Colt, "and whoever or whatever it was must have been possessed of almost superhuman strength to carry that heavy corpse into a tree and drop it upon us."

"The most uncanny feature of it to me," said Zora, "is the

fact that it was accomplished in absolute silence. I'll swear that not even a leaf rustled until just before the body hurtled down upon our table."

"It could have been only a man," said Zveri.

"Unquestionably," said Colt, "but what a man!"

As the company broke up later, repairing to their various tents, Zveri detained Zora with a gesture. "I want to talk to you a minute, Zora," he said, and the girl sank back into the chair she had just quitted. "What do you think of this American? You have had a good opportunity to size him up."

"He seems to be all right. He is a very likable fellow," replied the girl.

"He said or did nothing, then, that might arouse your suspicion?" demanded Zveri.

"No," said Zora, "nothing at all."

"You two have been alone here together for a number of days," continued Zveri. "Did he treat you with perfect respect?"

"He was certainly much more respectful than your friend, Raghunath Jafar."

"Don't mention that dog to me," said Zveri. "I wish that I had been here to kill him myself."

"I told him that you would when you got back, but someone beat you to it."

They were silent for several moments. It was evident that Zveri was trying to frame into words something that was upon his mind. At last he spoke. "Colt is a very prepossessing young man. See that you don't fall in love with him, Zora."

"And why not?" she demanded. "I have given my mind and my strength and my talent to the cause and, perhaps, most of my heart. But there is a corner of it that is mine to do with as I wish."

"You mean to say that you are in love with him?" demanded Zveri.

"Certainly not. Nothing of the kind. Such an idea had not entered my head. I just want you to know, Peter, that in matters of this kind you may not dictate to me."

"Listen, Zora. You know perfectly well that I love you, and what is more, I am going to have you. I get what I go after."

"Don't bore me, Peter. I have no time for anything so foolish as love now. When we are well through with this undertaking, perhaps I shall take the time to give it a little thought."

"I want you to give it a lot of thought right now, Zora," he insisted. "There are some details in relation to this expedition that I have not told you. I have not divulged them to anyone, but I am going to tell you now because I love you and you are going to become my wife. There is more at stake in this for us than you dream. After all the thought and all the risks and all the hardships, I do not intend to surrender all of the power and the wealth that I shall have gained to anyone."

"You mean not even to the cause?" she asked.

"I mean not even to the cause, except that I shall use them both for the cause."

"Then what do you intend? I do not understand you," she said.

"I intend to make myself Emperor of Africa," he declared, "and I intend to make you my empress."

"Peter!" she cried. "Are you crazy?"

"Yes, I am crazy for power, for riches, and for you."

"You can never do it, Peter. You know how far-reaching are the tentacles of the power we serve. If you fail it, if you turn traitor, those tentacles will reach you and drag you down to destruction."

"When I win my goal, my power will be as great as theirs, and then I may defy them."

"But how about these others with us, who are serving loyally the cause which they think you represent? They will tear you to pieces, Peter."

The man laughed. "You do not know them, Zora. They are all alike. All men and women are alike. If I offered to make them Grand Dukes and give them each a palace and a harem, they would slit their own mothers' throats to obtain such a prize."

The girl arose. "I am astounded, Peter. I thought that you, at least, were sincere."

He arose quickly and grasped her by the arm. "Listen, Zora," he hissed in her ear, "I love you, and because I love you I have put my life in your hands. But understand this, if you betray me, no matter how well I love you, I shall kill you. Do not forget that."

"You did not have to tell me that, Peter. I was perfectly well aware of it."

"And you will not betray me?" he demanded.

"I never betray a friend, Peter," she said.

The next morning Zveri was engaged in working out the

details of a second expedition to Opar based upon Romero's suggestions. It was decided that this time they would call for volunteers; and as the Europeans, the two Americans and the Filipino had already indicated their willingness to take part in the adventure, it remained now only to seek to enlist the services of some of the blacks and Arabs, and for this purpose Zveri summoned the entire company to a palaver. Here he explained just what they purposed doing. He stressed the fact that Comrade Romero had seen the inhabitants of the city and that they were only members of a race of stunted savages, armed only with sticks. Eloquently he explained how easily they might be overcome with rifles.

Practically the entire party was willing to go as far as the walls of Opar; but there were only ten warriors who would agree to enter the city with the white men, and all of these were from the askaris who had been left behind to guard camp and from those who had accompanied Colt from the Coast, none of whom had been subjected to the terrors of Opar. Not one of those who had heard the weird screams issuing from the ruins would agree to enter the city, and it was admitted among the whites that it was not at all unlikely that their ten volunteers might suddenly develop a change of heart when at last they stood before the frowning portals of Opar and heard the weird warning cry from its defenders.

Several days were spent in making careful preparations for the new expedition, but at last the final detail was completed; and early one morning Zveri and his followers set out once more upon the trail to Opar.

Zora Drinov had wished to accompany them, but as Zveri was expecting messages from a number of his various agents throughout Northern Africa, it had been necessary to leave her behind. Abu Batn and his warrors were left to guard the camp, and these, with a few black servants, were all who did not accompany the expedition.

Since the failure of the first expedition and the fiasco at the gates of Opar, the relations of Abu Batn and Zveri had been strained. The sheykh and his warriors, smarting under the charges of cowardice, had kept more to themselves than formerly; and though they would not volunteer to enter the city of Opar, they still resented the affront of their selection to remain behind as camp guards; and so it was that as the others departed, the Aarabs sat in the múk'aad of their sheykh's beyt es-sh'ar, whispering over their thick coffee, their swart scowling faces half hidden by their thorrîbs.

They did not deign even to glance at their departing comrades, but the eyes of Abu Batn were fixed upon the slender figure of Zora Drinov as the sheykh sat in silent meditation.

6

Betrayed

THE heart of little Nkima had been torn by conflicting emotions, as from the vantage point of the summit of the rocky hillock he had watched the departure of Miguel Romero from the city of Opar. Seeing these brave Tarmangani, armed with death-dealing thundersticks, driven away from the ruins, he was convinced that something terrible must have befallen his master within the grim recesses of that crumbling pile. His loyal heart prompted him to return and investigate, but Nkima was only a very little Manu —a little Manu who was very much afraid; and though he started twice again toward Opar, he could not muster his courage to the sticking point; and at last, whimpering pitifully, he turned back across the plains toward the grim forest, where, at least, the dangers were familiar ones.

* * *

The door of the gloomy chamber which Tarzan had entered swung inward, and his hands were still upon it as the menacing roar of the lion apprised him of the danger of his situation. Agile and quick is Numa, the lion, but with even greater celerity functioned the mind and muscles of Tarzan of the Apes. In the instant that the lion sprang toward him a picture of the whole scene flashed to the mind of the ape-man. He saw the gnarled priests of Opar advancing along the corridor in pursuit of him. He saw the heavy door that swung inward. He saw the charging lion, and he pieced these various factors together to create a situation far more to his advantage than

61

they normally presented. Drawing the door quickly inward, he stepped behind it as the lion charged, with the result that the beast, either carried forward by his own momentum or sensing escape, sprang into the corridor full in the faces of the advancing priests, and at the same instant Tarzan closed the door behind him.

Just what happened in the corridor without he could not see, but from the growls and screams that receded quickly into the distance he was able to draw a picture that brought a quiet smile to his lips; and an instant later a piercing shriek of agony and terror announced the fate of at least one of the fleeing Oparians.

Realizing that he would gain nothing by remaining where he was, Tarzan decided to leave the cell and seek a way out of the labyrinthine mazes of the pits beneath Opar. He knew that the lion upon its prey would doubtless bar his passage along the route he had been following when his escape had been interrupted by the priests and though, as a last resort, he might face Numa, he was of no mind to invite such an unnecessary risk; but when he sought to open the heavy door he found that he could not budge it, and in an instant he realized what had happened and that he was now in prison once again in the dungeons of Opar.

The bar that secured this particular door was not of the sliding type but, working upon a pin at the inner end, dropped into heavy wrought iron keepers bolted to the door itself and to its frame. When he had entered, he had raised the bar, which had dropped into place of its own weight when the door slammed to, imprisoning him as effectually as though the work had been done by the hand of man.

The darkness of the corridor without was less intense than that of the passage upon which his former cell had been located; and though not enough light entered the cell to illuminate its interior, there was sufficient to show him the nature of the ventilating opening in the door, which he found to consist of a number of small round holes, none of which was of sufficient diameter to permit him to pass his hand through in an attempt to raise the bar.

As Tarzan stood in momentary contemplation of his new predicament, the sound of stealthy movement came to him from the black recesses at the rear of the cell. He wheeled quickly, drawing his hunting knife from its sheath. He did not have to ask himself what the author of this sound might be, for he knew that the only other living creature that might have occupied this cell with its former inmate was another lion. Why it had not joined in the attack upon him, he could not guess, but that it would eventually seize him was a foregone conclusion. Perhaps even now it was preparing to sneak upon him. He wished that his eyes might penetrate the darkness, for if he could see the lion as it charged he might be better prepared to meet it. In the past he had met the charges of other lions, but always before he had been able to see their swift spring and to elude the sweep of their mighty talons as they reared upon their hind legs to seize him. Now it would be different, and for once in his life, Tarzan of the Apes felt death was inescapable. He knew that his time had come.

He was not afraid. He simply knew that he did not wish to die and that the price at which he would sell his life would cost his antagonist dearly. In silence he waited. Again he heard that faint, yet ominous sound. The foul air of the cell reeked with the stench of the carnivores. From somewhere in a distant corridor he heard the growling of a lion at its kill; and then a voice broke the silence.

"Who are you?" it asked. It was the voice of a woman, and it came from the back of the cell in which the ape-man was imprisoned.

"Where are you?" demanded Tarzan.

"I am here at the back of the cell," replied the woman.

"Where is the lion?"

"He went out when you opened the door," she replied.

"Yes, I know," said Tarzan, "but the other one. Where is he?"

"There is no other one. There was but one lion here and it is gone. Ah, now I know you!" she exclaimed. "I know the voice. It is Tarzan of the Apes."

"La!" exclaimed the ape-man, advancing quickly across the cell. "How could you be here with the lion and still live?"

"I am in an adjoining cell that is separated from this one by a door made of iron bars," replied La. Tarzan heard metal hinges creak. "It is not locked," she said. "It was not necessary to lock it, for it opens into this other cell where the lion was."

Groping forward through the dark, the two advanced until their hands touched one another.

La pressed close to the man. She was trembling. "I have been afraid," she said, "but I shall not be afraid now."

"I shall not be of much help to you," said Tarzan. "I also am a prisoner."

"I know it," replied La, "but I always feel safe when you are near."

"Tell me what has happened," demanded Tarzan. "How is it that Oah is posing as high priestess and you a prisoner in your own dungeons?"

"I forgave Oah her former treason when she conspired with Cadj to wrest my power from me," explained La, "but she could not exist without intrigue and duplicity. To further her ambitions, she made love to Dooth, who has been high priest since Jad-bal-ja killed Cadj. They spread stories about me through the city; and as my people have never forgiven me for my friendship for you, they succeeded in winning enough to their cause to overthrow and imprison me. All the ideas were Oah's, for Dooth and the other priests, as you well know, are stupid beasts. It was Oah's idea to imprison me thus with a lion for company, merely to make my suffering more terrible, until the time should come when she might prevail upon the priests to offer me in sacrifice to the Flaming God. In that she has had some difficulty, I know, as those who have brought my food have told me."

"How could they bring food to you here?" asked Tarzan. "No one could pass through the outer cell while the lion was there."

"There is another opening in the lion's cell, that leads into a low, narrow corridor into which they can drop meat from above. Thus they would entice the lion from this outer cell, after which they would lower a gate of iron bars across the opening of the small corridor into which he went, and while he was thus imprisoned they brought my food to me. But they did not feed him much. He was always hungry and often growling and pawing at the bars of my cell. Perhaps Oah hoped that some day he would batter them down."

"Where does this other corridor, in which they fed the lion, lead?" asked Tarzan.

"I do not know," replied La, "but I imagine that it is only a blind tunnel built in ancient times for this very purpose."

"We must have a look at it," said Tarzan. "It may offer a means of escape."

"Why not escape through the door by which you entered?" asked La; and when the ape-man had explained why this was impossible, she pointed out the location of the entrance to the small tunnel.

"We must get out of here as quickly as possible, if it is

possible at all," said Tarzan, "for if they are able to capture the lion, they will certainly return him to this cell."

"They will capture him," said La. "There is no question as to that."

"Then I had better hurry and make my investigation of the tunnel, for it might prove embarrassing were they to return him to the cell while I was in the tunnel, if it proved to be a blind one."

"I will listen at the outer door while you investigate," offered La. "Make haste."

Groping his way toward the section of the wall that La had indicated, Tarzan found a heavy grating of iron closing an aperture leading into a low and narrow corridor. Lifting the barrier, Tarzan entered and with his hands extended before him moved forward in a crouching position, since the low ceiling would not permit him to stand erect. He had progressed but a short distance when he discovered that the corridor made an abrupt right-angle turn to the left, and beyond the turn he saw at a short distance a faint luminosity. Moving quickly forward, he came to the end of the corridor, at the bottom of a vertical shaft, the interior of which was illuminated by subdued daylight. The shaft was constructed of the usual rough-hewn granite of the foundation walls of the city, but here set with no great nicety or precision, giving the interior of the shaft a rough and uneven surface.

As Tarzan was examining it, he heard La's voice coming along the tunnel from the cell in which he had left her. Her tone was one of excitement, and her message one that presaged a situation wrought with extreme danger to them both.

"Make haste, Tarzan. They are returning with the lion!"

The ape-man hurried quickly back to the mouth of the tunnel.

"Quick!" he cried to La, as he raised the gate that had fallen behind him after he had passed through.

"In there?" she demanded in an affrighted voice.

"It is our only chance of escape," replied the ape-man.

Without another word La crowded into the corridor beside him. Tarzan lowered the grating and, with La following closely behind him, returned to the opening leading into the shaft. Without a word, he lifted La in his arms and raised her as high as he could, nor did she need to be told what to do. With little difficulty she found both hand and footholds upon the rough surface of the interior of the shaft, and with

Tarzan just below her, assisting and steadying her, she made her way slowly aloft.

The shaft led directly upward into a room in the tower, which overlooked the entire city of Opar; and here, concealed by the crumbling walls, they paused to formulate their plans.

They both knew that their greatest danger lay in discovery by one of the numerous monkeys infesting the ruins of Opar, with which the inhabitants of the city are able to converse. Tarzan was anxious to be away from Opar that he might thwart the plans of the white men who had invaded his domain. But first he wished to bring about the downfall of La's enemies and reinstate her upon the throne of Opar, or if that should prove impossible, to insure the safety of her flight.

As he viewed her now in the light of day he was struck again by the matchlessness of her deathless beauty that neither time, nor care, nor danger seemed capable of dimming, and he wondered what he should do with her; where he could take her; where this savage priestess of the Flaming God could find a place in all the world, outside the walls of Opar, with the environments of which she would harmonize. And as he pondered, he was forced to admit to himself that no such place existed. La was of Opar, a savage queen born to rule a race of savage half-men. As well introduce a tigress to the salons of civilization as La of Opar. Two or three thousand years earlier she might have been a Cleopatra or a Sheba, but today she could be only La of Opar.

For some time they had sat in silence, the beautiful eyes of the high priestess resting upon the profile of the forest god. "Tarzan!" she said.

The man looked up. "What is it, La?" he asked.

"I still love you, Tarzan," she said in a low voice.

A troubled expression came into the eyes of the ape-man. "Let us not speak of that."

"I like to speak of it," she murmured. "It gives me sorrow, but it is a sweet sorrow—the only sweetness that has ever come into my life."

Tarzan extended a bronzed hand and laid it upon her slender, tapering fingers. "You have always possessed my heart, La," he said, "up to the point of love. If my affection goes no further than this, it is through no fault of mine nor yours."

La laughed. "It is certainly through no fault of mine, Tarzan," she said, "but I know that such things are not ordered by ourselves. Love is a gift of the gods. Sometimes it is awarded as a recompense; sometimes as a punishment. For me it has been a punishment, perhaps, but I would not have it otherwise. I had nurtured it in my breast since first I met you; and without that love, however hopeless it may be, I should not care to live."

Tarzan made no reply, and the two relapsed into silence, waiting for night to fall that they might descend into the city unobserved. Tarzan's alert mind was occupied with plans for reinstating La upon her throne, and presently they fell to discussing these.

"Just before the Flaming God goes to his rest at night," said La, "the priests and the priestesses all gather in the throne room. There they will be tonight before the throne upon which Oah will be seated. Then may we descend to the city."

"And then what?" asked Tarzan.

"If we can kill Oah in the throne room," said La, "and Dooth at the same time, they would have no leaders; and without leaders they are lost."

"I cannot kill a woman," said Tarzan.

"I can," returned La, "and you can attend to Dooth. You certainly would not object to killing him?"

"If he attacked, I would kill him," said Tarzan, "but not otherwise. Tarzan of the Apes kills only in self-defense and for food, or when there is no other way to thwart an enemy."

In the floor of the ancient room in which they were waiting were two openings; one was the mouth of the shaft through which they had ascended from the dungeons, the other opened into a similar but larger shaft, to the bottom of which ran a long wooden ladder set in the masonry of its sides. It was this shaft which offered them a means of escape from the tower, and as Tarzan sat with his eyes resting idly upon the opening, an unpleasant thought suddenly obtruded itself upon his consciousness.

He turned toward La. "We had forgotten," he said, "that whoever casts the meat down the shaft to the lion must ascend by this other shaft. We may not be as safe from detection here as we had hoped."

"They do not feed the lion very often," said La; "not every day."

"When did they feed him last?" asked Tarzan.

"I do not recall," said La. "Time drags so heavily in the darkness of the cell that I lost count of days."

"S-st!" cautioned Tarzan. "Someone is ascending now."

Silently the ape-man arose and crossed the floor to the opening, where he crouched upon the side opposite the ladder. La moved stealthily to his side, so that the ascending man, whose back would be toward them, as he emerged from the shaft, would not see them. Slowly the man ascended. They could hear his shuffling progress coming nearer and nearer to the top. He did not climb as the ape-like priests of Opar are wont to climb. Tarzan thought perhaps he was carrying a load either of such weight or cumbersomeness as to retard his progress, but when finally his head came into view the ape-man saw that he was an old man, which accounted for his lack of agility; and then powerful fingers closed about the throat of the unsuspecting Oparian, and he was lifted bodily out of the shaft.

"Silence!" said the ape-man. "Do as you are told and you will not be harmed."

La had snatched a knife from the girdle of their victim, and now Tarzan forced him to the floor of the room and slightly released his hold upon the fellow's throat, turning him around so that he faced them.

An expression of incredulity and surprise crossed the face of the old priest as his eyes fell upon La.

"Darus!" exclaimed La.

"All honor to the Flaming God who has ordered your escape!" exclaimed the priest.

La turned to Tarzan. "You need not fear Darus," she said; "he will not betray us. Of all the priests of Opar, there never lived one more loyal to his queen."

"That is right," said the old man, shaking his head.

"Are there many more loyal to the high priestess, La?" demanded Tarzan.

"Yes, very many," replied Darus, "but they are afraid. Oah is a she-devil and Dooth is a fool. Between the two of them there is no longer either safety or happiness in Opar."

"How many are there whom you absolutely know may be depended upon?" demanded La.

"Oh, very many," replied Darus.

"Gather them in the throne room tonight then, Darus; and as the Flaming God goes to his couch, be ready to strike at the enemies of La, your priestess."

"You will be there?" asked Darus.

"I shall be there," replied La. "This, your dagger, shall be the signal. When you see La of Opar plunge it into the breast of Oah, the false priestess, fall upon those who are the enemies of La."

"It shall be done, just as you say," Darus assured her, "and now I must throw this meat to the lion and be gone."

Slowly the old priest descended the ladder, gibbering and muttering to himself, after he had cast a few bones and scraps of meat into the other shaft to the lion.

"You are quite sure you can trust him, La?" demanded Tarzan.

"Absolutely," replied the girl. "Darus would die for me, and I know that he hates Oah and Dooth."

The slow remaining hours of the afternoon dragged on, the sun was low in the west, and now the two must take their greatest risk, that of descending into the city while it was still light and making their way to the throne room, although the risk was greatly minimized by the fact that the inhabitants of the city were all supposed to be congregated in the throne room at this time, performing the age-old rite with which they speeded the Flaming God to his night of rest. Without interruption they descended to the base of the tower, crossed the courtyard and entered the temple. Here, through devious and round-about passages, La led the way to a small doorway that opened into the throne room at the back of the dais upon which the throne stood. Here she paused, listening to the services being conducted within the great chamber, waiting for the cue that would bring them to a point when all within the room, except the high priestess, were prostrated with their faces pressed against the floor.

When that instant arrived, La swung open the door and leaped silently upon the dais behind the throne in which her victim sat. Close behind her came Tarzan, and in that first instant both realized that they had been betrayed, for the dais was swarming with priests ready to seize them.

Already one had caught La by an arm, but before he could drag her away Tarzan sprang upon him, seized him by the neck and jerked his head backward so suddenly and with such force that the sound of his snapping vertebra could be heard across the room. Then he raised the body high above his head and cast it into the faces of the priests charging upon him. As they staggered back, he seized La and swung her into the corridor along which they had approached the throne room.

It was useless to stand and fight, for he knew that even though he might hold his own for a while, they must eventually overcome him and that once they laid their hands upon La they would tear her limb from limb.

Down the corridor behind them came the yelling horde of priests, and in their wake, screaming for the blood of her victim, was Oah.

"Make for the outer walls by the shortest route, La," directed Tarzan, and the girl sped on winged feet, leading him through the labyrinthine corridors of the ruins, until they broke suddenly into the chamber of the seven pillars of gold, and then Tarzan knew the way.

No longer needing his guide, and realizing that the priests were overtaking them, being fleeter of foot than La, he swept the girl into his arms and sped through the echoing chambers of the temple toward the inner wall. Through that, across the courtyard and through the outer wall they passed, and still the priests pursued, urged on by screaming Oah. Out across the deserted valley they fled; and now the priests were losing ground, for their short, crooked legs could not compete with the speed of Tarzan's clean limbed stride, even though he was burdened by the weight of La.

The sudden darkness of the near tropics that follows the setting of the sun soon obliterated the pursuers from their sight; and a short time thereafter the sounds of pursuit ceased, and Tarzan knew that the chase had been abandoned, for the men of Opar have no love for the darkness of the outer world.

Then Tarzan paused and lowered La to the ground; but as he did so her soft arms encircled his neck and she pressed close to him, her cheek against his breast, and burst into tears.

"Do not cry, La," he said. "We shall come again to Opar, and when we do you shall be seated upon your throne again."

"I am not crying for that," she replied.

"Then why do you cry?" he asked.

"I am crying for joy," she said, "joy that perhaps I shall be alone with you now for a long time."

In pity, Tarzan pressed her to him for a moment, and then they set off once more toward the barrier cliff.

That night they slept in a great tree in the forest at the foot of the cliff, after Tarzan had constructed a rude couch for La between two branches, while he settled himself in a crotch of the tree a few feet below her.

It was dawn when Tarzan awoke. The sky was overcast, and he sensed an approaching storm. No food had passed his lips for many hours, and he knew that La had not eaten since the morning of the previous day. Food, therefore, was a prime essential and he must find it and return to La before the storm broke. Since it was meat that he craved, he knew that he must be able to make fire and cook it before La could eat it, though he himself still preferred it raw. He looked into La's cot and saw that she was still asleep. Knowing that she must be exhausted from all that she had passed through the previous day, he let her sleep on; and swinging to a nearby tree, he set out upon his search for food.

As he moved up wind through the middle terrace, every faculty of his delicately attuned senses was alert. Like the lion, Tarzan particularly relished the flesh of Pacco, the zebra, but either Bara, the antelope, or Horta, the boar, would have proven an acceptable substitute; but the forest seemed to be deserted by every member of the herds he sought. Only the scent spoor of the great cats assailed his nostrils, mingled with the lesser and more human odor of Manu, the monkey. Time means little to a hunting beast. It meant little to Tarzan, who, having set out in search of meat, would return only when he had found meat.

When La awakened, it was some time before she could place her surroundings; but when she did, a slow smile of happiness and contentment parted her lovely lips, revealing an even row of perfect teeth. She sighed, and then she whispered the name of the man she loved. "Tarzan!" she called.

There was no reply. Again she spoke his name, but this time louder, and again the only answer was silence. Slightly troubled, she arose upon an elbow and leaned over the side of her sleeping couch. The tree beneath her was empty.

She thought, correctly, that perhaps he had gone to hunt, but still she was troubled by his absence, and the longer she waited the more troubled she became. She knew that he did not love her and that she must be a burden to him. She knew, too, that he was as much a wild beast as the lions of the forest and that the same desire for freedom, which animated them, must animate him. Perhaps he had been unable to withstand the temptation longer and while she slept, he had left her.

There was not a great deal in the training or ethics of La of Opar that could have found exception to such conduct, for the life of her people was a life of ruthless selfishness and cruelty. They entertained few of the finer sensibilities of civilized man, or the great nobility of character that marked so many of the wild beasts. Her love for Tarzan had been the only soft spot in La's savage life, and realizing that she would think nothing of deserting a creature she did not love, she was fair enough to cast no reproaches upon Tarzan for having done the thing that she might have done, nor to her mind did it accord illy with her conception of his nobility of character.

As she descended to the ground, she sought to determine some plan of action for the future, and in this moment of her loneliness and depression she saw no alternative but to return to Opar, and so it was toward the city of her birth that she turned her steps; but she had not gone far before she realized the danger and futility of this plan, which could but lead to certain death while Oah and Dooth ruled in Opar. She felt bitterly toward Darus, who she believed had betrayed her; and accepting his treason as an index of what she might expect from others whom she had believed to be friendly to her, she realized the utter hopelessness of regaining the throne of Opar without outside help. La had no happy life to which she might look forward; but the will to live was yet strong within her, the result more, perhaps, of the courageousness of her spirit than of any fear of death, which, to her, was but another word for defeat.

She paused in the trail that she had reached a short distance from the tree in which she had spent the night; and there, with almost nothing to guide her, she sought to determine in what direction she should break a new trail into the future, for wherever she went, other than back to Opar, it would be a new trail, leading among peoples and experiences as foreign to her as though she had suddenly stepped from another planet, or from the long-lost continent of her progenitors.

It occurred to her that perhaps there might be other people in this strange world as generous and chivalrous as Tarzan. At least in this direction there lay hope. In Opar there was none, and so she turned back away from Opar; and above her black clouds rolled and billowed as the storm king marshalled his forces, and behind her a tawny beast with gleaming eyes slunk through the underbrush beside the trail that she followed.

7

In Futile Search

T ARZAN of the Apes, ranging far in search of food, caught
at length the welcome scent of Horta, the boar. The man
paused and, with a deep and silent inhalation, filled his
lungs with air until his great bronzed chest expanded to the
full. Already he was tasting the fruits of victory. The red
blood coursed through his veins, as every fiber of his being
reacted to the exhilaration of the moment—the keen delight
of the hunting beast that has scented its quarry. And then
swiftly and silently he sped in the direction of his prey.

Presently he came upon it, a young tusker, powerful and
agile, his wicked tusks gleaming as he tore bark from a
young tree. The ape-man was poised just above him, concealed by the foliage of a great tree.

A vivid flash of lightning broke from the billowing black
clouds above. Thunder crashed and boomed. The storm
broke, and at the same instant the man launched himself
downward upon the back of the unsuspecting boar, in one
hand the hunting knife of his long-dead sire.

The weight of the man's body crushed the boar to the
earth, and before it could struggle to its feet again, the keen
blade had severed its jugular. Its life blood gushing from the
wound, the boar sought to rise and turn to fight; but the steel
thews of the ape-man dragged it down, and an instant later,
with a last convulsive shudder, Horta died.

Leaping to his feet, Tarzan placed a foot upon the carcass
of his kill and, raising his face to the heavens, gave voice to
the victory cry of the bull-ape.

Faintly to the ears of marching men came the hideous scream. The blacks in the party halted, wide-eyed.

"What the devil was that?" demanded Zveri.

"It sounded like a panther," said Colt.

"That was no panther," said Kitembo. "It was the cry of a bull-ape who has made a kill, or——"

"Or what?" demanded Zveri.

Kitembo looked fearfully in the direction from which the sound had come. "Let us get away from here," he said.

Again the lightning flashed and the thunder crashed, and as the torrential rain deluged them, the party staggered on in the direction of the barrier cliffs of Opar.

* * *

Cold and wet, La of Opar crouched beneath a great tree that only partially protected her almost naked body from the fury of the storm, and in the dense underbrush a few yards from her a tawny carnivore lay with unblinking eyes fixed steadily upon her.

The storm, titanic in its brief fury, passed on, leaving the deep worn trail a tiny torrent of muddy water; and La, thoroughly chilled, hastened onward in an effort to woo new warmth to her chilled body.

She knew that trails must lead somewhere, and in her heart she hoped that this one would lead to the country of Tarzan. If she could live there, seeing him occasionally, she would be content. Even knowing that he was near her would be better than nothing. Of course she had no conception of the immensity of the world she trod. A knowledge of even the extent of the forest that surrounded her would have appalled her. In her imagination she visualized a small world, dotted with the remains of ruined cities like Opar, in which dwelt creatures like those she had known; gnarled and knotted men like the priests of Opar, white men like Tarzan, black men such as she had seen, and great shaggy gorillas like Bolgani, who had ruled in the Valley of the Palace of Diamonds.

And thinking these thoughts, she came at last to a clearing into which the unbroken rays of the warm sun poured without interruption. Near the center of the clearing was a small boulder; and toward this she made her way with the intention of basking in the warm rays of the sun until she should be thoroughly dried and warmed, for the dripping foliage of the forest had kept her wet and cold even after the rain had ceased.

As she seated herself she saw a movement at the edge of the clearing ahead of her, and an instant later a great leopard bounded into view. The beast paused at sight of the woman, evidently as much surprised as she; and then, apparently realizing the defenselessness of this unexpected prey, the creature crouched and with twitching tail slowly wormed itself forward.

La rose and drew from her girdle the knife that she had taken from Darus. She knew that flight was futile. In a few bounds the great beast could overtake her, and even had there been a tree that she could have reached before she was overtaken, it would have proven no sanctuary from a leopard. Defense, too, she knew to be futile, but surrender without battle was not within the fiber of La of Opar.

The metal discs, elaborately wrought by the hands of some long-dead goldsmith of ancient Opar, rose and fell above her firm breasts as her heart beat, perhaps a bit more rapidly, beneath them. On came the leopard. She knew that in an instant he would charge; and then of a sudden he rose to his feet, his back arched, his mouth grinning in a fearful snarl; and simultaneously a tawny streak whizzed by her from behind, and she saw a great lion leap upon her would-be destroyer.

At the last instant, but too late, the leopard had turned to flee; and the lion seized him by the back of the neck, and with his jaws and one great paw he twisted the head back until the spine snapped. Then, almost contemptuously, he cast the body from him and turned toward the girl.

In an instant La realized what had happened. The lion had been stalking her, and seeing another about to seize his prey, he had leaped to battle in its defense. She had been saved, but only to fall victim immediately to another and more terrible beast.

The lion stood looking at her. She wondered why he did not charge and claim his prey. She did not know that within that little brain the scent of the woman had aroused the memory of another day, when Tarzan had lain bound upon the sacrificial altar of Opar with Jad-bal-ja, the golden lion, standing guard above him. A woman had come—this same woman —and Tarzan, his master, had told him not to harm her, and she had approached and cut the bonds that secured him.

This Jad-bal-ja remembered, and he remembered, too, that

he was not to harm this woman; and if he was not to harm
her, then nothing must harm her. For this reason he had killed
Sheeta, the leopard.

But all this, La of Opar did not know, for she had not
recognized Jad-bal-ja. She merely wondered how much longer
it would be; and when the lion came closer she steeled herself, for still she meant to fight; yet there was something in his
attitude that she could not understand. He was not charging;
he was merely walking toward her, and when he was a couple
of yards from her he half turned away and lay down and
yawned.

For what seemed an eternity to the girl she stood there
watching him. He paid no attention to her. Could it be that,
sure of his prey and not yet hungry, he merely waited until he
was quite ready to make his kill? The idea was horrible, and
even La's iron nerves commenced to weaken beneath the
strain.

She knew that she could not escape, and so better instant
death than this suspense. She determined, therefore, to end
the matter quickly and to discover once and for all whether
the lion considered her already his prey or would permit
her to depart. Gathering all the forces of self-control that she
possessed, she placed the point of her dagger to her heart and
walked boldly past the lion. Should he attack her, she
would end the agony instantly by plunging the blade
into her heart.

Jad-bal-ja did not move, but with lazy, half-closed eyes he
watched the woman cross the clearing and disappear beyond
the turn of the trail that wound its way back into the jungle.

All that day La moved on with grim determination, looking
always for a ruined city like Opar, astonished by the immensity of the forest, appalled by its loneliness. Surely, she
thought, she must soon come to the country of Tarzan. She
found fruits and tubers to allay her hunger, and as the trail
descended a valley in which a river ran, she did not want for
water. But night came again, and still no sight of man or city.
Once again she crept into a tree to sleep, but this time there
was no Tarzan of the Apes to fashion a couch for her or to
watch over her safety.

* * *

After Tarzan had slain the boar, he cut off the hind
quarters and started back to the tree in which he had left La.

The storm made his progress much slower than it otherwise would have been, but notwithstanding this he realized long before he reached his destination that his hunting had taken him much farther afield than he had imagined.

When at last he reached the tree and found that La was not there, he was slightly disconcerted, but thinking that perhaps she had descended to stretch her limbs after the storm, he called her name aloud several times. Receiving no answer, he became genuinely apprehensive for her safety and, dropping to the ground, sought some sign of her spoor. It so happened that beneath the tree her footprints were still visible, not having been entirely obliterated by the rain. He saw that they led back in the direction of Opar, so that, although he lost them when they reached the trail, in which water still was running, he was none the less confident that he knew her intended destination; and so he set off in the direction of the barrier cliff.

It was not difficult for him to account for her absence and for the fact that she was returning to Opar, and he reproached himself for his thoughtlessness in having left her for so long a time without first telling her of his purpose. He guessed, rightly, that she had imagined herself deserted and had turned back to the only home she knew, to the only place in the world where La of Opar might hope to find friends; but that she would find them even there Tarzan doubted, and he was determined that she must not go back until she could do so with a force of warriors sufficiently great to insure the overthrow of her enemies.

It had been Tarzan's plan first to thwart the scheme of the party whose camp he had discovered in his dominion and then to return with La to the country of his Waziri, where he would gather a sufficient body of those redoubtable warriors to insure the safety and success of La's return to Opar. Never communicative, he had neglected to explain his purposes to La; and this he now regretted, since he was quite certain that had he done so she would not have felt it necessary to have attempted to return alone to Opar.

But he was not much concerned with the outcome since he was confident that he could overtake her long before she reached the city; and, enured as he was to the dangers of the forest and the jungle, he minimized their importance, as we do those which confront us daily in the ordinary course of our seemingly humdrum existence, where death threatens us quite as constantly as it does the denizens of the jungle.

At any moment expecting to catch sight of her whom he
sought, Tarzan traversed the back trail to the foot of the rocky
escarpment that guards the plain of Opar; and now he commenced to have his doubts, for it did not seem possible that La
could have covered so great a distance in so short a time.
He scaled the cliff and came out upon the summit of the flat
mountain that overlooked distant Opar. Here only a light
rain had fallen, the storm having followed the course of the
valley below, and plain in the trail were the footprints of
himself and La where they had passed down from Opar the
night before; but nowhere was there any sign of spoor to
indicate that the girl had returned, nor, as he looked out
across the valley, was there any moving thing in sight.

What had become of her? Where could she have gone? In
the great forest that spread below him there were countless
trails. Somewhere below, her spoor must be plain in the
freshly-wet earth, but he realized that even for him it might
prove a long and difficult task to pick it up again.

As he turned back rather sorrowfully to descend the barrier cliff, his attention was attracted by a movement at the
edge of the forest below. Dropping to his belly behind a low
bush, Tarzan watched the spot to which his attention had been
attracted; and as he did so the head of a column of men de-
bouched from the forest and moved toward the foot of the
cliff.

Tarzan had known nothing of what had transpired upon the
occasion of Zveri's first expedition to Opar, which had occurred while he had been incarcerated in the cell beneath the
city. The apparent mysterious disappearance of the party
that he had known to have been marching on Opar had
mystified him; but here it was again, and where it had been
in the meantime was of no moment.

Tarzan wished that he had his bow and arrow, which the
Oparians had taken from him and which he had not had an
opportunity to replace since he had escaped. But if he did not
have them, there were other ways of annoying the invaders.
From his position he watched them approach the cliff and
commence the ascent.

Tarzan selected a large boulder, many of which were
strewn about the flat top of the mountain, and when the
leaders of the party were about half way to the summit and
the others were strung out below them, the ape-man pushed
the rock over the edge of the cliff just above them. In its
descent it just grazed Zveri, struck a protuberance beyond

him, bounded over Colt's head, and carried two of Kitembo's warriors to death at the base of the escarpment.

The ascent stopped instantly. Several of the blacks who had accompanied the first expedition started a hasty retreat; and utter disorganization and rout faced the expedition, whose nerves had become more and more sensitive the nearer that they approached Opar.

"Stop the damn cowards!" shouted Zveri to Dorsky and Ivitch, who were bringing up the rear. "Who will volunteer to go over the top and investigate?"

"I'll go," said Romero.

"And I'll go with him," offered Colt.

"Who else?" demanded Zveri; but no one else volunteered, and already the Mexican and the American were climbing upward.

"Cover our advance with a few rifles," Colt shouted back to Zveri. "That ought to keep them away from the edge."

Zveri issued instructions to several of the askaris who had not joined in the retreat; and when their rifles commenced popping, it put new heart into those who had started to flee, and presently Dorsky and Ivitch had rallied the men and the ascent was resumed.

Perfectly well aware that he might not stop the advance single-handed, Tarzan had withdrawn quickly along the edge of the cliff to a spot where tumbled masses of granite offered concealment and where he knew that there existed a precipitous trail to the bottom of the cliff. Here he could remain and watch, or, if necessary, make a hasty retreat. He saw Romero and Colt reach the summit and immediately recognized the latter as the man he had seen in the base camp of the invaders. He had previously been impressed by the appearance of the young American, and now he acknowledged his unquestioned bravery and that of his companion in leading a party over the summit of the cliff in the face of an unknown danger.

Romero and Colt looked quickly about them, but there was no enemy in sight, and this word they passed back to the ascending company.

From his point of vantage Tarzan watched the expedition surmount the summit of the cliff and start on its march toward Opar. He believed that they could never find the treasure vaults; and now that La was not in the city, he was not concerned with the fate of those who had turned against her. Upon the bare and inhospitable Oparian plain, or in the

city itself, they could accomplish little in furthering the
objects of the expedition he had overheard Zora Drinov
explaining to Colt. He knew that eventually they must return
to their base camp, and in the meantime he would prosecute
his search for La; and so as Zveri led his expedition once
again toward Opar, Tarzan of the Apes slipped over the edge
of the barrier cliff and descended swiftly to the forest below.

Just inside the forest and upon the bank of the river was
an admirable camp site; and having noticed that the expedition
was accompanied by no porters, Tarzan naturally assumed
that they had established a temporary camp within striking
distance of the city, and it occurred to him that in this
camp he might find La a prisoner.

As he had expected, he found the camp located upon the
spot where, upon other occasions, he had camped with his
Waziri warriors. An old thorn boma that had encircled it for
years had been repaired by the newcomers, and within it a
number of rude shelters had been erected, while in the center
stood the tents of the white men. Porters were dozing in the
shade of the trees; a single askari made a pretense of standing
guard, while his fellows lolled at their ease, their rifles at their
sides; but nowhere could he see La of Opar.

He moved down wind from the camp, hoping to catch her
scent spoor if she was a prisoner there, but so strong was the
smell of smoke and the body odors of the blacks that he could
not be sure but that these drowned La's scent. He decided,
therefore, to wait until darkness had fallen when he might
make a more careful investigation, and he was further
prompted to this decision by the sight of weapons, which he
sorely needed. All of the warriors were armed with rifles, but
some, clinging through force of ancient habit to the weapons
of their ancestors, carried also bows and arrows, and in
addition there were many spears.

As a few mouthfuls of the raw flesh of Horta had constituted the only food that had passed Tarzan's lips for almost two
days, he was ravenously hungry. With the discovery that La
had disappeared, he had cached the hind quarter of the
boar in the tree in which they had spent the night and set
out upon his fruitless search for her; so now, while he waited
for darkness, he hunted again, and this time Bara, the antelope, fell a victim to his prowess, nor did he leave the
carcass of his kill until he had satisfied his hunger. Then he
lay up in a nearby tree and slept.

* * *

The anger of Abu Batn against Zveri was rooted deeply in his inherent racial antipathy for Europeans and their religion, and its growth was stimulated by the aspersions which the Russian had cast upon the courage of the Aarab and his followers.

"Dog of a Nasrâny!" ejaculated the sheykh. "He called us cowards, we Bedaùwy, and he left us here like old men and boys to guard the camp and the woman."

"He is but an instrument of Allah," said one of the Aarabs, "in the great cause that will rid Africa of all Nasrâny."

"Wellah-billah!" ejaculated Abu Batn. "What proof have we that these people will do as they promise? I would rather have my freedom on the desert and what wealth I can gather by myself than to lie longer in the same camp with these Nasrâny pigs."

"There is no good in them," muttered another.

"I have looked upon their woman," said the sheykh, "and I find her good. I know a city where she would bring many pieces of gold."

"In the trunk of the chief Nasrâny there are many pieces of gold and silver," said one of the men. "His boy told that to a Galla, who repeated it to me."

"The plunder of the camp is rich besides," suggested a swarthy warrior.

"If we do this thing, perhaps the great cause will be lost," suggested he who had first answered the sheykh.

"It is the cause of the Nasrâny," said Abu Batn, "and it is only for profit. Is not the huge pig always reminding us of the money, and the women, and the power that we shall have when we have thrown out the English? Man is moved only by his greed. Let us take our profits in advance and be gone."

Wamala was preparing the evening meal for his mistress. "Before, you were left with the brown bwana," he said, "and he was no good; nor do I like any better the sheykh Abu Batn. He is no good. I wish that Bwana Colt were here."

"So do I," said Zora. "It seems to me that the Aarabs have been sullen and surly ever since the expedition returned from Opar."

"They have sat all day in the tent of their chief talking together," said Wamala, "and often Abu Batn looked at you."

"That is your imagination, Wamala," replied the girl. "He would not dare to harm me."

"Who would have thought that the brown bwana would have dared to?" Wamala reminded her.

"Hush, Wamala, the first thing you know you will have me frightened," said Zora, and then suddenly, "Look, Wamala! Who is that?"

The black boy turned his eyes in the direction toward which his mistress was looking. At the edge of the camp stood a figure that might have wrung an exclamation of surprise from a Stoic. A beautiful woman stood there regarding them intently. She had halted just at the edge of camp—an almost naked woman whose gorgeous beauty was her first and most striking characteristic. Two golden discs covered her firm breasts, and a narrow stomacher of gold and precious stones encircled her hips, supporting in front and behind a broad strip of soft leather, studded with gold and jewels, which formed the pattern of a pedestal on the summit of which was seated a grotesque bird. Her feet were shod in sandals that were covered with mud, as were her shapely legs upward to above her knees. A mass of wavy hair, shot with golden bronze lights by the rays of the setting sun, half surrounded an oval face, and from beneath narrow penciled brows fearless gray eyes regarded them.

Some of the Aarabs had caught sight of her, too, and they were coming forward now toward her. She looked quickly from Zora and Wamala toward the others. Then the European girl arose quickly and approached her that she might reach her before the Arabs did; and as she came near the stranger with outstretched hands, Zora smiled. La of Opar came quickly to meet her as though sensing in the smile of the other an index to the friendly intent of this stranger.

"Who are you," asked Zora, "and what are you doing here alone in the jungle?"

La shook her head and replied in a language that Zora did not understand.

Zora Drinov was an accomplished linguist but she exhausted every language in her repertoire, including a few phrases from various Bantu dialects, and still found no means of communicating with the stranger, whose beautiful face and figure but added to the interest of the tantalizing enigma she presented to pique the curiosity of the Russian girl.

The Aarabs addressed her in their own tongue and Wamala

in the dialect of his tribe, but all to no avail. Then Zora put an arm about her and led her toward her tent; and there, by means of signs, La of Opar indicated that she would bathe. Wamala was directed to prepare a tub in Zora's tent, and by the time supper was prepared the stranger reappeared, washed and refreshed.

As Zora Drinov seated herself opposite her strange guest, she was impressed with the belief that never before had she looked upon so beautiful a woman, and she marvelled that one who must have felt so utterly out of place in her surroundings should still retain a poise that suggested the majestic bearing of a queen rather than of a stranger ill at ease.

By signs and gestures, Zora sought to converse with her guest until even the regal La found herself laughing; and then La tried it too until Zora knew that her guest had been threatened with clubs and knives and driven from her home, that she had walked a long way, that either a lion or a leopard had attacked her and that she was very tired.

When supper was over, Wamala prepared another cot for La in the tent with Zora, for something in the faces of the Aarabs had made the European girl fear for the safety of her beautiful guest.

"You must sleep outside the tent door tonight, Wamala," she said. "Here is an extra pistol."

In his goat hair beyt Abu Batn, the sheykh, talked long into the night with the principal men of his tribe. "The new one," he said, "will bring a price such as has never been paid before."

* * *

Tarzan awoke and glanced upward through the foliage at the stars. He saw that the night was half gone, and he arose and stretched himself. He ate again sparingly of the flesh of Bara and slipped silently into the shadows of the night.

The camp at the foot of the barrier cliff slept. A single askari kept guard and tended the beast fire. From a tree at the edge of the camp two eyes watched him, and when he was looking away a figure dropped silently into the shadows. Behind the huts of the porters it crept, pausing occasionally to test the air with dilated nostrils. It came at last, among the shadows, to the tents of the Europeans, and one by one it ripped a hole in each rear wall and entered. It was Tarzan searching for La, but he did not find her and, disappointed, he turned to another matter.

Making a half circuit of the camp, moving sometimes only inch by inch as he wormed himself along on his belly, lest the askari upon guard might see him, he made his way to the shelters of the other askaris, and there he selected a bow and arrows, and a stout spear, but even yet he was not done.

For a long time he crouched waiting—waiting until the askari by the fire should turn in a certain direction.

Presently the sentry arose and threw some dry wood upon the fire, after which he walked toward the shelter of his fellows to awaken the man who was to relieve him. It was this moment for which Tarzan had been waiting. The path of the askari brought him close to where Tarzan lay in hiding. The man approached and passed, and in the same instant Tarzan leaped to his feet and sprang upon the unsuspecting black. A strong arm encircled the fellow from behind and swung him to a broad, bronzed shoulder. As Tarzan had anticipated, a scream of terror burst from the man's lips, awakening his fellows; and then he was borne swiftly through the shadows of the camp away from the beast fire as, with his prey struggling futilely in his grasp, the ape-man leaped the thorn boma and disappeared into the black jungle beyond.

So sudden and violent was the attack, so complete the man's surprise, that he had loosened his grasp upon his rifle in an effort to clutch his antagonist as he was thrown lightly to the shoulder of his captor.

His screams, echoing through the forest, brought his terrified companions from their shelters in time to see an indistinct form leap the boma and vanish into the darkness. They stood temporarily paralyzed by fright, listening to the diminishing cries of their comrade. Presently these ceased as suddenly as they had commenced. Then the headman found his voice.

"Simba!" he said.

"It was not Simba," declared another. "It ran high upon two legs, like a man. I saw it."

Presently from the dark jungle came a hideous, long-drawn cry. "That is the voice of neither man nor lion," said the headman.

"It is a demon," whispered another, and then they huddled about the fire, throwing dry wood upon it until its blaze had crackled high into the air.

In the darkness of the jungle Tarzan paused and laid aside his spear and bow, possession of which had permitted him to use but one hand in his abduction of the sentry. Now the fingers of his free hand closed upon the throat of his victim, putting a sudden period to his screams. Only for an instant did Tarzan choke the man; and when he relaxed his grasp upon the fellow's throat, the black made no further outcry, fearing to invite again the ungentle grip of those steel fingers. Quickly Tarzan jerked the fellow to his feet, relieved him of his knife and, grasping him by his thick wool, pushed him ahead of him into the jungle, after stooping to retrieve his spear and bow. It was then that he voiced the victory cry of the bull-ape, for the value of the effect that it would have not only upon his victim, but upon his fellows in the camp behind them.

Tarzan had no intention of harming the fellow. His quarrel was not with the innocent black tools of the white men; and, while he would not have hesitated to take the life of the black had it been necessary, he knew them well enough to know that he might effect his purpose with them as well without bloodshed as with it.

The whites could not accomplish anything without their black allies, and if Tarzan could successfully undermine the morale of the latter, the schemes of their masters would be as effectually thwarted as though he had destroyed them, since he was confident that they would not remain in a district where they were constantly reminded of the presence of a malign, supernatural enemy. Furthermore, this policy accorded better with Tarzan's grim sense of humor and, therefore, amused him, which the taking of life never did.

For an hour he marched his victim ahead of him in an utter silence, which he knew would have its effect upon the nerves of the black man. Finally he halted him, stripped his remaining clothing from him, and taking the fellow's loin cloth bound his wrists and ankles together loosely. Then, appropriating his cartridge belt and other belongings, Tarzan left him, knowing that the black would soon free himself from his bonds; yet, believing that he had made his escape, would remain for life convinced that he had narrowly eluded a terrible fate.

Satisfied with his night's work, Tarzan returned to the tree in which he had cached the carcass of Bara, ate once more and lay up in sleep until morning, when he again took up his search for La, seeking trace of her up the valley beyond the barrier cliff of Opar, in the general direction that her spoor had indicated she had gone, though, as a matter of fact, she had gone in precisely the opposite direction, down the valley.

8

The Treachery of Abu Batn

NIGHT was falling when a frightened little monkey took refuge in a tree top. For days he had been wandering through the jungle, seeking in his little mind a solution for his problem during those occasional intervals that he could concentrate his mental forces upon it. But in an instant he might forget it to go swinging and scampering through the trees, or again a sudden terror would drive it from his consciousness, as one or another of the hereditary menaces to his existence appeared within the range of his perceptive faculties.

While his grief lasted, it was real and poignant, and tears welled in the eyes of little Nkima as he thought of his absent master. Lurking always within him upon the borderland of conviction was the thought that he must obtain succor for Tarzan. In some way he must fetch aid to his master. The great black Gomangani warriors, who were also the servants of Tarzan, were many darknesses away, but yet it was in the general direction of the country of the Waziri that he drifted. Time was in no sense the essence of the solution of this or any other problem in the mind of Nkima. He had seen Tarzan enter Opar alive. He had not seen him destroyed, nor had he seen him come out of the city; and, therefore, by the standards of his logic Tarzan must still be alive and in the city, but because the city was filled with enemies Tarzan must be in danger. As conditions were they would remain. He could not readily visualize any change that he did not actually witness, and so, whether he found and fetched the Waziri today or tomorrow would have little effect upon the result. They

would go to Opar and kill Tarzan's enemies, and then little
Nkima would have his master once more, and he would not
have to be afraid of Sheeta, or Sabor, or Histah.

Night fell, and in the forest Nkima heard a gentle tapping.
He aroused himself and listened intently. The tapping grew in
volume until it rolled and moved through the jungle. Its source
was at no great distance, and as Nkima became aware of this,
his excitement grew.

The moon was well up in the heavens, but the shadows of
the jungle were dense. Nkima was upon the horns of a
dilemma, between his desire to go to the place from which
the drumming emanated and his fear of the dangers that
might lie along the way; but at length the urge prevailed over
his terror, and keeping well up in the relatively greater safety
of the tree tops, he swung quickly in the direction from which
the sound was coming to halt at last, above a little natural
clearing that was roughly circular in shape.

Below him, in the moonlight, he witnessed a scene that he
had spied upon before, for here the great apes of To-yat were
engaged in the death dance of the Dum-Dum. In the center
of the amphitheater was one of those remarkable earthen
drums, which from time immemorial primitive man has heard,
but which few have seen. Before the drum were seated two
old shes, who beat upon its resounding surface with short
sticks. There was a rough rhythmic cadence to their beating,
and to it, in a savage circle, danced the bulls; while encircling
them in a thin outer line, the females and the young squatted
upon their haunches, enthralled spectators of the savage
scene. Close beside the drum lay the dead body of Shetta,
the leopard, to celebrate whose killing the Dum-Dum had been
organized.

Presently the dancing bulls would rush in upon the body
and beat it with heavy sticks and, leaping out again, resume
their dance. When the hunt, and the attack, and the death
had been depicted at length, they would cast away their
bludgeons and with bared fangs leap upon the carcass, tearing
and rending it as they fought among themselves for large
pieces or choice morsels.

Now Nkima and his kind are noted neither for their tact
nor judgment. One wiser than little Nkima would have remained silent until the dance and the feast were over and
until a new day had come and the great bulls of the tribe of
To-yat had recovered from the hysterical frenzy that the
drum and the dancing always induced within them. But little

Nkima was only a monkey. What he wanted, he wanted immediately, not being endowed with that mental poise which results in patience, and so he swung by his tail from an overhanging branch and scolded at the top of his voice in an effort to attract the attention of the great apes below.

"To-yat! Ga-yat! Zu-tho!" he cried. "Tarzan is in danger! Come with Nkima and save Tarzan!"

A great bull stopped in the midst of the dancing and looked up. "Go away, Manu," he growled. "Go away or we kill!" But little Nkima thought that they could not catch him, and so he continued to swing from the branch and yell and scream at them until finally To-yat sent a young ape, who was not too heavy, to clamber into the upper branches of the tree, to catch little Nkima and kill him.

Here was an emergency which Nkima had not foreseen. Like many people, he had believed that everyone would be as interested in what interested him as he; and when he had first heard the booming of the drums of the Dum-Dum, he thought that the moment the apes learned of Tarzan's peril they would set out upon the trail to Opar.

Now, however, he knew differently, and as the real menace of his mistake became painfully apparent with the leaping of a young ape into the tree below him, little Nkima emitted a loud shriek of terror and fled through the night; nor did he pause until, panting and exhausted, he had put a good mile between himself and the tribe of To-yat.

When La of Opar awoke in the tent of Zora Drinov she looked about her, taking in the unfamiliar objects that surrounded her, and presently her gaze rested upon the face of her sleeping hostess. These, indeed, she thought, must be the people of Tarzan, for had they not treated her with kindness and courtesy? They had offered her no harm and had fed her and given her shelter. A new thought crossed her mind now and her brows contracted, as did the pupils of her eyes into which there came a sudden, savage light. Perhaps this woman was Tarzan's mate. La of Opar grasped the hilt of Darus' knife where it lay ready beside her. But then, as suddenly as it had come, the mood passed, for in her heart she knew that she could not return evil for good, nor could she harm whom Tarzan loved, and when Zora opened her eyes La greeted her with a smile.

If the European girl was a cause for astonishment to La, she herself filled the other with profoundest wonder and mystification. Her scant, yet rich and gorgeous apparel harked back to an ancient age, and the gleaming whiteness of her skin seemed as much out of place in the heart of an African jungle as did her trappings in the twentieth century. Here was a mystery that nothing in the past experience of Zora Drinov could assist in solving. How she wished that she could converse with her, but all that she could do was to smile back at the beautiful creature regarding her so intently.

La, accustomed as she had been to being waited upon all her life by the lesser priestesses of Opar, was surprised by the facility with which Zora Drinov attended to her own needs as she rose to bathe and dress, the only service she received being in the form of a pail of hot water that Wamala fetched and poured into her folding tub; yet though La had never before been expected to lift a hand in the making of her toilet, she was far from helpless, and perhaps she found pleasure in the new experience of doing for herself.

Unlike the customs of the men of Opar, those of its women required scrupulous bodily cleanliness, so that in the past much of La's time had been devoted to her toilet, to the care of her nails, and her teeth, and her hair, and to the massaging of her body with aromatic unguents—customs, handed down from a cultured civilization of antiquity, to take on in ruined Opar the significance of religious rites.

By the time the two girls were ready for breakfast, Wamala was prepared to serve it; and as they sat outside the tent beneath the shade of a tree, eating the coarse fare of the camp, Zora noted unwonted activity about the beyts of the Aarabs, but she gave the matter little thought, as they had upon other occasions moved their tents from one part of the camp to another.

Breakfast over, Zora took down her rifle, wiped out the bore and oiled the breech mechanism, for today she was going out after fresh meat, the Aarabs having refused to hunt. La watched her with evident interest and later saw her depart with Wamala and two of the black porters; but she did not attempt to accompany her since, although she had looked for it, she had received no sign to do so.

Ibn Dammuk was the son of a sheykh of same tribe as Abu Batn, and upon this expedition he was the latter's right-hand man. With the fold of his thôb drawn across the lower part of his face, leaving only his eyes exposed, he had been watching the two girls from a distance. He saw Zora Drinov quit the camp with a gun-bearer and two porters and knew that she had gone to hunt.

For some time after she had departed he sat in silence with two companions. Then he arose and sauntered across the camp toward La of Opar, where she sat buried in reverie in a camp chair before Zora's tent. As the three men approached, La eyed them with level gaze, her natural suspicion of strangers aroused in her breast. As they came closer and their features became distinct, she felt a sudden distrust of them. They were crafty, malign looking men, not at all like Tarzan, and instinctively she distrusted them.

They halted before her and Ibn Dammuk, the son of a sheykh, addressed her. His voice was soft and oily, but it did not deceive her.

La eyed him haughtily. She did not understand him and she did not wish to, for the message that she read in his eyes disgusted her. She shook her head to signify that she did not understand and turned away to indicate that the interview was terminated, but Ibn Dammuk stepped closer and laid a hand familiarly upon her naked shoulder.

Her eyes flaming with anger, La leaped to her feet, one hand moving swiftly to the hilt of her dagger. Ibn Dammuk stepped back, but one of his men leaped forward to seize her.

Misguided fool! Like a tigress she was upon him; and before his friends could intervene, the sharp blade of the knife of Darus, the priest of the Flaming God, had sunk thrice into his breast, and with a gasping scream he had slumped to the ground dead.

With flaming eyes and bloody knife, the high priestess of Opar stood above her kill, while Abu Batn and the other Aarabs, attracted by the death cry of the stricken man, ran hurriedly toward the little group.

"Stand back!" cried La. "Lay no profaning hand upon the person of the high priestess of the Flaming God."

They did not understand her words, but they understood her flashing eyes and her dripping blade. Jabbering volubly, they gathered around her, but at a safe distance. "What means this, Ibn Dammuk?" demanded Abu Batn.

"Dogman did but touch her, and she flew at him like el adrea, lord of the broad head."

"A lioness she may be," said Abu Batn, "but she must not be harmed."

"Wullah!" exclaimed Ibn Dammuk, "but she must be tamed."

"Her taming we may leave to him who will pay many

pieces of gold for her," replied the sheykh. "It is necessary only for us to cage her. Surround her, my children, and take the knife from her. Make her wrists secure behind her back, and by the time the other returns we shall have struck camp and be ready to depart."

A dozen brawny men leaped upon La simultaneously. "Do not harm her! Do not harm her!" screamed Abu Batn, as, fighting like a lioness indeed, La sought to defend herself. Slashing right and left with her dagger, she drew blood more than once before they overpowered her; nor did they accomplish it before another Aarab fell with a pierced heart, but at length they succeeded in wrenching the blade from her and securing her wrists.

Leaving two warriors to guard her, Abu Batn turned his attention to gathering up the few black servants that remained in camp. These he forced to prepare loads of such of the camp equipment and provisions as he required. While this work was going on under Ibn Dammuk's supervision, the sheykh ransacked the tents of the Europeans, giving special attention to those of Zora Drinov and Zveri, where he expected to find the gold that the leader of the expedition was reputed to have in large quantities; nor was he entirely disappointed since he found in Zora's tent a box containing a considerable amount of money, though by no means the great quantity that he had expected, a fact which was due to the foresight of Zveri, who had personally buried the bulk of his funds beneath the floor of his tent.

Zora met with unexpected success in her hunting, for within a little more than an hour of her departure from camp she had come upon antelope, and two quick shots had dropped as many members of the herd. She waited while the porters skinned and dressed them and then returned leisurely toward camp. Her mind was occupied to some extent with the disquieting attitude of the Aarabs, but she was not at all prepared for the reception that she met when she approached camp about noon.

She was walking in advance, immediately followed by Wamala, who was carrying both of her rifles, while behind them were the porters, staggering under their heavy loads. Just as she was about to enter the clearing, Aarabs leaped from the underbrush on either side of the trail. Two of them seized Wamala and wrenched the rifles from his grasp, while others laid heavy hands upon Zora. She tried to free herself from them and draw her revolver, but the attack had taken her so by surprise that before she could accomplish anything in defense, she was overpowered and her hands bound at her back.

"What is the meaning of this?" she demanded. "Where is Abu Batn, the sheykh?"

The men laughed at her. "You shall see him presently," said one. "He has another guest whom he is entertaining, so he could not come to meet you," at which they all laughed again.

As she stepped into the clearing where she could obtain an unobstructed view of the camp, she was astounded by what she saw. Every tent had been struck. The Aarabs were leaning on their rifles ready to march, each of them burdened with a small pack, while the few black men, who had been left in camp, were lined up before heavy loads. All the rest of the paraphernalia of the camp, which Abu Batn had not men enough to transport, was heaped in a pile in the center of the clearing, and even as she looked she saw men setting torches to it.

As she was led across the clearing toward the waiting Aarabs, she saw her erstwhile guest between two warriors, her wrists confined by thongs even as her own. Near her, scowling malevolently, was Abu Batn.

"Why have you done this thing, Abu Batn?" demanded Zora.

"Allah was wroth that we should betray our land to the Nasrâny," said the sheykh. "We have seen the light, and we are going back to our own people."

"What do you intend to do with this woman and with me?" asked Zora.

"We shall take you with us for a little way," replied Abu Batn. "I know a kind man who is very rich, who will give you both a good home."

"You mean that you are going to sell us to some black sultan?" demanded the girl.

The sheykh shrugged. "I would not put it that way," he said. "Rather let us say that I am making a present to a great and good friend and saving you and this other woman from certain death in the jungle should we depart without you."

"Abu Batn, you are a hypocrite and a traitor," cried Zora, her voice vibrant with contempt.

"The Nasrâny like to call names," said the sheykh with a

sneer. "Perhaps if the pig, Zveri, had not called us names, this would not have happened."

"So this is your revenge," asked Zora, "because he reproached you for your cowardice at Opar?"

"Enough!" snapped Abu Batn. "Come, my children, let us be gone."

As the flames licked at the edges of the great pile of provisions and equipment that the Aarabs were forced to leave behind, the deserters started upon their march toward the West.

The girls marched near the head of the column, the feet of the Aarabs and the carriers behind them totally obliterating their spoor from the motley record of the trail. They might have found some comfort in their straits had they been able to converse with one another; but La could understand no one and Zora found no pleasure in speaking to the Aarabs, while Wamala and the other blacks were so far toward the rear of the column that she could not have communicated with them had she cared to.

To pass the time away, Zora conceived the idea of teaching her companion in misery some European language, and because in the original party there had been more who were familiar with English than any other tongue, she selected that language for her experiment.

She began by pointing to herself and saying "woman" and then to La and repeating the same word, after which she pointed to several of the Arabs in succession and said "man" in each instance. It was evident that La understood her purpose immediately, for she entered into the spirit of it with eagerness and alacrity, repeating the two words again and again, each time indicating either a man or a woman.

Next the European girl again pointed to herself and said "Zora." For a moment La was perplexed, and then she smiled and nodded.

"Zora," she said, pointing to her companion, and then, swiftly, she touched her own breast with a slender forefinger and said, "La."

And this was the beginning. Each hour La learned new words, all nouns at first, that described each familiar object that appeared oftenest to their view. She learned with remarkable celerity, evidencing an alert and intelligent mind and a retentive memory, for once she learned a word she never forgot it. Her pronunciation was not always perfect,

for she had a decidedly foreign accent that was like nothing
Zora Drinov ever had heard before, and so altogether
captivating that the teacher never tired of hearing her pupil
recite.

As the march progressed, Zora realized that there was
little likelihood that they would be mistreated by their captors,
it being evident to her that the sheykh was impressed with the
belief that the better the condition in which they could be
presented to their prospective purchaser the more handsome
the return that Abu Batn might hope to receive.

Their route lay to the northwest through a section of the
Galla country of Abyssinia, and from scraps of conversation
Zora overhead she learned that Abu Batn and his followers
were apprehensive of danger during this portion of the journey.
And well they may have been, since for ages the Arabs
have conducted raids in Galla territory for the purpose of
capturing slaves, and among the Negroes with them was a
Galla slave that Abu Batn had brought with him from his
desert home.

After the first day the prisoners had been allowed the
freedom of their hands, but always Aarab guards surrounded
them, though there seemed little likelihood that an unarmed
girl would take the risk of escaping into the jungle, where
she would be surrounded by the dangers of wild beasts or
almost certain starvation. However, could Abu Batn have
read their thoughts, he might have been astonished to learn
that in the mind of each was a determination to escape to
any fate rather than to march docilely on to an end that the
European girl was fully conscious of and which La of Opar
unquestionably surmised in part.

La's education was progressing nicely by the time the party
approached the border of the Galla country, but in the
meantime both girls had become aware of a new menace
threatening La of Opar. Ibn Dammuk marched often beside
her, and in his eyes, when he looked at her, was a message
that needed no words to convey. But when Abu Batn was
near, Ibn Dammuk ignored the fair prisoner, and this caused
Zora the most apprehension, for it convinced her that the
wily Ibn was but biding his time until he might find conditions
favorable to the carrying out of some scheme that he already
had decided upon, nor did Zora harbor any doubts as to the
general purpose of his plan.

At the edge of the Galla country they were halted by a river
in flood. They could not go north into Abyssinia proper,

and they dared not go south, where they might naturally have expected pursuit to follow. So perforce they were compelled to wait where they were.

And while they waited Ibn Dammuk struck.

9

In the Death Cell of Opar

O NCE again Peter Zveri stood before the walls of Opar, and once again the courage of his black soldiers was dissipated by the weird cries of the inmates of the city of mystery. The ten warriors, who had not been to Opar before and who had volunteered to enter the city, halted trembling as the first of the blood-curdling screams rose, shrill and piercing, from the forbidding ruins.

Miguel Romero once more led the invaders, and directly behind him was Wayne Colt. According to the plan the blacks were to have followed closely behind these two, with the rest of the whites bringing up the rear, where they might rally and encourage the Negroes, or if necessary, force them on at the points of their pistols. But the blacks would not even enter the opening of the outer wall, so demoralized were they by the uncanny warning screams which their superstitious minds attributed to malignant demons, against which there could be no defense and whose animosity meant almost certain death for those who disregarded their wishes.

"In with you, you dirty cowards!" cried Zveri, menacing the blacks with his revolver in an effort to force them into the opening.

One of the warriors raised his rifle threateningly. "Put away your weapon, white man," he said. "We will fight men, but we will not fight the spirits of the dead."

"Lay off, Peter," said Dorsky. "You will have the whole bunch on us in a minute and we shall all be killed."

Zveri lowered his pistol and commenced to plead with the warriors, promising them rewards that amounted to riches to them if they would accompany the whites into the city; but the volunteers were obdurate—nothing could induce them to venture into Opar.

Seeing failure once again imminent and with a mind already obsessed by the belief that the treasures of Opar would make him fabulously wealthy and insure the success of his secret scheme of empire, Zveri determined to follow Romero and Colt with the remainder of his aides, which consisted only of Dorsky, Ivitch and the Filipino boy. "Come on," he said, "we will have to make a try at it alone, if these yellow dogs won't help us."

By the time the four men had passed through the outer wall, Romero and Colt were already out of sight beyond the inner wall. Once again the warning scream broke menacingly upon the brooding silence of the ruined city.

"God!" ejaculated Ivitch. "What do you suppose it could be?"

"Shut up," exclaimed Zveri irritably. "Stop thinking about it, or you'll go yellow like those damn blacks."

Slowly they crossed the court toward the inner wall, nor was there much enthusiasm manifest among them other than for an evident desire in the breast of each to permit one of the others the glory of leading the advance. Tony had reached the opening when a bedlam of noise from the opposite side of the wall burst upon their ears—a hideous chorus of war cries, mingled with the sound of rushing feet. There was a shot, and then another and another.

Tony turned to see if his companions were following him. They had halted and were standing with blanched faces, listening.

Then Ivitch turned. "To hell with the gold!" he said, and started back toward the outer wall at a run.

"Come back, you lousy cur," cried Zveri, and took after him with Dorsky at his heels. Tony hesitated for a moment and then scurried in pursuit, nor did any of them halt until they were beyond the outer wall. There Zveri overtook Ivitch and seized him by the shoulder. "I ought to kill you," he cried in a trembling voice.

"You were as glad to get out of there as I was," growled Ivitch. "What was the sense of going in there? We should only have been killed like Colt and Romero. There were too many of them. Didn't you hear them?"

"I think Ivitch is right," said Dorsky. "It's all right to be brave, but we have got to remember the cause—if we are killed everything is lost."

"But the gold!" exclaimed Zveri. "Think of the gold!"

"Gold is no good to dead men," Dorsky reminded him.

"How about our comrades?" asked Tony. "Are we to leave them to be killed?"

"To hell with the Mexican," said Zveri, "and as for the American I think his funds will still be available as long as we can keep the news of his death from getting back to the Coast."

"You are not even going to try to rescue them?" asked Tony.

"I cannot do it alone," said Zveri.

"I will go with you," said Tony.

"Little good two of us can accomplish," mumbled Zveri, and then in one of his sudden rages, he advanced menacingly upon the Filipino, his great figure towering above that of the other.

"Who do you think you are anyway?" he demanded. "I am in command here. When I want your advice I'll ask for it."

When Romero and Colt passed through the inner wall, that part of the interior of the temple which they could see appeared deserted, and yet they were conscious of movement in the darker recesses and the apertures of the ruined galleries that looked down into the courtway.

Colt glanced back. "Shall we wait for the others?" he asked.

Romero shrugged. "I think we are going to have this glory all to ourselves, comrade," he said with a grin.

Colt smiled back at him. "Then let's get on with the business," he said. "I don't see anything very terrifying yet."

"There is something in there though," said Romero. "I've seen things moving."

"So have I," said Colt.

With their rifles ready, they advanced boldly into the temple; but they had not gone far when, from shadowy archways and from numerous gloomy doorways there rushed a horde of horrid men, and the silence of the ancient city was shattered by hideous war cries.

Colt was in advance and now he kept on moving forward, firing a shot above the heads of the grotesque warrior priests of Opar. Romero saw a number of the enemy running along the side of the great room which they had entered, with the evident intention of cutting off their retreat. He swung about and fired, but not over their heads. Realizing the gravity of their position, he shot to kill, and now Colt did the same, with the result that the screams of a couple of wounded men mingled now with the war cries of their fellows.

Romero was forced to drop back a few steps to prevent the Oparians from surrounding him. He shot rapidly now and succeeded in checking the advance around their flank. A quick glance at Colt showed him standing his ground, and at the same instant he saw a hurled club strike the American on the head. The man dropped like a log, and instantly his body was covered by the terrible little men of Opar.

Miguel Romero realized that his companion was lost, and even if not now already dead, he, singlehanded, could accomplish nothing toward his rescue. If he escaped with his own life he would be fortunate, and so, keeping up a steady fire, he fell back toward the aperture in the inner wall.

Having captured one of the invaders, seeing the other falling back, and fearing to risk further the devastating fire of the terrifying weapon in the hand of their single antagonist, the Oparians hesitated.

Romero passed through the inner wall, turned and ran swiftly to the outer and a moment later had joined his companions upon the plain.

"Where is Colt?" demanded Zveri.

"They knocked him out with a club and captured him," said Romero. "He is probably dead by this time."

"And you deserted him?" asked Zveri.

The Mexican turned upon his chief in fury. "You ask me that?" he demanded. "You turned pale and ran even before you saw the enemy. If you fellows had backed us up Colt might not have been lost, but to let us go in there alone the two of us didn't have a Chinaman's chance with that bunch of wild men. And you accuse me of cowardice?"

"I didn't do anything of the kind," said Zveri sullenly. "I never said you were a coward."

"You meant to imply it though," snapped Romero, "but let me tell you, Zveri, that you can't get away with that with me or anyone else who has been to Opar with you."

From behind the walls rose a savage cry of victory; and while it still rumbled through the tarnished halls of Opar, Zveri turned dejectedly away from the city. "It's no use," he said. "I can't capture Opar alone. We are returning to camp."

The little priests, swarming over Colt, stripped him of his weapons and secured his hands behind his back. He was still unconscious, and so they lifted him to the shoulder of one of their fellows and bore him away into the interior of the temple.

When Colt regained consciousness he found himself lying on the floor of a large chamber. It was the throne room of the temple of Opar, where he had been fetched that Oah, the high priestess, might see the prisoner.

Perceiving that their captive had regained consciousness, his guards jerked him roughly to his feet and pushed him forward toward the foot of the dais upon which stood Oah's throne.

The effect of the picture bursting suddenly upon him imparted to Colt the definite impression that he was the victim of an hallucination or a dream. The outer chamber of the ruin, in which he had fallen, had given no suggestion of the size and semi-barbaric magnificence of this great chamber, the grandeur of which was scarcely dimmed by the ruin of ages.

He saw before him, upon an ornate throne, a young woman of exceptional physical beauty, surrounded by the semi-barbaric grandeur of an ancient civilization. Grotesque and hairy men and beautiful maidens formed her entourage. Her eyes, resting upon him, were cold and cruel; her mien haughty and contemptuous. A squat warrior, more ape-like in his conformation than human, was addressing her in a language unfamiliar to the American.

When he had finished, the girl rose from the throne and, drawing a long knife from her girdle, raised it high above her head as she spoke rapidly and almost fiercely, her eyes fixed upon the prisoner.

From among a group of priestesses at the right of Oah's throne, a girl, just come into womanhood, regarded the prisoner through half-closed eyes, and beneath the golden plates that confined her smooth, white breasts, the heart of Nao palpitated to the thoughts that contemplation of this strange warrior engendered within her.

When Oah had finished speaking, Colt was lead away, quite ignorant of the fact that he had been listening to the sentence of death imposed upon him by the high priestess of the Flaming God. His guards conducted him to a cell just within the entrance of a tunnel leading from the sacrificial court to the pits beneath the city, and because it was not entirely below ground, fresh air and light had access to it through a window and the grated bars of its doorway. Here the escort left him, after removing the bonds from his wrists.

Through the small window in his cell Wayne Colt looked out upon the inner court of the Temple of the Sun at Opar.

He saw the surrounding galleries rising tier upon tier to the summit of a lofty wall. He saw the stone altar standing in the center of the court, and the brown stains upon it and upon the pavement at its foot told him what the unitelligible words of Oah had been unable to convey. For an instant he felt his heart sink within his breast, and a shudder passed through his frame as he contemplated his inability to escape the fate which confronted him. There could be no mistaking the purpose of that altar when viewed in connection with the grinning skulls of former human sacrifices which stared through eyeless sockets upon him from their niches in the surrounding walls.

Fascinated by the horror of his situation, he stood staring at the altar and skulls, but presently he gained control of himself and shook the terror from him, yet the hopelessness of his situation continued to depress him. His thoughts turned to his companion. He wondered what Romero's fate had been. There, indeed, had been a brave and gallant comrade, in fact, the only member of the party who had impressed Colt favorably, or in whose society he had found pleasure. The others had seemed either ignorant fanatics or avaricious opportunists, while the manner and speech of the Mexican had stamped him as a light-hearted soldier of fortune, who might gayly offer his life in any cause which momentarily seized his fancy with an eye more singly for excitement and adventure than for any serious purpose. He did not know, of course, that Zveri and the others had deserted him; but he was confident that Romero had not before his cause had become utterly hopeless, or until the Mexican himself had been killed or captured.

In lonely contemplation of his predicament, Colt spent the rest of the long afternoon. Darkness fell, and still there came no sign from his captors. He wondered if they intended leaving him there without food or water, or if, perchance, the ceremony that was to see him offered in sacrifice upon that grim, brown-stained altar was scheduled to commence so soon that they felt it unnecessary to minister to his physical needs.

He had lain down upon the hard cement-like surface of the cell floor and was trying to find momentary relief in sleep, when his attention was attracted by the shadow of a sound coming from the courtyard where the altar stood. As he listened he was positive that someone was approaching, and rising quietly he went to the window and looked out. In the shadowy darkness of the night, relieved only by the faint light of distant stars, he saw something moving across the courtyard toward his cell, but whether man or beast he could not distinguish; and then, from somewhere high up among the lofty ruins, there pealed out upon the silent night the long drawn scream, which seemed now to the American as much a part of the mysterious city of Opar as the crumbling ruins themselves.

* * *

It was a sullen and discouraged party that made its way back to the camp at the edge of the forest below the barrier cliffs of Opar, and when they arrived it was to find only further disorganization and discouragement.

No time was lost in narrating to the members of the returning expedition the story of the sentry who had been carried off into the jungle at night by a demon, from whom the man had managed to escape before being devoured. Still fresh in their minds was the uncanny affair of the death of Raghunath Jafar, nor were the nerves of those who had been before the walls of Opar inclined to be at all steadied by that experience, so that it was a nervous company that bivouacked that night beneath the dark trees at the edge of the gloomy forest and, with sighs of relief, witnessed the coming of dawn.

Later, after they had taken up the march toward the base camp, the spirit of the blacks gradually returned to normal and presently the tension under which they had been laboring for days was relieved by song and laughter, but the whites were gloomy and sullen. Zveri and Romero did not speak to one another, while Ivitch, like all weak characters, nursed a grievance against everyone because of his own display of cowardice during the fiasco at Opar.

From the interior of a hollow tree in which he had been hiding, little Nkima saw the column pass; and after it was safely by he emerged from his retreat and, dancing up and down upon a limb of the tree, shouted dire threats after them and called them many names.

* * *

Tarzan of the Apes lay stretched upon his belly upon the back of Tantor, the elephant, his elbows upon the broad head, his chin resting in his cupped hands. Futile had been his search for the spoor of La of Opar. Had the Earth opened and swallowed her she could not more effectually have disappeared.

Today Tarzan had come upon Tantor and, as had been his custom from childhood, he had tarried for that silent communion with the sagacious old patriarch of the forest, which seemed always to impart to the man something of the beast's great strength of character and poise. There was an atmosphere of restful stability about Tantor that filled the ape-man with a peace and tranquillity that he found restful; and Tantor, upon his part, welcomed the companionship of the Lord of the Jungle, whom, alone, of all two legged creatures, he viewed with friendship and affection.

The beasts of the jungle acknowledge no master, least of all the cruel tyrant that drives civilized man throughout his headlong race from the cradle to the grave—Time, the master of countless millions of slaves. Time, the measurable aspect of duration, was measureless to Tarzan and Tantor. Of all the vast resources that Nature had placed at their disposal, she had been most profligate with Time, since she had awarded to each all that he could use during his lifetime, no matter how extravagant of it he might be. So great was the supply of it that it could not be wasted, since there was always more, even up to the moment of death, after which it ceased, with all things, to be essential to the individual. Tantor and Tarzan, therefore, were wasting no time as they communed together in silent meditation; but though Time and space go on forever, whether in curves or straight lines, all other things must end; and so the quiet and the peace that the two friends were enjoying were suddenly shattered by the excited screams of a diminutive monkey in the foliage of a great tree above them.

It was Nkima. He had found his Tarzan, and his relief and joy aroused the jungle to the limit of his small, shrill voice. Lazily Tarzan rolled over and looked up at the jabbering simian above him; and then Nkima, satisfied now beyond peradventure of a doubt that this was, indeed, his master, launched himself downward to alight upon the bronzed body of the ape-man. Slender, hairy little arms went around Tarzan's neck as Nkima hugged close to this haven of refuge which imparted to him those brief moments in his life when he might enjoy the raptures of a temporary superiority complex. Upon Tarzan's shoulder he felt almost fearless and could, with impunity, insult the entire world.

"Where have you been, Nkima?" asked Tarzan.

"Looking for Tarzan," replied the monkey.

"What have you seen since I left you at the walls of Opar?" demanded the ape-man.

"I have seen many things. I have seen the great Mangani dancing in the moonlight around the dead body of Sheeta. I have seen the enemies of Tarzan marching through the forest. I have seen Histah, gorging himself on the carcass of Bara."

"Have you seen a Tarmangani she?" demanded Tarzan.

"No," replied Nkima. "There were no shes among the Gomangani and Tarmangani enemies of Tarzan. Only bulls, and they marched back toward the place where Nkima first saw them."

"When was this?" asked Tarzan.

"Kudu had climbed into the heavens but a short distance out of the darkness when Nkima saw the enemies of Tarzan marching back to the place where he first saw them."

"Perhaps we had better see what they are up to," said the ape-man. He slapped Tantor affectionately with his open palm in farewell, leaped to his feet and swung nimbly into the overhanging branches of a tree; while far away Zveri and his party plodded through the jungle toward their base camp.

Tarzan of the Apes follows no earth-bound trails where the density of the forest offers him the freedom of leafy highways, and thus he moves from point to point with a speed that has often been disconcerting to his enemies.

Now he moved in an almost direct line so that he overtook the expedition as it made camp for the night. As he watched them from behind a leafy screen of high-flung foliage, he noticed, though with no surprise, that they were not burdened with any treasure from Opar.

As the success and happiness of jungle dwellers, nay, even life itself, is largely dependent upon their powers of observation, Tarzan had developed his to a high degree of perfection. At his first encounter with this party he had made himself familiar with the faces, physiques and carriages of all of its principals and of many of its humble warriors and porters, with the result that he was immediately aware that Colt was no longer with the expedition. Experience permitted Tarzan to draw a rather accurate picture of what had happened at Opar and of the probable fate of the missing man.

Years ago he had seen his own courageous Waziri turn and flee upon the occasion of their first experience of the weird warning screams from the ruined city, and he could easily guess that Colt, attempting to lead the invaders into the city, had been deserted and found either death or capture within the gloomy interior. This, however, did not greatly concern Tarzan. While he had been rather drawn toward Colt by that tenuous and invisible power known as personality, he still considered him as one of his enemies, and if he were either dead or captured Tarzan's cause was advanced by that much.

From Tarzan's shoulder Nkima looked down upon the camp, but he kept silent as Tarzan had instructed him to do. Nkima saw many things that he would have liked to have possessed, and particularly he coveted a red calico shirt worn by one of the askaris. This, he thought, was very grand, indeed, being set off as it was by the unrelieved nakedness of the majority of the blacks. Nkima wished that his master would descend and slay them all, but particularly the man with the red shirt; for, at heart, Nkima was bloodthirsty, which made it fortunate for the peace of the jungle that he had not been born a gorilla. But Tarzan's mind was not set upon carnage. He had other means for thwarting the activities of these strangers. During the day he had made a kill, and now he withdrew to a safe distance from the camp and satisfied his hunger, while Nkima searched for birds' eggs, fruit, and insects.

And so night fell and when it had enveloped the jungle in impenetrable darkness, relieved only by the beast fires of the camp, Tarzan returned to a tree where he could overlook the activities of the bivouacked expedition. He watched them in silence for a long time, and then suddenly he raised his voice in a long scream that perfectly mimicked the hideous warning cry of Opar's defenders.

The effect upon the camp was instantaneous. Conversation, singing, and laughter ceased. For a moment the men sat as in a paralysis of terror. Then, seizing their weapons, they came closer to the fire.

With the shadow of a smile upon his lips, Tarzan melted away into the jungle.

10

The Love of a Priestess

IBN DAMMUK had bided his time and now, in the camp by the swollen river at the edge of the Galla country, he at last found the opportunity he had so long awaited. The surveillance over the two prisoners had somewhat relaxed, due largely to the belief entertained by Abu Batn that the women would not dare to invite the perils of the jungle by attempting to escape from captors who were, at the same time, their protectors from even greater dangers. He had, however, reckoned without a just estimation of the courage and resourcefulness of his two captives, who, had he but known it, were constantly awaiting the first opportunity for escape. It was this fact, as well, that played into the hands of Ibn Dammuk.

With great cunning he enlisted the services of one of the blacks who had been forced to accompany them from the base camp and who was virtually a prisoner. By promising him his liberty Ibn Dammuk had easily gained the man's acquiescence in the plan that he had evolved.

A separate tent had been pitched for the two women, and before it sat a single sentry, whose presence Abu Batn considered more than sufficient for this purpose, which was, perhaps, even more to protect the women from his own followers than to prevent a very remotely possible attempt at escape.

This night, which Ibn Dammuk had chosen for his villainy, was one for which he had been waiting, since it found upon duty before the tent of the captives one of his own men, a member of his own tribe, who was bound by laws of hereditary loyalty to serve and obey him. In the forest, just beyond the camp, waited Ibn Dammuk, with two more of his own tribesmen, four slaves that they had brought from the desert and the black porter who was to win his liberty by this night's work.

The interior of the tent that had been pitched for Zora and La was illuminated by a paper lantern, in which a candle burned dimly; and in this subdued light the two sat talking in La's newly acquired English, which was at best most fragmentary and broken. However, it was far better than no means of communication and gave the two girls the only pleasure that they enjoyed. Perhaps it was not a remarkable coincidence that this night they were speaking of escape and planning to cut a hole in the back of their tent through which they might sneak away into the jungle after the camp had settled down for the night and their sentry should be dozing at his post. And while they conversed, the sentry before their tent rose and strolled away, and a moment later they heard a scratching upon the back of the tent. Their conversation ceased, and they sat with eyes riveted upon the point where the fabric of the tent moved to the pressure of the scratching without.

Presently a voice spoke in a low whisper. "Memsahib Drinov!"

"Who is it? What do you want?" asked Zora in a low voice.

"I have found a way to escape. I can help you if you wish."

"Who are you?" demanded Zora.

"I am Bukula," and Zora at once recognized the name as that of one of the blacks that Abu Batn had forced to accompany him from the base camp.

"Put out your lantern," whispered Bukula. "The sentry has gone away. I will come in and tell you my plans."

Zora arose and blew out the candle, and a moment later the two captives saw Bukula crawling into the interior of the tent. "Listen, Memsahib," he said, "the boys that Abu Batn stole from Bwana Zveri are running away tonight. We are going back to the safari. We will take you two with us, if you want to come."

"Yes," said Zora, "we will come."

"Good!" said Bukula. "Now listen well to what I tell you. The sentry will not come back, but we cannot all go out at once. First I will take this other Memsahib with me out into the jungle where the boys are waiting; then I will return for you. You can make talk to her. Tell her to follow me and to make no noise."

Zora turned to La. "Follow Bukula," she said. "We are going tonight. I will come after you."

"I understand," replied La.

"It is all right, Bukula," said Zora. "She understands."

Bukula stepped to the entrance to the tent and looked quickly about the camp. "Come!" he said, and, followed by La, disappeared quickly from Zora's view.

The European girl fully realized the risk that they ran in going into the jungle alone with these half-savage blacks, yet she trusted them far more implicitly than she did the Aarabs and, too, she felt that she and La together might circumvent any treachery upon the part of any of the Negroes, the majority of whom she knew would be loyal and faithful. Waiting in the silence and loneliness of the darkened tent, it seemed to Zora that it took Bukula an unnecessarily long time to return for her; but when minute after minute dragged slowly past until she felt that she had waited for hours and there was no sign either of the black or the sentry, her fears were aroused in earnest. Presently she determined not to wait any longer for Bukula, but to go out into the jungle in search of the escaping party. She thought that perhaps Bukula had been unable to return without risking detection and that they were all waiting just beyond the camp for a favorable opportunity to return to her. As she arose to put her decision into action, she heard footsteps approaching the tent, and thinking that they were Bukula's, she waited; but instead she saw the flapping robe and the long-barreled musket of an Aarab silhouetted against the lesser darkness of the exterior as the man stuck his head inside the tent. "Where is Hajellan?" he demanded, giving the name of the departed sentry.

"How should we know?" retorted Zora in a sleepy voice. "Why do you awaken us thus in the middle of the night? Are we the keepers of your fellows?"

The fellow grumbled something in reply and then, turning, called aloud across the camp, announcing to all who might hear that Hajellan was missing and inquiring if any had seen him. Other warriors strolled over then, and there was a great deal of speculation as to what had become of Hajellan. The name of the missing man was called aloud many times, but there was no response, and finally the sheykh came and questioned everyone. "The women are in the tent yet?" he demanded of the new sentry.

"Yes," replied the man. "I have talked with them."

"It is strange," said Abu Batn, and then, "Ibn Dammuk!"

he cried. "Where art thou, Ibn? Hajellan was one of thy men." There was no answer. "Where is Ibn Dammuk?"

"He is not here," said a man standing near the sheykh.

"Nor are Fodil and Dareyem," said another.

"Search the camp and see who is missing," commanded Abu Batn; and when the search had been made they found that Ibn Dammuk, Hajellan, Fodil, and Dareyem were missing with five of the blacks.

"Ibn Dammuk has deserted us," said Abu Batn. "Well, let it go. There will be fewer with whom to share the reward we shall reap when we are paid for the two women," and thus reconciling himself to the loss of four good fighting men, Abu Batn repaired to his tent and resumed his interrupted slumber.

Weighted down by apprehension as to the fate of La and disappointment occasioned by her own failure to escape, Zora spent an almost sleepless night, yet fortunate for her peace of mind was it that she did not know the truth.

Bukula moved silently into the jungle, followed by La; and when they had gone a short distance from the camp, the girl saw the dark forms of men standing in a little group ahead of them. The Arabs, in their tell-tale thôbs, were hidden in the underbrush, but their slaves had removed their own white robes and, with Bukula, were standing naked but for G strings, thus carrying conviction to the mind of the girl that only black prisoners of Abu Batn awaited her. When she came among them, however, she learned her mistake; but too late to save herself, for she was quickly seized by many hands and effectually gagged before she could give the alarm. The Ibn Dammuk and his Aarab companions appeared, and silently the party moved on down the river through the dark forest, though not before they had subdued the enraged high priestess of the Flaming God, secured her wrists behind her back, and placed a rope about her neck.

All night they fled, for Ibn Dammuk well guessed what the wrath of Abu Batn would be when, in the morning, he discovered the trick that had been played upon him; and when morning dawned they were far away from camp, but still Ibn Dammuk pushed on, after a brief halt for a hurried breakfast.

Long since had the gag been removed from La's mouth, and now Ibn Dammuk walked beside her, gloating upon his prize. He spoke to her, but La could not understand him and only strode on in haughty disdain, biding her time against the moment when she might be revenged and inwardly sorrowing over her separation from Zora, for whom a strange affection had been aroused in her savage breast.

Toward noon the party withdrew from the game trail which they had been following and made camp near the river. It was here that Ibn Dammuk made a fatal blunder. Goaded to passion by close proximity to the beautiful woman for whom he had conceived a mad infatuation, the Aarab gave way to his desire to be alone with her; and leading her along a little trail that paralleled the river, he took her away out of sight of his companions; and when they had gone perhaps a hundred yards from camp, he seized her in his arms and sought to kiss her lips.

With equal safety might Ibn Dammuk have embraced a lion. In the heat of his passion he forgot many things, among them the dagger that hung always at his side. But La of Opar did not forget. With the coming of daylight she had noticed that dagger, and ever since she had coveted it; and now as the man pressed her close, her hand sought and found its hilt. For an instant she seemed to surrender. She let her body go limp in his arms, while her own, firm and beautifully rounded, crept about him, one to his right shoulder, the other beneath his left arm. But as yet she did not give him her lips, and then as he struggled to possess them the hand upon his shoulder seized him suddenly by the throat. The long, tapered fingers that seemed so soft and white were suddenly claws of steel that closed upon his windpipe; and simultaneously the hand that had crept so softly beneath his left arm drove his own long dagger into his heart from beneath his shoulder blade.

The single cry that he might have given was choked in his throat. For an instant the tall form of Ibn Dammuk stood rigidly erect; then it slumped forward, and the girl let it slip to the earth. She spurned it once with her foot, then removed from it the girdle and sheath for the dagger, wiped the bloody blade upon the man's thôb and hurried on up the little river trail until she found an opening in the underbrush that led away from the stream. On and on she went until exhaustion overtook her; and then, with her remaining strength, she climbed into a tree in search of much needed rest.

*   *   *

Wayne Colt watched the shadowy figure approach the

mouth of the corridor where his cell lay. He wondered if this was a messenger of death, coming to lead him to sacrifice. Nearer and nearer it came until presently it stopped before the bars of his cell door; and then a soft voice spoke to him in a low whisper and in a tongue which he could not understand, and he knew that his visitor was a woman.

Prompted by curiosity, he came close to the bars. A soft hand reached in and touched him, almost caressingly. A full moon rising above the high walls that ring the sacrificial court suddenly flooded the mouth of the corridor and the entrance to Colt's cell in silvery light, and in it the American saw the figure of a young girl pressed against the cold iron of the grating. She handed him food, and when he took it she caressed his hand and drawing it to the bars pressed her lips against it.

Wayne Colt was nonplussed. He could not know that Nao, the little priestess, had been the victim of love at first sight, that to her mind and eyes, accustomed to the sight of males only in the form of the hairy, grotesque priests of Opar, this stranger appeared a god indeed.

A slight noise attracted Nao's attention toward the court and, as she turned, the moonlight flooded her face, and the American saw that she was very lovely. Then she turned back toward him, her dark eyes wells of adoration, her full, sensitive lips trembling with emotion as, still clinging to his hand, she spoke rapidly in low liquid tones.

She was trying to tell Colt that at noon of the second day he was to be offered in sacrifice to the Flaming God, that she did not wish him to die and if it were possible she would help him, but that she did not know how that would be possible.

Colt shook his head. "I cannot understand you, little one," he said, and Nao, though she could not interpret his words, sensed the futility of her own. Then, raising one of her hands from his, she made a great circle in a vertical plane from east to west with a slender index finger, indicating the path of the sun across the heavens; and then she started a second circle, which she stopped at zenith, indicating high noon of the second day. For an instant her raised hand poised dramatically aloft; and then, the fingers closing as though around the hilt of an imaginary sacrificial knife, she plunged the invisible point deep into her bosom.

"Thus will Oah destroy you," she said, reaching through the bars and touching Colt over the heart.

The American thought that he understood the meaning

of her pantomime, which he then repeated, plunging the imaginary blade into his own breast and looking questioningly at Nao.

In reply she nodded sadly, and the tears welled to her eyes.

As plainly as though he had understood her words, Colt realized that here was a friend who would help him if she could, and reaching through the bars, he drew the girl gently toward him and pressed his lips against her forehead. With a low sob Nao encircled his neck with her arms and pressed her face to his. Then, as suddenly, she released him and, turning, hurried away on silent feet, to disappear in the gloomy shadows of an archway at one side of the court of sacrifice.

Colt ate the food that she had brought him and for a long time lay pondering the inexplicable forces which govern the acts of men. What train of circumstances leading down out of a mysterious past had produced this single human being in a city of enemies in whom, all unsuspecting, there must always have existed a germ of potential friendship for him, an utter stranger and alien, of whose very existence she could not possibly have dreamed before this day. He tried to convince himself that the girl had been prompted to her act by pity for his plight, but he knew in his heart that a more powerful motive impelled her.

Colt had been attracted to many women, but he had never loved; and he wondered if that was the way that love came and if some day it would seize him as it had seized this girl; and he wondered also if, had conditions been different, he might have been as strongly attracted to her. If not, then there seemed to be something wrong in the scheme of things; and still puzzling over this riddle of the ages, he fell asleep upon the hard floor of his cell.

With morning a hairy priest came and gave him food and water, and during the day others came and watched him, as though he were a wild beast in a menagerie. And so the long day dragged on, and once again night came—his last night.

He tried to picture what the final ceremony would be like. It seemed almost incredible that in the twentieth century he was to be offered as a human sacrifice to some heathen deity, but yet the pantomime of the girl and the concrete evidence of the bloody altar and the grinning skulls assured him that such must be the very fate awaiting him upon the morrow. He thought of his family and his friends at home; they would never know what had become of him. He weighed his sacrifice against the mission that he had undertaken and he had no regret, for he knew that it had not been in vain. Far away, already near the Coast, was the message he had dispatched by the runner. That would insure that he had not failed in his part for the sake of a great principle for which, if necessary, he was glad to lay down his life. He was glad that he had acted promptly and sent the message when he had, for now, upon the morrow, he could go to his death without vain regrets.

He did not want to die, and he made many plans during the day to seize upon the slightest opportunity that might be presented to him to escape.

He wondered what had become of the girl and if she would come again now that it was dark. He wished that she would, for he craved the companionship of a friend during his last hours; but as the night wore on, he gave up the hope and sought to forget the morrow in sleep.

As Wayne Colt moved restlessly upon his hard couch, Firg, a lesser priest of Opar, snored upon his pallet of straw in the small, dark recess that was his bed chamber. Firg was the keeper of the keys, and so impressed was he with the importance of his duties that he never would permit anyone even to touch the sacred emblems of his trust, and probably because it was well known that Firg would die in defense of them they were entrusted to him. Not with justice could Firg have laid any claim to intellectuality, if he had known that such a thing existed. He was only an abysmal brute of a man and, like many men, far beneath the so-called brutes in many of the activities of mind. When he slept, all his faculties were asleep, which is not true of wild beasts when they sleep.

Firg's cell was in one of the upper stories of the ruins that still remained intact. It was upon a corridor that encircled the main temple court—a corridor that was now in dense shadow, since the moon, touching it early in the night, had now passed on; so that the figure creeping stealthily toward the entrance to Firg's chamber would have been noticeable only to one who happened to be quite close. It moved silently, but without hesitation, until it came to the entrance beyond which Firg lay. There it paused, listening, and when it heard Firg's noisy snoring, it entered quickly. Straight to the side of the sleeping man it moved, and there it knelt, searching with one hand lightly over his body, while the other grasped a long, sharp knife that hovered constantly above the hairy chest of the priest.

Presently it found what it wanted—a great ring, upon which were strung several enormous keys. A leather thong fastened the ring to Firg's girdle, and with the keen blade of the dagger the nocturnal visitor sought to sever the thong. Firg stirred, and instantly the creature at his side froze to immobility. Then the priest moved restlessly and commenced to snore again, and once more the dagger sawed at the leather thong. It passed through the strand unexpectedly and touched the metal of the ring lightly, but just enough to make the keys jangle ever so slightly.

Instantly Firg was awake, but he did not rise. He was never to rise again.

Silently, swiftly, before the stupid creature could realize his danger, the keen blade of the dagger had pierced his heart.

Soundlessly, Firg collapsed. His slayer hesitated a moment with poised dagger as though to make certain that the work had been well done. Then, wiping the tell-tale stains from the dagger's blade with the victim's loin cloth, the figure arose and hurried from the chamber, in one hand the great keys upon their golden ring.

Colt stirred uneasily in his sleep and then awakened with a start. In the waning moonlight he saw a figure beyond the grating of his cell. He heard a key turn in the massive lock. Could it be that they were coming for him? He rose to his feet, the urge of his last conscious thought strong upon him— escape. And then as the door swung open, a soft voice spoke, and he knew that the girl had returned.

She entered the cell and threw her arms about Colt's neck, drawing his lips down to hers. For a moment she clung to him, and then she released him and, taking one of his hands in hers, urged him to follow her; nor was the American loath to leave the depressing interior of the death cell.

On silent feet Nao led the way across the corner of the sacrificial court, through a dark archway into a gloomy corridor. Winding and twisting, keeping always in dark shadows, she led him along a circuitous route through the ruins, until, after what seemed an eternity to Colt, the girl opened a low, strong, wooden door and led him into the great entrance hall of the temple, through the mighty portal of which he could see the inner wall of the city.

Here Nao halted, and coming close to the man looked up into his eyes. Again her arms stole about his neck, and again she pressed her lips to his. Her cheeks were wet with tears, and her voice broke with little sobs that she tried to stifle as she poured her love into the ears of the man who could not understand.

She had brought him here to offer him his freedom, but she could not let him go yet. She clung to him, caressing him and crooning to him.

For a quarter of an hour she held him there, and Colt had not the heart to tear himself away, but at last she released him and pointed toward the opening in the inner wall.

"Go!" she said, "taking the heart of Nao with you. I shall never see you again, but at least I shall always have the memory of this hour to carry through life with me."

Wayne stooped and kissed her hand, the slender, savage little hand that had but just killed that her lover might live. Though of that, Wayne knew nothing.

She pressed her dagger with its sheath upon him that he might not go out into the savage world unarmed, and then he turned away from her and moved slowly toward the inner wall. At the entrance of the opening he paused and turned about. Dimly, in the moonlight, he saw the figure of the little priestess standing very erect in the shadows of the ancient ruins. He raised his hand and waved a final, silent farewell.

A great sadness depressed Colt as he passed through the inner wall and crossed the court to freedom, for he knew that he had left behind him a sad and hopeless heart, in the bosom of one who must have risked death, perhaps, to save him—a perfect friend of whom he could but carry a vague memory of a half-seen lovely face, a friend whose name he did not know, the only tokens of whom he had carried away with him were the memory of hot kisses and a slender dagger.

And thus, as Wayne Colt walked across the moonlit plain of Opar, the joy of his escape was tempered by sadness as he recalled the figure of the forlorn little priestess standing in the shadows of the ruins.

11

Lost in the Jungle

I T WAS some time after the uncanny scream had disturbed the camp of the conspirators before the men could settle down to rest again.

Zveri believed that they had been followed by a band of Oparian warriors, who might be contemplating a night attack, and so he placed a heavy guard about the camp; but his blacks were confident that that unearthly cry had broken from no human throat.

Depressed and dispirited, the men resumed their march the following morning. They made an early start and by dint of much driving arrived at the base camp just before dark. The sight that met their eyes there filled them with consternation. The camp had disappeared, and in the center of the clearing where it had been pitched a pile of ashes suggested that disaster had overtaken the party that had been left behind.

This new misfortune threw Zveri into a maniacal rage, but there was no one present upon whom he might lay the blame, and so he was reduced to the expedient of trampling back and forth while he cursed his luck in loud tones and several languages.

From a tree Tarzan watched him. He, too, was at a loss to understand the nature of the disaster that seemed to have overtaken the camp during the absence of the main party, but as he saw that it caused the leader intense anguish, the ape-man was pleased.

The blacks were confident that this was another manifestation of the anger of the malign spirit that had been haunting them, and they were all for deserting the ill-starred white man, whose every move ended in failure or disaster.

Zveri's powers of leadership deserve full credit, since from the verge of almost certain mutiny he forced his men by means of both cajolery and threat to remain with him. He set them to building shelters for the entire party, and immediately he dispatched messengers to his various agents, urging them to forward necessary supplies at once. He knew that certain things he needed already were on the way from the Coast— uniforms, rifles, ammunition. But now he particularly needed provisions and trade goods. To insure discipline, he kept the men working constantly, either in adding to the comforts of the camp, enlarging the clearing, or hunting fresh meats.

And so the days passed and became weeks, and meanwhile Tarzan watched in waiting. He was in no hurry, for hurry is not a characteristic of the beasts. He roamed the jungle often at a considerable distance from Zveri's camp, but occasionally he would return, though not to molest them, preferring to let them lull themselves into a stupor of tranquil security, the shattering of which in his own good time would have dire effect upon their morale. He understood the psychology of terror, and it was with terror that he would defeat them.

* * *

To the camp of Abu Batn, upon the border of the Galla country, word had come from spies that he had sent out that the Galla warriors were gathering to prevent his passage through their territory. Being weakened by the desertion of so many men, the sheykh dared not defy the bravery and numbers of the Galla warriors, but he knew that he must make some move, since it seemed inevitable that pursuit must overtake him from the rear, if he remained where he was much longer.

At last scouts that he had sent far up the river on the opposite side returned to report that a way to the west seemed clear along a more northerly route, and so breaking camp, Abu Batn moved north with his lone prisoner.

Great had been his rage when he discovered that Ibn Dammuk had stolen La, and now he redoubled his precaution to prevent the escape of Zora Drinov. So closely was she guarded that any possibility of escape seemed almost hopeless. She had learned the fate for which Abu Batn was reserving her, and now, depressed and melancholy, her mind was occupied with plans for self-destruction. For a time she had harbored the hope that Zveri would overtake the Aarabs and rescue her, but this she had long since discarded, as day after day passed without bringing the hoped for succor.

She could not know, of course, the straits in which Zveri had found himself. He had not dared to detach a party of his men to search for her, fearing that, in their mutinous state of mind, they might murder any of his lieutenants that he placed in charge of them and return to their own tribe, where, through the medium of gossip, word of his expedition and its activities might reach his enemies; nor could he lead all of his force upon such an expedition in person, since he must remain at the base camp to receive the supplies that he knew would presently be arriving.

Perhaps, had he known definitely the danger that confronted Zora, he would have cast aside every other consideration and gone to her rescue; but being naturally suspicious of the loyalty of all men, he had persuaded himself that Zora had deliberately deserted him—a half-hearted conviction that had at least the effect of rendering his naturally unpleasant disposition infinitely more unbearable, so that those who should have been his companions and his support in his hour of need contrived as much as possible to keep out of his way.

And while these things were transpiring, little Nkima sped through the jungle upon a mission. In the service of his beloved master, little Nkima could hold to a single thought and a line of action for considerable periods of time at a stretch; but eventually his attention was certain to be attracted by some extraneous matter and then, for hours perhaps, he would forget all about whatever duty had been imposed upon him; but when it again occurred to him, he would carry on entirely without any appreciation of the fact that there had been a break in the continuity of his endeavor.

Tarzan, of course, was entirely aware of this inherent weakness in his little friend; but he knew, too, from experience that, however many lapses might occur, Nkima would never entirely abandon any design upon which his mind had been fixed; and having himself none of civilized man's slavish subservience to time, he was prone to overlook Nkima's erratic performance of a duty as a fault of almost negligible consequence. Some day Nkima would arrive at his destination. Perhaps it would be too late. If such a thought occurred at all to the ape-man, doubtless he passed it off with a shrug.

But time is of the essence of many things to civilized man. He fumes, and frets, and reduces his mental and physical efficiency if he is not accomplishing something concrete during the passage of every minute of that medium which seems to him like a flowing river, the waters of which are utterly wasted if they are not utilized as they pass by.

Imbued by some such insane conception of time, Wayne Colt sweated and stumbled through the jungle, seeking his companions as though the very fate of the universe hung upon the slender chance that he should reach them without the loss of a second.

The futility of his purpose would have been entirely apparent to him could he have known that he was seeking his companions in the wrong direction. Wayne Colt was lost. Fortunately for him he did not know it; at least not yet. That stupefying conviction was to come later.

Days passed and still his wanderings revealed no camp. He was hard put to it to find food, and his fare was meager and often revolting, consisting of such fruits as he had already learned to know and of rodents, which he managed to bag only with the greatest difficulty and an appalling waste of that precious time which he still prized above all things. He had cut himself a stout stick and would lie in wait along some tiny runway where observation had taught him he might expect to find his prey, until some unwary little creature came within striking distance. He had learned that dawn and dusk were the best hunting hours for the only animals that he could hope to bag, and he learned other things as he moved through the grim jungle, all of which pertained to his struggle for existence. He had learned, for instance, that it was wiser for him to take to the trees whenever he heard a strange noise. Usually the animals got out of his way as he approached; but once a rhinoceros charged him, and again he almost stumbled upon a lion at his kill. Providence intervened in each instance and he escaped unkilled, but thus he learned caution.

About noon one day he came to a river that effectually blocked his further progress in the direction that he had been travelling. By this time the conviction was strong upon him that he was utterly lost, and not knowing which direction he should take, he decided to follow the line of least resistance and travel down hill with the river, upon the shore of which he was positive that sooner or later he must discover a native village.

He had proceeded no great distance in the new direction, following a hard-packed trail, worn deep by the countless feet of many beasts, when his attention was arrested by a sound that reached his ears dimly from a distance. It came from somewhere ahead of him, and his hearing, now far more acute than it ever had been before, told him that something was approaching. Following the practice that he had found most conducive to longevity since he had been wandering alone and ill-armed against the dangers of the jungle, he flung himself quickly into a tree and sought a point of vantage from where he could see the trail below him. He could not see it for any distance ahead, so tortuously did it wind through the jungle. Whatever was coming would not be visible until it was almost directly beneath him, but that now was of no importance. This experience of the jungle had taught him patience, and perchance he was learning, too, a little of the valuelessness of time, for he settled himself comfortably to wait at his ease.

The noise that he heard was little more than an imperceptible rustling, but presently it assumed a new volume and a new significance, so that now he was sure that it was someone running rapidly along the trail, and not one but two—he distinctly heard the footfalls of the heavier creature mingling with those he had first heard.

And then he heard a man's voice cry "Stop!" and now the sounds were very close to him, just around the first bend ahead. The sound of running feet stopped, to be followed by that of a scuffle and strange oaths in a man's voice.

And then a woman's voice spoke, "Let me go! You will never get me where you are taking me alive."

"Then I'll take you for myself now," said the man.

Colt had heard enough. There had been something familiar in the tones of the woman's voice. Silently he dropped to the trail, drawing his dagger, and stepped quickly toward the sounds of the altercation. As he rounded the bend in the trail, he saw just before him only a man's back—by thôb and thorîb an Arab—but beyond the man and in his clutches Colt knew the woman was hidden by the flowing robes of her assailant.

Leaping forward, he seized the fellow by the shoulder and jerked him suddenly about; and as the man faced him Colt saw that it was Abu Batn, and now, too, he saw why the voice of the woman had seemed familiar—she was Zora Drinov.

Abu Batn purpled with rage at the interruption, but great as was his anger so, too, was his surprise as he recognized the American. Just for an instant he thought that possibly this was the advance guard of a party of searchers and avengers from Zveri's camp, but when he had time to observe the unkempt, disheveled, unarmed condition of Colt he realized that the man was alone and doubtless lost.

"Dog of a Nasrâny!" he cried, jerking away from Colt's grasp. "Lay not your filthy hand upon a true believer." At the same time he moved to draw his pistol, but in that instant Colt was upon him again, and the two men went down in the narrow trail, the American on top.

What happened then, happened very quickly. As Abu Batn drew his pistol, he caught the hammer in the folds of his thôb, so that the weapon was discharged. The bullet went harmlessly into the ground, but the report warned Colt of his imminent danger, and in self defense he ran his blade through the sheykh's throat.

As he rose slowly from the body of the sheykh, Zora Drinov grasped him by the arm. "Quick!" she said. "That shot will bring the others. They must not find us."

He did not wait to question her, but, stooping, quickly salvaged Abu Batn's weapons and ammunition, including a long musket that lay in the trail beside him; and then with Zora in the lead they ran swiftly up the trail down which he had just come.

Presently, hearing no indication of pursuit, Colt halted the girl.

"Can you climb?" he asked.

"Yes," she replied. "Why?"

"We are going to take to the trees," he said. "We can go into the jungle a short distance and throw them off the trail."

"Good!" she said, and with his assistance clambered into the branches of a tree beneath which they stood.

Fortunately for them, several large trees grew close together so that they were able to make their way with comparative ease a full hundred feet from the trail, where, climbing high into the branches of a great tree, they were effectually hidden from sight in all directions.

When at last they were seated side by side in a great crotch, Zora turned toward Colt. "Comrade Colt!" she said. "What has happened? What are you doing here alone? Were you looking for me?"

The man grinned. "I was looking for the whole party," he said. "I have seen no one since we entered Opar. Where is the camp, and why was Abu Batn pursuing you?"

"We are a long way from the camp," replied Zora. "I do not know how far, though I could return to it, if it were not for the Arabs." And then briefly she told the story of Abu Batn's treachery and of her captivity. "The sheykh made a temporary camp shortly after noon today. The men were very tired, and for the first time in days they relaxed their vigilance over me. I realized that at last the moment I had been awaiting so anxiously had arrived, and while they slept I escaped into the jungle. My absence must have been discovered shortly after I left, and Abu Batn overtook me. The rest you witnessed."

"Fate functioned deviously and altogether wonderfully," he said. "To think that your only chance of rescue hinged upon the contingency of my capture at Opar!"

She smiled. "Fate reaches back further than that," she said. "Suppose you had not been born?"

"Then Abu Batn would have carried you off to the harem of some black sultan, or perhaps another man would have been captured at Opar."

"I am glad that you were born," said Zora.

"Thank you," said Colt.

While listening for signs of pursuit, they conversed in low tones, Colt narrating in detail the events leading up to his capture, though some of the details of his escape he omitted through a sense of loyalty to the nameless girl who had aided him. Neither did he stress Zveri's lack of control over his men, or what Colt considered his inexcusable cowardice in leaving himself and Romero to their fate within the walls of Opar without attempting to succor them, for he believed that the girl was Zveri's sweetheart and he did not wish to offend her.

"What became of Comrade Romero?" she asked.

"I do not know," he said. "The last I saw of him he was standing his ground, fighting off those crooked little demons."

"Alone?" she asked.

"I was pretty well occupied myself," he said.

"I do not mean that," she replied. "Of course, I know you were there with Romero, but who else?"

"The others had not arrived," said Colt.

"You mean you two went in alone?" she asked.

Colt hesitated. "You see," he said, "the blacks refused to

enter the city, so the rest of us had to go in or abandon the attempt to get the treasures."

"But only you and Miguel did go in. Is that not true?" she demanded.

"I passed out so soon, you see," he said with a laugh, "that really I do not know exactly what did happen."

The girl's eyes narrowed. "It was beastly," she said.

As they talked, Colt's eyes were often upon the girl's face. How lovely she was, even beneath the rags and the dirt that were the outward symbols of her captivity among the Aarabs. She was a little thinner than when he had last seen her, and her eyes were tired and her face drawn from privation and worry. But, perhaps, by very contrast her beauty was the more startling. It seemed incredible that she could love the coarse, loud-mouthed Zveri, who was her antithesis in every respect.

Presently she broke a short silence. "We must try to get back to the base camp," she said. "It is vital that I be there. So much must be done, so much that no one else can do."

"You think only of the cause," he said; "never of yourself. You are very loyal."

"Yes," she said in a low voice. "I am loyal to the thing I have sworn to accomplish."

"I am afraid," he said, "that for the past few days I have been thinking more of my own welfare than of that of the proletariat."

"I am afraid that at heart you are still bourgeois," she said, "and that you cannot yet help looking upon the proletariat with contempt."

"What makes you say that?" he asked. "I am sure that I said nothing to warrant it."

"Often a slight unconscious inflection in the use of a word alters the significance of a whole statement, revealing a speaker's secret thoughts."

Colt laughed good naturedly. "You are a dangerous person to talk to," he said. "Am I to be shot at sunrise?"

She looked at him seriously. "You are different from the others," she said. "I think you could never imagine how suspicious they are. What I have said is only in the way of warning you to watch your every word when you are talking with them. Some of them are narrow and ignorant, and they are already suspicious of you because of your antecedents. They are sensitively jealous of a new importance which they believe their class has attained."

"Their class?" he asked. "I thought you told me once that you were of the proletariat?"

If he had thought that he had surprised her and that she would show embarrassment, he was mistaken. She met his eyes squarely and without wavering. "I am," she said, "but I can still see the weaknesses of my class."

He looked at her steadily for a long moment, the shadow of a smile touching his lips. "I do not believe——"

"Why do you stop?" she asked. "What is it that you do not believe?"

"Forgive me," he said. "I was starting to think aloud."

"Be careful, Comrade Colt," she warned him. "Thinking aloud is sometimes fatal"; but she tempered her words with a smile.

Further conversation was interrupted by the sound of the voices of men in the distance. "They are coming," said the girl.

Colt nodded, and the two remained silent, listening to the sounds of approaching voices and footsteps. The men came abreast of them and halted; and Zora, who understood the Aarab tongue, heard one of them say, "The trail stops here. They have gone into the jungle."

"Who can the man be who is with her?" asked another.

"It is a Nasrâny. I can tell by the imprint of his feet," said another.

"They would go toward the river," said a third. "That is the way that I should go if I were trying to escape."

"Wullah! You speak words of wisdom," said the first speaker. "We will spread out here and search toward the river; but look out for the Nasrâny. He has the pistol and the musket of the sheykh."

The two fugitives heard the sound of pursuit diminishing in the distance as the Aarabs forced their way into the jungle toward the river. "I think we had better get out of this," said Colt; "and while it may be pretty hard going, I believe that we had better stick to the brush for awhile and keep on away from the river."

"Yes," replied Zora, "for that is the general direction in which the camp lies." And so they commenced their long and weary march in search of their comrades.

They were still pushing through dense jungle when night overtook them. Their clothes were in rags and their bodies scratched and torn, mute and painful reminders of the thorny way that they had traversed.

Hungry and thirsty they made a dry camp among the branches of a tree, where Colt built a rude platform for the girl, while he prepared to sleep upon the ground at the foot of the great bole. But to this, Zora would not listen.

"That will not do at all," she said. "We are in no position to permit ourselves to be the victims of every silly convention that would ordinarily order our lives in civilized surroundings. I appreciate your thoughtful consideration, but I would rather have you up here in the tree with me than down there where the first hunting lion that passed might get you." And so with the girl's help Colt built another platform close to the one that he had built for her; and as darkness fell, they stretched their tired bodies on their rude couches and sought to sleep.

Presently Colt dozed, and in his dream he saw the slender figure of a star-eyed goddess, whose cheeks were wet with tears, but when he took her in his arms and kissed her he saw that she was Zora Drinov; and then a hideous sound from the jungle below awakened him with a start, so that he sat up, seizing the musket of the sheykh in readiness.

"A hunting lion," said the girl in a low voice.

"Phew!" exclaimed Colt. "I must have been asleep, for that certainly gave me a start."

"Yes, you were asleep," said the girl. "I heard you talking," and he felt that he detected laughter in her voice.

"What was I saying?" asked Colt.

"Maybe you wouldn't want to hear. It might embarrass you," she told him.

"No. Come ahead. Tell me."

"You said 'I love you.' "

"Did I, really?"

"Yes. I wonder whom you were talking to," she said, banteringly.

"I wonder," said Colt, recalling that in his dream the figure of one girl had merged into that of another.

The lion, hearing their voices, moved away growling. He was not hunting the hated man-things.

12

Down Trails of Terror

S LOW days dragged by for the man and woman searching for their comrades—days filled with fatiguing effort, most of which was directed toward the procuring of food and water for their sustenance. Increasingly was Colt impressed by the character and personality of his companion. With apprehension he noticed that she was gradually weakening beneath the strain of fatigue and the scant and inadequate food that he had been able to procure for her. But yet she kept a brave front and tried to hide her condition from him. Never once had she complained. Never by word or look had she reproached him for his inability to procure sufficient food, a failure which he looked upon as indicative of inefficiency. She did not know that he himself often went hungry that she might eat, telling her when he returned with food that he had eaten his share where he had found it, a deception that was made possible by the fact that when he hunted he often left Zora to rest in some place of comparative security, that she might not be subjected to needless exertion.

He had left her thus today, safe in a great tree beside a winding stream. She was very tired. It seemed to her that now she was always tired. The thought of continuing the march appalled her, and yet she knew that it must be undertaken. She wondered how much longer she could go on before she sank exhausted for the last time. It was not, however, for herself that she was most concerned, but for this man—this scion of wealth, and capitalism, and power, whose constant consideration and cheerfulness and tenderness had been

127

a revelation to her. She knew that when she could go no
further, he would not leave her and that thus his chances
of escape from the grim jungle would be jeopardized and
perhaps lost forever because of her. She hoped, for his sake,
that death would come quickly to her that, thus relieved of
responsibility, he might move on more rapidly in search of
that elusive camp that seemed to her now little more than
a meaningless myth. But from the thought of death she
shrank, not because of the fear of death, as well might have
been the case, but for an entirely new reason, the sudden
realization of which gave her a distinct shock. The tragedy
of this sudden self-awakening left her numb with terror. It
was a thought that must be put from her, one that she must
not entertain even for an instant; and yet it persisted—persisted with a dull insistency that brought tears to her eyes.

Colt had gone farther afield than usual this morning in
his search for food, for he had sighted an antelope; and, his
imagination inflamed by the contemplation of so much meat
in a single kill and what it would mean for Zora, he clung
doggedly to the trail, lured further on by an occasional
glimpse of his quarry in the distance.

The antelope was only vaguely aware of an enemy, for
he was upwind from Colt and had not caught his scent,
while the occasional glimpses he had had of the man had
served mostly to arouse his curiosity; so that though he
moved away he stopped often and turned back in an effort
to satisfy his wonderment. But presently he waited a moment
too long. In his desperation, Colt chanced a long shot; and
as the animal dropped, the man could not stifle a loud cry
of exultation.

As time, that she had no means of measuring, dragged
on, Zora grew increasingly apprehensive on Colt's account.
Never before had he left her for so long a time, so that she
began to construct all sorts of imaginary calamities that
might have overtaken him. She wished now that she had gone
with him. If she had thought it possible to track him, she
would have followed him; but she knew that that was impossible. However, her forced inactivity made her restless.
Her cramped position in the tree became unendurable; and
then, suddenly assailed by thirst, she lowered herself to the
ground and walked toward the river.

When she had drunk and was about to return to the tree,
she heard the sound of something approaching from the
direction in which Colt had gone. Instantly her heart leaped

with gladness, her depression and even much of her fatigue seemed to vanish, and she realized suddenly how very lonely she had been without him. How dependent we are upon the society of our fellow-men, we seldom realize until we become the victims of enforced solitude. There were tears of happiness in Zora Drinov's eyes as she advanced to meet Colt. Then the bushes before her parted, and there stepped into view, before her horrified gaze, a monstrous, hairy ape.

To-yat, the king, was as much surprised as the girl, but his reactions were almost opposite. It was with no horror that he viewed this soft, white she-Mangani. To the girl there was naught but ferocity in his mien, though in his breast was an entirely different emotion. He lumbered toward her; and then, as though released from a momentary paralysis, Zora turned to flee. But how futilely, she realized an instant later as a hairy paw gripped her roughly by the shoulder. For an instant she had forgotten the sheykh's pistol that Colt always left with her for self-protection. Jerking it from its holster, she turned upon the beast; but To-yat, seeing in the weapon a club with which she intended to attack him, wrenched it from her grasp and hurled it aside; and then, though she struggled and fought to regain her freedom, he lifted her lightly to his hip and lumbered off into the jungle in the direction that he had been going.

Colt tarried at his kill only long enough to remove the feet, the head and the viscera, that he might by that much reduce the weight of the burden that he must carry back to camp, for he was quite well aware that his privation had greatly reduced his strength.

Lifting the carcass to his shoulder, he started back toward camp, exulting in the thought that for once he was returning with an ample quantity of strength-giving flesh. As he staggered along beneath the weight of the small antelope, he made plans that imparted a rosy hue to the future. They would rest now until their strength returned; and while they were resting they would smoke all of the meat of his kill that they did not eat at once, and thus they would have a reserve supply of food that he felt would carry them a great distance. Two days' rest with plenty of food would, he was positive, fill them with renewed hope and vitality.

As he started laboriously along the back trail, he commenced to realize that he had come much farther than he had thought, but it had been well worth while. Even though he reached Zora in a state of utter exhaustion, he did not fear for a minute but that he would reach her, so confident was he of his own powers of endurance and the strength of his will.

As he staggered at last to his goal, he looked up into the tree and called her by name. There was no reply. In that first brief instant of silence, a dull and sickening premonition of disaster crept over him. He dropped the carcass of the deer and looked hurriedly about.

"Zora! Zora!" he cried; but only the silence of the jungle was his answer. Then his searching eyes found the pistol of Abu Batn where To-yat had dropped it; and his worst fears were substantiated, for he knew that if Zora had gone away of her own volition she would have taken the weapon with her. She had been attacked by something and carried off, of that he was positive; and presently as he examined the ground closely he discovered the imprints of a great man-like foot.

A sudden madness seized Wayne Colt. The cruelty of the jungle, the injustice of Nature aroused within his breast a red rage. He wanted to kill the thing that had stolen Zora Drinov. He wanted to tear it with his hands and rend it with his teeth. All the savage instincts of primitive man were reborn within him as, forgetting the meat that the moment before had meant so much to him, he plunged headlong into the jungle upon the faint spoor of To-yat, the king ape.

* * *

La of Opar made her way slowly through the jungle after she had escaped from Ibn Dammuk and his companions. Her native city called to her, though she knew that she might not enter it in safety; but what place was there in all the world that she might go to? Something of a conception of the immensity of the great world had been impressed upon her during her wandering since she had left Opar, and the futility of searching further for Tarzan had been indelibly impressed upon her mind. So she would go back to the vicinity of Opar, and perhaps some day again Tarzan would come there. That great dangers beset her way she did not care, for La of Opar was indifferent to life that had never brought her much of happiness. She lived because she lived; and it is true that she would strive to prolong life because such is the law of Nature, which imbues the most miserable unfortunates with as powerful an urge to prolong their misery as it gives to the fortunate few who are happy and contented a similar desire to live.

Presently she became aware of pursuit, and so she increased her speed and kept ahead of those who were following her. Finding a trail, she followed it, knowing that if it permitted her to increase her speed it would permit her pursuers also to increase theirs, nor would she be able to hear them now as plainly as she had before, when they were forcing their way through the jungle. Still she was confident that they could not overtake her; but as she was moving swiftly on, a turn in the trail brought her to a sudden stop, for there, blocking her retreat, stood a great, maned lion. This time La remembered the animal, not as Jad-bal-ja, the hunting mate of Tarzan, but as the lion that had rescued her from the leopard, after Tarzan had deserted her.

Lions were familiar creatures to La of Opar, where they were often captured by the priests while cubs, and where it was not unusual to raise some of them occasionally as pets until their growing ferocity made them unsafe. Therefore, La knew that lions could associate with people without devouring them; and, having had experience of this lion's disposition and having as little sense of fear as Tarzan himself, she quickly made her choice between the lion and the Aarabs pursuing her and advanced directly toward the great beast, in whose attitude she saw there was no immediate menace. She was sufficiently a child of nature to know that death came quickly and painlessly in the embrace of a lion, and so she had no fear, but only a great curiosity.

Jad-bal-ja had long had the scent spoor of La in his nostrils, as she had moved with the wind along the jungle trails; and so he had awaited her, his curiosity aroused by the fainter scent spoor of the men who trailed her. Now as she came toward him along the trail, he stepped to one side that she might pass and, like a great cat, rubbed his maned neck against her legs.

La paused and laid a hand upon his head and spoke to him in low tones in the language of the first man—the language of the great apes that was the common language of her people, as it was Tarzan's language.

Hajellan, leading his men in pursuit of La, rounded a bend in the trail and stopped aghast. He saw a great lion facing him, a lion that bared its fangs now in an angry snarl; and beside the lion, one hand tangled in its thick black mane, stood the white woman.

The woman spoke a single word to the lion in a language that Hajellan did not understand. "Kill!" said La in the language of the great apes.

So accustomed was the high priestess of the Flaming God to command that it did not occur to her that Numa might do other than obey; and so, although she did not know that it was thus that Tarzan had been accustomed to command Jad-bal-ja, she was not surprised when the lion crouched and charged.

Fodil and Dareyem had pushed close behind their companion as he halted, and great was their horror when they saw the lion leap forward. They turned and fled, colliding with the blacks behind them; but Hajellan only stood paralyzed with fright as Jad-bal-ja reared upon his hind feet and seized him, his great jaws crunching through the man's head and shoulders, cracking his skull like an egg shell. He gave the body a vicious shake and dropped it. Then he turned and looked inquiringly at La.

In the woman's heart was no more sympathy for her enemies than in the heart of Jad-bal-ja; she only wished to be rid of them. She did not care whether they lived or died, and so she did not urge Jad-bal-ja after those who had escaped. She wondered what the lion would do now that he had made his kill; and knowing that the vicinity of a feeding lion was no safe place, she turned and moved on along the trail. But Jad-bal-ja was no eater of man, not because he had any moral scruples, but because he was young and active and had no difficulty in killing prey that he relished far more than he did the salty flesh of man. Therefore, he left Hajellan lying where he had fallen and followed La along the shadowy jungle trails.

A black man, naked but for a G string, bearing a message from the Coast for Zveri, paused where two trails crossed. From his left the wind was blowing, and to his sensitive nostrils it bore the faint stench that announced the presence of a lion. Without a moment's hesitation, the man vanished into the foliage of a tree that overhung the trail. Perhaps Simba was not hungry, perhaps Simba was not hunting; but the black messenger was taking no chances. He was sure that the lion was approaching, and he would wait here where he could see both trails until he discovered which one Simba took.

Watching with more or less indifference because of the

safety of his sanctuary, the Negro was ill-prepared for the shock which the sight that presently broke upon his vision induced. Never in the lowest steps of his superstition had he conceived such a scene as he now witnessed, and he blinked his eyes repeatedly to make sure that he was awake; but, no, there could be no mistake. It was indeed a white woman almost naked but for golden ornaments and a soft strip of leopard skin beneath her narrow stomacher—a white woman who walked with the fingers of one hand tangled in the black mane of a great golden lion.

Along the trail they came, and at the crossing they turned to the left into the trail that he had been following. As they disappeared from his view, the black man fingered the fetish that was suspended from a cord about his neck and prayed to Mulungo, the god of his people; and when he again set out toward his destination he took another and more circuitous route.

Often, after darkness had fallen, Tarzan had come to the camp of the conspirators and, perched in a tree above them, listened to Zveri outlining his plans to his companions; so that the ape-man was familiar with what they intended, down to the minutest detail.

Now, knowing that they would not be prepared to strike for some time, he was roaming the jungle far away from the sight and stench of man, enjoying to the full the peace and freedom that were his life. He knew that Nkima should have reached his destination by this time and delivered the message that Tarzan had dispatched by him. He was still puzzled by the strange disappearance of La and piqued by his inability to pick up her trail. He was genuinely grieved by her disappearance, for already he had his plans well formulated to restore her to her throne and punish her enemies; but he gave himself over to no futile regrets as he swung through the trees in sheer joy of living, or when hunger overtook him, stalked his prey in the grim and terrible silence of the hunting beast.

Sometimes he thought of the good-looking young American, to whom he had taken a fancy in spite of the fact that he considered him an enemy. Had he known of Colt's now almost hopeless plight, it is possible that he would have gone to his rescue, but he knew nothing of it.

So, alone and friendless, sunk to the uttermost depths of despair, Wayne Colt stumbled through the jungle in search

of Zora Drinov and her abductor. But already he had lost
the faint trail; and To-yat, far to his right, lumbered along
with his captive safe from pursuit.

Weak from exhaustion and shock, thoroughly terrified now
by the hopelessness of her hideous position, Zora had lost
consciousness. To-yat feared that she was dead; but he carried
her on, nevertheless, that he might at least have the satisfaction of exhibiting her to his tribe as evidence of his prowess
and, perhaps, to furnish an excuse for another Dum-Dum.
Secure in his might, conscious of few enemies that might
with safety to themselves molest him, To-yat did not take
the precaution of silence, but wandered on through the jungle
heedless of all dangers.

Many were the keen ears and sensitive nostrils that carried
the message of his passing to their owners, but to only one
did the strange mingling of the scent spoor of the bull ape
with that of a she-Mangani suggest a condition worthy of
investigation. So as To-yat pursued his careless way, another
creature of the jungle, moving silently on swift feet, bore
down upon him; and when, from a point of vantage, keen
eyes beheld the shaggy bull and the slender, delicate girl, a
lip curled in a silent snarl. A moment later To-yat, the king
ape, was brought to a snarling, bristling halt as the giant
figure of a bronzed Tarmangani dropped lightly into the trail
before him, a living threat to his possession of his prize.

The wicked eyes of the bull shot fire and hate. "Go away,"
he said. "I am To-yat. Go away or I kill."

"Put down the she," demanded Tarzan.

"No," bellowed To-yat. "She is mine."

"Put down the she," repeated Tarzan, "and go your way;
or I kill. I am Tarzan of the Apes, Lord of the Jungle!"

Tarzan drew the hunting knife of his father and crouched
as he advanced toward the bull. To-yat snarled; and seeing
that the other meant to give battle, he cast the body of the
girl aside that he might not be handicapped. As they circled,
each looking for an advantage, there came a sudden, terrific
crashing sound in the jungle down wind from them.

Tantor, the elephant, asleep in the security of the depth
of the forest, had been suddenly awakened by the growling
of the two beasts. Instantly his nostrils caught a familiar
scent spoor—the scent spoor of his beloved Tarzan—and his
ears told him that he was facing in battle the great Mangani,
whose scent was also strong in the nostrils of Tantor.

To the snapping and bending of trees, the great bull rushed through the forest; and as he emerged suddenly, towering above them, To-yat, the king ape, seeing death in those angry eyes and gleaming tusks, turned and fled into the jungle.

13

The Lion-Man

P ETER ZVERI was, in a measure, regaining some of the confidence that he had lost in the ultimate success of his plan, for his agents were succeeding at last in getting to him some of his much needed supplies, together with contingents of disaffected blacks wherewith to recruit his forces to sufficient numbers to insure the success of his contemplated invasion of Italian Somaliland. It was his plan to make a swift and sudden incursion, destroying native villages and capturing an outpost or two, then retreating quickly across the border, pack away the French uniforms for possible future use and undertake the overthrow of Ras Tafari in Abyssinia, where his agents had assured him conditions were ripe for a revolution. With Abyssinia under his control to serve as a rallying point, his agents assured him that the native tribes of all Northern Africa would flock to his standards.

In distant Bokhara a fleet of two hundred planes—bombers, scouts, and fighting planes—made available through the greed of American capitalists, were being mobilized for a sudden dash across Persia and Arabia to his base in Abyssinia. With these to support his great native army, he felt that his position would be secure, the malcontents of Egypt would join forces with him and, with Europe embroiled in a war that would prevent any concerted action against him, his dream of empire might be assured and his position made impregnable for all time.

Perhaps it was a mad dream; perhaps Peter Zveri was mad—but, then, what great world conqueror has not been a little mad?

He saw his frontiers pushed toward the south as, little by little, he extended his dominion, until one day he should rule a great continent—Peter I, Emperor of Africa.

"You seem happy, Comrade Zveri," said little Antonio Mori.

"Why should I not be, Tony?" demanded the dreamer. "I see success just before us. We should all be happy, but we are going to be very much happier later on."

"Yes," said Tony, "when the Philippines are free, I shall be very happy. Do you not think that I should be a very big man back there, then, Comrade Zveri?"

"Yes," said the Russian, "but you can be a bigger man if you stay here and work for me. How would you like to be a Grand Duke, Tony?"

"A Grand Duke!" exclaimed the Filipino. "I thought there were no more Grand Dukes."

"But perhaps there may be again."

"They were wicked men who ground down the working classes," said Tony.

"To be a Grand Duke who grinds down the rich and takes money from them might not be so bad," said Peter. "Grand Dukes are very rich and powerful. Would you not like to be rich and powerful, Tony?"

"Well, of course, who would not?"

"Then always do as I tell you, Tony; and some day I shall make you a Grand Duke," said Zveri.

The camp was filled with activity now at all times, for Zveri had conceived the plan of whipping his native recruits into some semblance of military order and discipline. Romero, Dorsky, and Ivitch having had military experience, the camp was filled with marching men, deploying, charging and assembling, practicing the Manual of Arms, and being instructed in the rudiments of fire discipline.

The day following his conversation with Zveri, Tony was assisting the Mexican, who was sweating over a company of black recruits.

During a period of rest, as the Mexican and Filipino were enjoying a smoke, Tony turned to his companion. "You have travelled much, Comrade," said the Filipino. "Perhaps you can tell me what sort of uniform a Grand Duke wears."

"I have heard," said Romero, "that in Hollywood and New York many of them wear aprons."

Tony grimaced. "I do not think," he said, "that I want to be a Grand Duke."

The blacks in the camp, held sufficiently interested and busy in drills to keep them out of mischief, with plenty of food and with the prospects of fighting and marching still in the future, were a contented and happy lot. Those who had undergone the harrowing experiences of Opar and those other untoward incidents that had upset their equanimity had entirely regained their self confidence, a condition for which Zveri took all the credit to himself, assuming that it was due to his remarkable gift for leadership. And then a runner arrived in camp with a message for him and with a weird story of having seen a white woman hunting in the jungle with a black-maned golden lion. This was sufficient to recall to the blacks the other weird occurrences and to remind them that there were supernatural agencies at work in this territory, that it was peopled by ghosts and demons, and that at any moment some dire calamity might befall them.

But if this story upset the equanimity of the blacks, the message that the runner brought to Zveri precipitated an emotional outbreak in the Russian that bordered closely upon the frenzy of insanity. Blaspheming in a loud voice, he strode back and forth before his tent; nor would he explain to any of his lieutenants the cause of his anger.

And while Zveri fumed, other forces were gathering against him. Through the jungle moved a hundred ebon warriors, their smooth, sleek skin, their rolling muscles and elastic step bespeaking their physical fitness. They were naked but for narrow loin cloths of leopard or lion skin and a few of those ornaments that are dear to the hearts of savages— anklets and arm bands of copper and necklaces of the claws of lions or leopards—while above the head of each floated a white plume. But here the primitiveness of their equipment ceased, for their weapons were the weapons of modern fighting men; high-powered service rifles, revolvers, and bandoleers of cartridges. It was, indeed, a formidable appearing company that swung steadily and silently through the jungle, and upon the shoulder of the black chief who led them rode a little monkey.

*　　*　　*

Tarzan was relieved when Tantor's sudden and unexpected charge drove To-yat into the jungle; for Tarzan of the Apes found no pleasure in quarreling with the Mangani, which he considered above all other creatures his brothers. He never forgot that he had been nursed at the breast of Kala, the she-ape, nor that he had grown to manhood in the tribe of Kerchak, the king. From infancy to manhood he had thought of himself only as an ape, and even now it was often easier for him to understand and appreciate the motives of the great Mangani than those of man.

At a signal from Tarzan, Tantor stopped; and assuming again his customary composure, though still alert to any danger that might threaten his friend, he watched while the ape-man turned and knelt beside the prostrate girl. Tarzan had at first thought her dead, but he soon discovered that she was only in a swoon. Lifting her in his arms, he spoke a half dozen words to the great pachyderm, who turned about and, putting down his head, started off straight into the dense jungle, making a pathway along which Tarzan bore the unconscious girl.

Straight as an arrow moved Tantor, the elephant, to halt at last upon the bank of a considerable river. Beyond this was a spot that Tarzan had in mind to which he wished to convey To-yat's unfortunate captive, whom he had recognized immediately as the young woman he had seen in the base camp of the conspirators and a cursory examination of whom convinced him was upon the verge of death from starvation, shock, and exposure.

Once again he spoke to Tantor; and the great pachyderm, twining his trunk around their bodies, lifted the two gently to his broad back. Then he waded into the river and set out for the opposite shore. The channel in the center was deep and swift, and Tantor was swept off his feet and carried down stream for a considerable distance before he found footing again, but eventually he won to the opposite bank. Here again he went ahead, making trail, until at last he broke into a broad, well marked game trail.

Now Tarzan took the lead, and Tantor followed. While they moved thus silently toward their destination, Zora Drinov opened her eyes. Instantly recollection of her plight filled her consciousness; and then almost simultaneously she realized that her cheek, resting upon the shoulder of her captor, was not pressing against a shaggy coat, but against the smooth skin of a human body, and then she turned her head and looked at the profile of the creature that was carrying her.

She thought at first that she was the victim of some

strange hallucination of terror; for, of course, she could not measure the time that she had been unconscious, nor recall any of the incidents that had occurred during that period. The last thing that she remembered was that she had been in the arms of a great ape, who was carrying her off to the jungle. She had closed her eyes; and when she opened them again, the ape had been transformed into a handsome demigod of the forest.

She closed her eyes and turned her head so that she faced back over the man's shoulder. She thought that she would keep her eyes tightly closed for a moment, then open them and turn them stealthily once more toward the face of the creature that was carrying her so lightly along the jungle trail. Perhaps this time he would be an ape again, and then she would know that she was indeed mad, or dreaming.

And when she did open her eyes, the sight that met them convinced her that she was experiencing a nightmare; for plodding along the trail directly behind her, was a giant bull elephant.

Tarzan, apprised of her returning consciousness by the movement of her head upon his shoulder, turned his own to look at her and saw her gazing at Tantor in wide-eyed astonishment. Then she turned toward him, and their eyes met.

"Who are you?" she asked in a whisper. "Am I dreaming?" But the ape-man only turned his eyes to the front and made no reply.

Zora thought of struggling to free herself; but realizing that she was very weak and helpless, she at last resigned herself to her fate and let her cheek fall again to the bronzed shoulder of the ape-man.

When Tarzan finally stopped and laid his burden upon the ground, it was in a little clearing through which ran a tiny stream of clear water. Immense trees arched overhead, and through their foliage the great sun dappled the grass beneath them.

As Zora Drinov lay stretched upon the soft turf, she realized for the first time how weak she was; for when she attempted to rise, she found that she could not. As her eyes took in the scene about her, it seemed more than ever like a dream—the great bull elephant standing almost above her and the bronzed figure of an almost naked giant squatting upon his haunches beside the little stream. She saw him fold a great leaf into the shape of a cornucopia and, after filling it with water, rise and come toward her. Without a word he stooped, and putting an arm beneath her shoulders and raising her to a sitting position, he offered her the water from his improvised cup.

She drank deeply, for she was very thirsty. Then, looking up into the handsome face above her, she voiced her thanks; but when the man did not reply, she thought, naturally, that he did not understand her. When she had satisfied her thirst and he had lowered her gently to the ground again, he swung lightly into a tree and disappeared into the forest. But above her the great elephant stood, as though on guard, his huge body swaying gently to and fro.

The quiet and peace of her surroundings tended to soothe her nerves, but deeply rooted in her mind was the conviction that her situation was most precarious. The man was a mystery to her; and while she knew, of course, that the ape that had stolen her had not been transformed miraculously into a handsome forest god, yet she could not account in any way for his presence or for the disappearance of the ape, except upon the rather extravagant hypothesis that the two had worked together, the ape having stolen her for this man, who was its master. There had been nothing in the man's attitude to suggest that he intended to harm her, and yet so accustomed was she to gauge all men by the standards of civilized society that she could not conceive that he had other than ulterior designs.

To her analytical mind the man presented a paradox that intrigued her imagination, seeming, as he did, so utterly out of place in this savage African jungle; while at the same time he harmonized perfectly with his surroundings, in which he seemed absolutely at home and assured of himself, a fact that was still further impressed upon her by the presence of the wild bull elephant, to which the man paid no more attention than one would to a lap dog. Had he been unkempt, filthy, and degraded in appearance, she would have catalogued him immediately as one of those social outcasts, usually half demented, who are occasionally found far from the haunts of men, living the life of wild beasts, whose high standards of decency and cleanliness they uniformly fail to observe. But this creature had suggested more the trained athlete in whom cleanliness was a fetish, nor did his well shaped head and intelligent eyes even remotely suggest mental or moral degradation.

And as she pondered him, the man returned, bearing a

great load of straight branches, from which the twigs and leaves had been removed. With a celerity and adeptness that bespoke long years of practice, he constructed a shelter upon the bank of the rivulet. He gathered broad leaves to thatch its roof, and leafy branches to enclose it upon three sides, so that it formed a protection against the prevailing winds. He floored it with leaves and small twigs and dry grasses. Then he came and, lifting the girl in his arms, bore her to the rustic bower he had fabricated.

Once again he left her; and when he returned he brought a little fruit, which he fed to her sparingly, for he guessed that she had been long without food and knew that he must not overtax her stomach.

Always he worked in silence; and though no word had passed between them, Zora Drinov felt growing within her consciousness a conviction of his trustworthiness.

The next time that he left her he was gone a considerable time, but still the elephant stood in the clearing, like some titanic sentinel upon guard.

When next the man returned, he brought the carcass of a deer; and then Zora saw him make fire, after the manner of primitive men. As the meat roasted above it, the fragrant aroma came to her nostrils, bringing consciousness of a ravening hunger. When the meat was cooked, the man came and squatted beside her, cutting small pieces with his keen hunting knife and feeding her as though she had been a helpless baby. He gave her only a little at a time, making her rest often; and while she ate he spoke for the first time, but not to her, nor in any language that she had ever heard. He spoke to the great elephant, and the huge pachyderm wheeled slowly about and entered the jungle, where she could hear the diminishing noise of his passage until it was lost in the distance. Before the meal was over, it was quite dark; and she finished it in the fitful light of the fire that shone redly on the bronzed skin of her companion and shot back from mysterious gray eyes that gave the impression of seeing everything, even her inmost thoughts. Then he brought her a drink of water, after which he squatted down outside her shelter and proceeded to satisfy his own hunger.

Gradually the girl had been lulled to a feeling of security by the seeming solicitude of her strange protector. But now distinct misgivings assailed her, and suddenly she felt a strange new fear of the silent giant in whose power she was; for when he ate she saw that he ate his meat raw, tearing the flesh like a wild beast. When there came the sound of something moving in the jungle just beyond the fire light and he raised his head and looked and there came a low and savage growl of warning from his lips, the girl closed her eyes and buried her face in her arms in sudden terror and revulsion. From the darkness of the jungle there came an answering growl; but the sound moved on, and presently all was silent again.

It seemed a long time before Zora dared open her eyes again, and when she did she saw that the man had finished his meal and was stretched out on the grass between her and the fire. She was afraid of him, of that she was quite certain; yet, at the same time, she could not deny that his presence there imparted to her a feeling of safety that she had never before felt in the jungle. As she tried to fathom this, she dozed and presently was asleep.

The young sun was already bringing renewed warmth to the jungle when she awoke. The man had replenished the fire and was sitting before it, grilling small fragments of meat. Beside him were some fruits, which he must have gathered since he had awakened. As she watched him, she was still further impressed by his great physical beauty, as well as by a certain marked nobility of bearing that harmonized well with the dignity of his poise and the intelligence of his keen gray eyes. She wished that she had not seen him devour his meat like a—ah, that was it—like a lion. How much like a lion he was, in his strength, and dignity, and majesty, and with all the quiet suggestion of ferocity that pervaded his every act. And so it was that she came to think of him as her lion-man and, while trying to trust him, always fearing him not a little.

Again he fed her and brought her water before he satisfied his own hunger; but before he started to eat, he arose and voiced a long, low call. Then once more he squatted upon his haunches and devoured his food. Although he held it in his strong, brown hands and ate the flesh raw, she saw now that he ate slowly and with the same quiet dignity that marked his every act, so that presently she found him less revolting. Once again she tried to talk with him, addressing him in various languages and several African dialects, but as for any sign he gave that he understood her she might as well have been addressing a dumb brute. Doubtless her disappointment would have been replaced by anger could she have known that she was addressing an English lord, who understood per-

fectly every word that she uttered, but who, for reasons
which he himself best knew, preferred to remain the dumb
brute to this woman whom he looked upon as an enemy.

However, it was well for Zora Drinov that he was what he
was, for it was the prompting of the English lord and not that
of the savage carnivore that had moved him to succor her
because she was alone, and helpless, and a woman. The beast
in Tarzan would not have attacked her, but would merely
have ignored her, letting the law of the jungle take its course
as it must with all her creatures.

Shortly after Tarzan had finished his meal, a crashing in
the jungle announced the return of Tantor; and when he
appeared in the little clearing, the girl realized that the great
brute had come in response to the call of the man, and
marvelled.

And so the days wore on; and slowly Zora Drinov regained
her strength, guarded by night by the silent forest god and
by day by the great bull elephant. Her only apprehension
now was for the safety of Wayne Colt, who was seldom
from her thoughts. Nor was her apprehension groundless,
for the young American had fallen upon bad days.

Almost frantic with concern for the safety of Zora, he had
exhausted his strength in futile search for her and her abductor, forgetful of himself until hunger and fatigue had taken
their toll of his strength. He had awakened at last to the
realization that his condition was dangerous; and now when
he needed food most, the game that he had formerly found
reasonably plentiful seemed to have deserted the country.
Even the smaller rodents that had once sufficed to keep him
alive were either too wary for him or not present at all.
Occasionally he found fruits that he could eat, but they
seemed to impart little or no strength to him; and at last
he was forced to the conviction that he had reached
the end of his endurance and his strength and that nothing
short of a miracle could preserve him from death. He was
so weak that he could stagger only a few steps at a time
and then, sinking to the ground, was forced to lie there for
a long time before he could arise again; and always there
was the knowledge that eventually he would not arise.

Yet he would not give up. Something more than the urge
to live drove him on. He could not die, he must not die
while Zora Drinov was in danger. He had found a well
beaten trail at last where he was sure that sooner or later
he must meet a native hunter, or, perhaps, find his way to

the camp of his fellows. He could only crawl now, for he had not the strength to rise; and then suddenly the moment came that he had striven so long to avert—the moment that marked the end, though it came in a form that he had only vaguely anticipated as one of several that might ring the curtain upon his earthly existence.

As he lay in the trail resting before he dragged himself on again, he was suddenly conscious that he was not alone. He had heard no sounds, for doubtless his hearing had been dulled by exhaustion; but he was aware through the medium of that strange sense, the possession of which each of us has felt at some time in his existence, that told him eyes were upon him.

With an effort he raised his head and looked, and there, before him in the trail, stood a great lion, his lips drawn back in an angry snarl, his yellow-green eyes glaring balefully.

14

Shot Down

ARZAN went almost daily to watch the camp of his enemy, moving swiftly through the jungle by trails unknown
to man. He saw that preparations for the first bold
stroke were almost completed, and finally he saw uniforms
being issued to all members of the party—uniforms which
he recognized as those of French Colonial Troops—and he
realized that the time had come when he must move. He
hoped that little Nkima had carried his message safely, but
if not, Tarzan would find some other way.

Zora Drinov's strength was slowly returning. Today she
had arisen and taken a few steps out into the sunlit clearing.
The great elephant regarded her. She had long since ceased to
fear him, as she had ceased to fear the strange white man
who had befriended her. Slowly the girl approached the great
bull, and Tantor regarded her out of his little eyes as he
waved his trunk to and fro.

He had been so docile and harmless all the days that he
had guarded her that it had grown to be difficult for Zora
to conceive him capable of inflicting injury upon her. But
as she looked into his little eyes now, there was an expression
there that brought her to a sudden halt; and as she realized
that after all he was only a wild bull elephant, she suddenly
appreciated the rashness of her act. She was already so close
to him that she could have reached out and touched him,
as had been her intention, having thought that she would
thus make friends with him.

It was in her mind to fall back with dignity, when the
waving trunk shot suddenly out and encircled her body. Zora

146

Drinov did not scream. She only closed her eyes and waited. She felt herself lifted from the ground, and a moment later the elephant had crossed the little clearing and deposited her in her shelter. Then he backed off slowly and resumed his post of duty.

He had not hurt her. A mother could not have lifted her baby more gently, but he had impressed upon Zora Drinov that she was a prisoner and that he was her keeper. As a matter of fact, Tantor was only carrying out Tarzan's instructions, which had nothing to do with the forcible restraint of the girl, but were only a measure of precaution to prevent her wandering into the jungle where other dangers might overtake her.

Zora had not fully regained her strength, and the experience left her trembling. Though she now realized that her sudden fears for her safety had been groundless, she decided that she would take no more liberties with her mighty warden.

It was not long after, that Tarzan returned, much earlier in the day than was his custom. He spoke only to Tantor; and the great beast, touching him almost caressingly with his trunk, turned and lumbered off into the forest. Then Tarzan advanced to where Zora sat in the opening of her shelter. Lightly he lifted her from the ground and tossed her to his shoulder; and then, to her infinite surprise at the strength and agility of the man, he swung into a tree and was off through the jungle in the wake of the pachyderm.

At the edge of the river that they had crossed before, Tantor was awaiting them, and once more he carried Zora and Tarzan safely to the other bank.

Tarzan himself had crossed the river twice a day since he had made the camp for Zora; but when he went alone he needed no help from Tantor or any other, for he swam the swift stream, his eye alert and his keen knife ready should Gimla, the crocodile, attack him. But for the crossing of the woman, he had enlisted the services of Tantor that she might not be subjected to the danger and hardship of the only other means of crossing that was possible.

As Tantor clambered up the muddy bank, Tarzan dismissed him with a word, as with the girl in his arms he leaped into a nearby tree.

That flight through the jungle was an experience that might long stand vividly in the memory of Zora Drinov. That a human being could possess the strength and agility of the creature that carried her seemed unbelievable, and she might easily have attributed a supernatural origin to him had she not felt the life in the warm flesh that was pressed against hers. Leaping from branch to branch, swinging across breathless voids, she was borne swiftly through the middle terrace of the forest. At first she had been terrified, but gradually fear left her, to be replaced by that utter confidence which Tarzan of the Apes has inspired in many a breast. At last he stopped and, lowering her to the branch upon which he stood, pointed through the surrounding foliage ahead of them. Zora looked and to her astonishment saw the camp of her companions lying ahead and below her. Once more the ape-man took her in his arms and dropped lightly to the ground into a wide trail that swept past the base of the tree in which he had halted. With a wave of his hand he indicated that she was free to go to the camp.

"Oh, how can I thank you!" exclaimed the girl. "How can I ever make you understand how splendid you have been and how I appreciate all that you have done for me?" But his only reply was to turn and swing lightly into the tree that spread its green foliage above them.

With a rueful shake of her head, Zora Drinov started along the trail toward camp, while above her Tarzan followed through the trees to make certain that she arrived in safety.

Paul Ivitch had been hunting, and he was just returning to camp when he saw something move in a tree at the edge of the clearing. He saw the spots of a leopard, and raising his rifle, he fired; so that at the moment that Zora entered the camp, the body of Tarzan of the Apes lunged from a tree almost at her side, blood trickling from a bullet wound in his head as the sunshine played upon the leopard spots of his loin cloth.

*   *   *

The sight of the lion growling above him might have shaken the nerves of a man in better physical condition than was Wayne Colt, but the vision of a beautiful girl running quickly toward the savage beast from the rear was the final stroke that almost overwhelmed him.

Through his brain ran a medley of recollection and conjecture. In a brief instant he recalled that men had borne witness to the fact that they had felt no pain while being mauled by a lion—neither pain nor fear—and he also recalled that men went mad from thirst and hunger. If he were to die, then, it would not be painful, and of that he was glad; but if he were not to die, then surely he was mad, for the lion and the girl must be the hallucination of a crazed mind.

Fascination held his eyes fixed upon the two. How real they were! He heard the girl speak to the lion, and then he saw her brush past the great savage beast and come and bend over him where he lay helpless in the trail. She touched him, and then he knew that she was real.

"Who are you?" she asked, in limping English that was beautiful with a strange accent. "What has happened to you?"

"I have been lost," he said, "and I am about done up. I have not eaten for a long while," and then he fainted.

Jad-bal-ja, the golden lion, had conceived a strange affection for La of Opar. Perhaps it was the call of one kindred savage spirit to another. Perhaps it was merely the recollection that she was Tarzan's friend. But be that as it may, he seemed to find the same pleasure in her company that a faithful dog finds in the company of his master. He had protected her with fierce loyalty, and when he made his kill he shared the flesh with her. She, however, after cutting off a portion that she wanted, had always gone away a little distance to build her primitive fire and cook the flesh; nor ever had she ventured back to the kill after Jad-bal-ja had commenced to feed, for a lion is yet a lion, and the grim and ferocious growls that accompanied his feeding warned the girl against presuming too far upon the new found generosity of the carnivore.

They had been feeding, when the approach of Colt had attracted Numa's attention and brought him into the trail from his kill. For a moment La had feared that she might not be able to keep the lion from the man, and she had wanted to do so; for something in the stranger's appearance reminded her of Tarzan, whom he more nearly resembled than he did the grotesque priests of Opar. Because of this fact she thought that possibly the stranger might be from Tarzan's country. Perhaps he was one of Tarzan's friends and if so, she must protect him. To her relief, the lion had obeyed her when she had called upon him to halt, and now he evinced no further desire to attack the man.

When Colt regained consciousness, La tried to raise him to his feet; and, with considerable difficulty and some slight assistance from the man, she succeeded in doing so. She put one of his arms across her shoulders and, supporting him thus, guided him back along the trail, while Jad-bal-ja followed at their heels. She had difficulty in getting him through the brush to the hidden glen where Jad-bal-ja's kill lay and her little fire was burning a short distance away. But at last she succeeded and when they had come close to her fire, she lowered the man to the ground, while Jad-bal-ja turned once more to his feeding and his growling.

La fed the man tiny pieces of the meat that she had cooked, and he ate ravenously all that she would give him. A short distance away ran the river, where La and the lion would have gone to drink after they had fed; but doubting whether she could get the man so great a distance through the jungle, she left him there with the lion and went down to the river; but first she told Jad-bal-ja to guard him, speaking in the language of the first men, the language of the Mangani, that all creatures of the jungle understand to a greater or lesser extent. Near the river La found what she sought—a fruit with a hard rind. With her knife she cut an end from one of these fruits and scooped out the pulpy interior, producing a primitive but entirely practical cup, which she filled with water from the river.

The water, as much as the food, refreshed and strengthened Colt; and though he lay but a few yards from a feeding lion, it seemed an eternity since he had experienced such a feeling of contentment and security, clouded only by his anxiety concerning Zora.

"You feel stronger now?" asked La, her voice tinged with concern.

"Very much," he replied.

"Then tell me who you are and if this is your country."

"This is not my country," replied Colt. "I am an American. My name is Wayne Colt."

"You are perhaps a friend of Tarzan of the Apes?" she asked.

He shook his head. "No," he said. "I have heard of him, but I do not know him."

La frowned. "You are his enemy, then?" she demanded.

"Of course not," replied Colt. "I do not even know him."

A sudden light flashed in La's eyes. "Do you know Zora?" she asked.

Colt came to his elbow with a sudden start. "Zora Drinov?" he demanded. "What do you know of her?"

"She is my friend," said La.

"She is my friend also," said Colt.

"She is in trouble," said La.

"Yes, I know it; but how did you know?"

"I was with her when she was taken prisoner by the men of the desert. They took me also, but I escaped."

"How long ago was that?"

"The Flaming God has gone to rest many times since I saw Zora," replied the girl.

"Then I have seen her since."

"Where is she?"

"I do not know. She was with the Aarabs when I found her. We escaped from them; and then, while I was hunting in the jungle something came and carried her away. I do not know whether it was a man or a gorilla; for though I saw its footprints, I could not be sure. I have been searching for her for a long time; but I could not find food, and it has been some time since I have had water; so I lost my strength, and you found me as I am."

"You shall not want for food nor water now," said La, "for Numa, the lion, will hunt for us; and if we can find the camp of Zora's friends, perhaps they will go out and search for her."

"You know where the camp is?" he asked. "Is it near?"

"I do not know where it is. I have been searching for it to lead her friends after the men of the desert."

Colt had been studying the girl as they talked. He had noted her strange, barbaric apparel and the staggering beauty of her face and figure. He knew almost intuitively that she was not of the world that he knew, and his mind was filled with curiosity concerning her.

"You have not told me who you are," he said.

"I am La of Opar," she replied, "high priestess of the Flaming God."

Opar! Now indeed he knew that she was not of his world. Opar, the city of mystery, the city of fabulous treasures. Could it be that the same city that housed the grotesque warriors with whom he and Romero had fought produced also such beautiful creatures as Nao and La, and only these? He wondered why he had not connected her with Opar at once, for now he saw that her stomacher was similar to that of Nao and of the priestess that he had seen upon the throne in the great chamber of the ruined temple. Recalling his attempt to enter Opar and loot it of its treasures, he deemed it expedient to make no mention of any familiarity with the city of the girl's birth, for he guessed that Opar's women might be as primitively fierce in their vengeance as he had found Nao in her love.

The lion, and the girl, and the man lay up that night beside Jad-bal-ja's kill, and in the morning Colt found that his strength had partially returned. During the night Numa had finished his kill; and after the sun had risen, La found fruits which she and Colt ate, while the lion strolled to the river to drink, pausing once to roar, that the world might know the king was there.

"Numa will not kill again until tomorrow," she said, "so we shall have no meat until then, unless we are fortunate enough to kill something ourselves."

Colt had long since abandoned the heavy rifle of the Aarabs, to the burden of which his growing weakness had left his muscles inadequate; so he had nothing but his bare hands and La only a knife with which they might make a kill.

"Then I guess we shall eat fruit until the lion kills again," he said. "In the meantime we might as well be trying to find the camp."

She shook her head. "No," she said, "you must rest. You were very weak when I found you, and it is not well that you should exert yourself until you are strong again. Numa will sleep all day. You and I will cut some sticks and lie beside a little trail, where the small things go. Perhaps we shall have luck; but if we do not, Numa will kill again tomorrow, and this time I shall take a whole hind quarter."

"I cannot believe that a lion would let you do that," said the man.

"At first I did not understand it myself," said La, "but after a while I remembered. It is because I am Tarzan's friend that he does not harm me."

* * *

When Zora Drinov saw her lion-man lying lifeless on the ground, she ran quickly to him and knelt at his side. She had heard the shot, and now seeing the blood running from the wound upon his head, she thought that someone had killed him intentionally and when Ivitch came running out, his rifle in his hand, she turned upon him like a tigress.

"You have killed him," she cried. "You beast! He was worth more than a dozen such as you."

The sound of the shot and the crashing of the body to the

ground had brought men running from all parts of the camp;
so that Tarzan and the girl were soon surrounded by a curious
and excited throng of blacks, among whom the remaining
whites were pushing their way.

Ivitch was stunned, not only by the sight of the giant white
man lying apparently dead before him, but also by the presence of Zora Drinov, whom all within the camp had given up
as irretrievably lost. "I had no idea, Comrade Drinov," he
explained, "that I was shooting at a man. I see now what
caused my mistake. I saw something moving in a tree and
thought that it was a leopard, but instead it was the leopard
skin that he wears about his loins."

By this time Zveri had elbowed his way to the center of
the group. "Zora!" he cried in astonishment as he saw the
girl. "Where did you come from? What has happened? What
is the meaning of this?"

"It means that this fool, Ivitch, has killed the man who
saved my life," cried Zora.

"Who is he?" asked Zveri.

"I do not know," replied Zora. "He has never spoken to
me. He does not seem to understand any language with which
I am familiar."

"He is not dead," cried Ivitch. "See, he moved."

Romero knelt and examined the wound in Tarzan's head.
"He is only stunned," he said. "The bullet struck him a
glancing blow. There are no indications of a fracture of the
skull. I have seen men hit thus before. He may be unconscious
for a long time, or he may not, but I am sure that he will
not die."

"Who the devil do you suppose he is?" asked Zveri.

Zora shook her head. "I have no idea," she said. "I only
know that he is as splendid as he is mysterious."

"I know who he is," said a black, who had pushed forward to where he could see the figure of the prostrate man,
"and if he is not already dead, you had better kill him, for he
will be your worst enemy."

"What do you mean?" demanded Zveri. "Who is he?"

"He is Tarzan of the Apes."

"You are certain?" snapped Zveri.

"Yes, Bwana," replied the black. "I saw him once before,
and one never forgets Tarzan of the Apes."

"Yours was a lucky shot, Ivitch," said the leader, "and
now you may as well finish what you started."

"Kill him, you mean?" demanded Ivitch.

"Our cause is lost and our lives with it, if he lives," replied Zveri. "I thought that he was dead, or I should never have come here; and now that Fate has thrown him into our hands we would be fools to let him escape, for we could not have a worse enemy than he."

"I cannot kill him in cold blood," said Ivitch.

"You always were a weak minded fool," said Zveri, "but I am not. Stand aside, Zora," and as he spoke he drew his revolver and advanced toward Tarzan.

The girl threw herself across the ape-man, shielding his body with hers. "You cannot kill him," she cried. "You must not."

"Don't be a fool, Zora," snapped Zveri.

"He saved my life and brought me back here to camp. Do you think I am going to let you murder him?" she demanded.

"I am afraid you can't help yourself, Zora," replied the man. "I do not like to do it, but it is his life or the cause. If he lives, we fail."

The girl leaped to her feet and faced Zveri. "If you kill him, Peter, I shall kill you—I swear it by everything that I hold most dear. Hold him prisoner if you will, but as you value your life, do not kill him."

Zveri went pale with anger. "Your words are treason," he said. "Traitors to the cause have died for less than what you have said."

Zora Drinov realized that the situation was extremely dangerous. She had little reason to believe that Zveri would make good his threat toward her, but she saw that if she would save Tarzan she must act quickly. "Send the others away," she said to Zveri. "I have something to tell you before you kill this man."

For a moment the leader hesitated. Then he turned to Dorsky, who stood at his side. "Have the fellow securely bound and taken to one of the tents," he commanded. "We shall give him a fair trial after he has regained consciousness and then place him before a firing squad," and then to the girl, "Come with me, Zora, and I will listen to what you have to say."

In silence the two walked to Zveri's tent. "Well?" inquired Zveri, as the girl halted before the entrance. "What have you to say to me that you think will change my plans relative to your lover?"

Zora looked at him for a long minute, a faint sneer of contempt curling her lips. "*You* would think such a thing," she said, "but you are wrong. However you may think, though, you shall not kill him."

"And why not?" demanded Zveri.

"Because if you do I shall tell them all what your plans are; that you yourself are a traitor to the cause, and that you have been using them all to advance your own selfish ambition to make yourself Emperor of Africa."

"You would not dare," cried Zveri; "nor would I let you; for as much as I love you, I shall kill you here on the spot, unless you promise not to interfere in any way with my plans."

"You do not dare kill me," taunted the girl. "You have antagonized every man in the camp, Peter, and they all like me. Some of them, perhaps, love me a little. Do you think that I should not be avenged within five minutes after you had killed me? You will have to think of something else, my friend; and the best thing that you can do is to take my advice. Keep Tarzan of the Apes a prisoner if you will, but on your life do not kill him or permit anyone else to do so."

Zveri sank into a camp chair. "Everyone is against me," he said. "Even you, the woman I love, turn against me."

"I have not changed toward you in any respect, Peter," said the girl.

"You mean that?" he asked, looking up.

"Absolutely," she replied.

"How long were you alone in the jungle with that man?" he demanded.

"Don't start that, Peter," she said. "He could not have treated me differently if he had been my own brother; and certainly, all other considerations aside, you should know me well enough to know that I have no such weakness in the direction that your tone implied."

"You have never loved me—that is the reason," he declared. "But I would not trust you or any other woman with a man she loves or with whom she was temporarily infatuated."

"That," she said, "has nothing to do with what we are discussing. Are you going to kill Tarzan of the Apes, or are you not?"

"For your sake, I shall let him live," replied the man, "even though I do not trust you," he added. "I trust no one. How can I? Look at this," and he took a code message from his pocket and handed it to her. "This came a few days ago—the damn traitor. I wish I could get my hands on him. I should like to have killed him myself, but I suppose I shall have no such luck, as he is probably already dead."

Zora took the paper. Below the message, in Zveri's scrawling hand, it had been decoded in Russian script. As she read it, her eyes grew large with astonishment. "It is incredible," she cried.

"It is the truth, though," said Zveri. "I always suspected the dirty hound," and he added with an oath, "I think that damn Mexican is just as bad."

"At least," said Zora, "his plan has been thwarted, for I take it that his message did not get through."

"No," said Zveri. "By error it was delivered to our agents instead of his."

"Then no harm has been done."

"Fortunately, no; but it has made me suspicious of everyone, and I am going to push the expedition through at once before anything further can occur to interfere with my plans."

"Everything is ready, then?" she asked.

"Everything is ready," he replied. "We march tomorrow morning. And now tell me what happened while I was at Opar. Why did the Aarabs desert, and why did you go with them?"

"Abu Batn was angry and resentful because you left him to guard the camp. The Aarabs felt that it was a reflection upon their courage, and I think that they would have deserted you anyway, regardless of me. Then, the day after you left, a strange woman wandered into camp. She was a very beautiful white woman from Opar; and Abu Batn, conceiving the idea of profiting through the chance that Fate had sent him, took us with him with the intention of selling us into captivity on his return march to his own country."

"Are there no honest men in the world?" demanded Zveri.

"I am afraid not," replied the girl; but as he was staring moodily at the ground, he did not see the contemptuous curl of her lip that accompanied her reply.

She described the luring of La from Abu Batn's camp and of the sheykh's anger at the treachery of Ibn Dammuk; and then she told him of her own escape, but she did not mention Wayne Colt's connection with it and led him to believe that she wandered alone in the jungle until the great ape had captured her. She dwelt at length upon Tarzan's kindness and consideration and told of the great elephant who had guarded her by day.

"Sounds like a fairy story," said Zveri, "but I have heard

enough about this ape-man to believe almost anything concerning him, which is one reason why I believe we shall never be safe while he lives."

"He cannot harm us while he is our prisoner; and certainly, if you love me as you say you do, the man who saved my life deserves better from you than ignominious death."

"Speak no more of it," said Zveri. "I have already told you that I would not kill him," but in his treacherous mind he was formulating a plan whereby Tarzan might be destroyed while still he adhered to the letter of his promise to Zora.

15

"Kill, Tantor, Kill!"

EARLY the following morning the expedition filed out of camp, the savage black warriors arrayed in the uniforms of French Colonial Troops; while Zveri, Romero, Ivitch, and Mori wore the uniforms of French officers. Zora Drinov accompanied the marching column; for though she had asked to be permitted to remain and nurse Tarzan, Zveri would not permit her to do so, saying that he would not again let her out of his sight. Dorsky and a handful of blacks were left behind to guard the prisoner and watch over the store of provisions and equipment that were to be left in the base camp.

As the column had been preparing to march, Zveri gave his final instructions to Dorsky. "I leave this matter entirely in your hands," he said. "It must appear that he escaped, or, at worst, that he met an accidental death."

"You need give the matter no further thought, Comrade," replied Dorsky. "Long before you return, this stranger will have been removed."

A long and difficult march lay before the invaders, their route lying across southeastern Abyssinia into Italian Somaliland, along five hundred miles of rough and savage country. It was Zveri's intention to make no more than a demonstration in the Italian colony, merely sufficient to arouse the anger of the Italians still further against the French and to give the fascist dictator the excuse which Zveri believed was all that he awaited to carry his mad dream of Italian conquest across Europe.

Perhaps Zveri was a little mad, but then he was a disciple

of mad men whose greed for power wrought distorted images in their minds, so that they could not differentiate between the rational and the bizarre; and then, too, Zveri had for so long dreamed his dream of empire that he saw now only his goal and none of the insurmountable obstacles that beset his path. He saw a new Roman emperor ruling Europe, and himself as Emperor of Africa making an alliance with his new European power against all the balance of the world. He pictured two splendid golden thrones; upon one of them sat the Emperor Peter I, and upon the other the Empress Zora; and so he dreamed through the long, hard marches toward the east.

* * *

It was the morning of the day following that upon which he had been shot before Tarzan regained consciousness. He felt weak and sick, and his head ached horribly. When he tried to move, he discovered that his wrists and ankles were securely bound. He did not know what had happened, and at first he could not imagine where he was; but, as recollection slowly returned and he recognized about him the canvas walls of a tent, he understood that in some way his enemies had captured him. He tried to wrench his wrists free from the cords that held them, but they resisted his every effort.

He listened intently and sniffed the air, but he could detect no evidence of the teeming camp that he had seen when he had brought the girl back. He knew, however, that at least one night had passed; for the shadows that he could see through the tent opening indicated that the sun was high in the heavens, whereas it had been low in the west when last he saw it. Hearing voices, he realized that he was not alone, though he was confident that there must be comparatively few men in camp.

Deep in the jungle he heard an elephant trumpeting, and once, from far off, came faintly the roar of a lion. Tarzan strove again to snap the bonds that held him, but they would not yield. Then he turned his head so that he faced the opening in the tent, and from his lips burst a long, low cry; the cry of a beast in distress.

Dorsky, who was lolling in a chair before his own tent, leaped to his feet. The blacks, who had been talking animatedly, before their own shelters, went quickly quiet and seized their weapons.

"What was that?" Dorsky demanded of his black boy.

The fellow, wide-eyed and trembling, shook his head. "I do not know, Bwana," he said. "Perhaps the man in the tent has died, for such a noise may well have come from the throat of a ghost."

"Nonsense," said Dorsky. "Come, we'll have a look at him." But the black held back, and the white man went on alone.

The sound, which had come apparently from the tent in which the captive lay, had had a peculiar effect upon Dorsky, causing the flesh of his scalp to creep and a strange foreboding to fill him; so that as he neared the tent, he went more slowly and held his revolver ready in his hand.

When he entered the tent, he saw the man lying where he had been left; but now his eyes were open, and when they met those of the Russian, the latter had a sensation similar to that which one feels when he comes eye to eye with a wild beast that has been caught in a trap.

"Well," said Dorsky, "so you have come to, have you? What do you want?" The captive made no reply, but his eyes never left the other's face. So steady was the unblinking gaze that Dorsky became uneasy beneath it. "You had better learn to talk," he said gruffly, "if you know what is good for you." Then it occurred to him that perhaps the man did not understand him so he turned in the entrance and called to some of the blacks, who had advanced, half in curiosity, half in fear, toward the tent of the prisoner. "One of you fellows come here," he said.

At first no one seemed inclined to obey, but presently a stalwart warrior advanced. "See if this fellow can understand your language. Come in and tell him that I have a proposition to make to him and that he had better listen to it."

"If this is indeed Tarzan of the Apes," said the black, "he can understand me," and he came warily to the entrance of the tent.

The black repeated the message in his own dialect, but by no sign did the ape-man indicate that he understood.

Dorsky lost his patience. "You damned ape," he said. "You needn't try to make a fool of me. I know perfectly well that you understand this fellow's gibberish, and I know, too, that you are an Englishman and that you understand English. I'll give you just five minutes to think this thing over, and then I am coming back. If you have not made up your mind to talk by that time, you can take the consequences." Then he turned on his heel and left the tent.

* * *

Little Nkima had travelled far. Around his neck was a stout thong, supporting a little bag of leather, in which reposed a message. This eventually he had brought to Muviro, war chief of the Waziri; and when the Waziri had started out upon their long march, Nkima had ridden proudly upon the shoulder of Muviro. For some time he had remained with the black warriors; but then, at last, moved perhaps by some caprice of his erratic mind, or by a great urge that he could not resist, he had left them and, facing alone all the dangers that he feared most, had set out by himself upon business of his own.

Many and narrow were the escapes of Nkima as he swung through the giants of the forest. Could he have resisted temptation, he might have passed with reasonable safety, but that he could not do; and so he was forever getting himself into trouble by playing pranks upon strangers, who, if they possessed any sense of humor themselves, most certainly failed to appreciate little Nkima's. Nkima could not forget that he was friend and confidant of Tarzan, Lord of the Jungle, though he seemed often to forget that Tarzan was not there to protect him when he hurled taunts and insults at other monkeys less favored. That he came through alive speaks more eloquently for his speed than for his intelligence or courage. Much of the time he was fleeing in terror, emitting shrill screams of mental anguish; yet he never seemed to learn from experience, and having barely eluded one pursuer intent upon murdering him he would be quite prepared to insult or annoy the next creature he met, especially selecting, it would seem, those that were larger and stronger than himself.

Sometimes he fled in one direction, sometimes in another, so that he occupied much more time than was necessary in making his journey. Otherwise he would have reached his master in time to be of service to him at a moment that Tarzan needed a friend as badly, perhaps, as ever he had needed one before in his life.

And now, while far away in the forest Nkima fled from an old dog baboon, whom he had hit with a well-aimed stick, Michael Dorsky approached the tent where Nkima's master lay bound and helpless. The five minutes were up, and Dorsky had come to demand Tarzan's answer. He came alone, and as he entered the tent his simple plan of action was well formulated in his mind.

The expression upon the prisoner's face had changed. He seemed to be listening intently. Dorsky listened then, too, but could hear nothing; for by comparison with the hearing of Tarzan of the Apes Michael Dorsky was deaf. What Tarzan heard filled him with quiet satisfaction.

"Now," said Dorsky, "I have come to give you your last chance. Comrade Zveri has led two expeditions to Opar in search of the gold that we know is stored there. Both expeditions failed. It is well known that you know the location of the treasure vaults of Opar and can lead us to them. Agree that you will do this when Comrade Zveri returns, and not only will you not be harmed, but you will be released as quickly as Comrade Zveri feels that it would be safe to have you at liberty. Refuse and you die." He drew a long, slender stiletto from its sheath at his belt. "If you refuse to answer me, I shall accept that as evidence that you have not accepted my proposition." And as the ape-man maintained his stony silence, the Russian held the thin blade low before his eyes. "Think well, ape," he said, "and remember that when I slip this between your ribs there will be no sound. It will pierce your heart, and I shall leave it there until the blood has ceased to flow. Then I shall remove it and close the wound. Later in the day you will be found dead, and I shall tell the blacks that you died from the accidental gunshot. Thus your friends will never learn the truth. You will not be avenged, and you will have died uselessly." He paused for a reply, his evil eyes glinting menacingly into the cold, grey eyes of the ape-man.

The dagger was very near Tarzan's face now; and of a sudden, like a wild beast, he raised his body, and his jaws closed like a steel trap upon the wrist of the Russian. With a scream of pain, Dorsky drew back. The dagger dropped from his nerveless fingers. At the same instant Tarzan swung his legs around the feet of the would-be assassin; and as Dorsky rolled over on his back, he dragged Tarzan of the Apes on top of him.

The ape-man knew from the snapping of Dorsky's wrist bones between his teeth that the man's right hand was useless; and so he released it. Then to the Russian's horror, the ape-man's jaws sought his jugular as, from his throat, there rumbled the growl of a savage beast at bay.

Screaming for his men to come to his assistance, Dorsky tried to reach the revolver at his right hip with his left hand, but he soon saw that unless he could rid himself of Tarzan's body he would be unable to do so.

Already he heard his men running toward the tent, shouting among themselves, and then he heard exclamations of surprise and screams of terror. The next instant the tent vanished from above them, and Dorsky saw a huge bull elephant towering above him and his savage antagonist.

Instantly Tarzan ceased his efforts to close his teeth on Dorsky's throat and at the same time rolled quickly from the body of the Russian. As he did so, Dorsky's hand found his revolver.

"Kill, Tantor!" shouted the ape-man. "Kill!"

The sinuous trunk of the pachyderm twined around the Russian. The little eyes of the elephant flamed red with hate, and he trumpeted shrilly as he raised Dorsky high above his head and, wheeling about, hurled him out into the camp; while the terrified blacks, casting affrighted glances over their shoulders, fled into the jungle. Then Tantor charged his victim. With his great tusks he gored him; and then, in a frenzy of rage, trumpeting and squealing, he trampled him until nothing remained of Michael Dorsky but a bloody pulp.

From the moment that Tantor had seized the Russian, Tarzan had sought ineffectually to stay the great brute's fury, but Tantor was deaf to commands until he had wreaked his vengeance upon this creature that had dared to attack his friend. But when his rage had spent its force and nothing remained against which to vent it, he came quietly to Tarzan's side and at a word from the ape-man lifted his brown body gently in his powerful trunk and bore him away into the forest.

Deep into the jungle to a hidden glade, Tantor carried his helpless friend, and there he placed him gently on soft grasses beneath the shade of a tree. Little more could the great bull do other than to stand guard. As a result of the excitement attending the killing of Dorsky and his concern for Tarzan, Tantor was nervous and irritable. He stood with upraised ears, alert for any menacing sound, waving his sensitive trunk to and fro, searching each vagrant air current for the scent of danger.

The pain of his wound annoyed Tarzan far less than the pangs of thirst.

To little monkeys watching him from the trees he called, "Come, Manu, and untie the thongs that bind my wrists."

"We are afraid," said an old monkey.

"I am Tarzan of the Apes," said the man reassuringly. "Tarzan has been your friend always. He will not harm you."

"We are afraid," repeated the old monkey. "Tarzan deserted us. For many moons the jungle has not known Tarzan; but other Tarmangani and strange Gomangani came and with thundersticks they hunted little Manu and killed him. If Tarzan had still been our friend, he would have driven these strange men away."

"If I had been here, the strange men-things would not have harmed you," said Tarzan. "Still would Tarzan have protected you. Now I am back, but I cannot destroy the strangers or drive them away until the thongs are taken from my wrists."

"Who put them there?" asked the monkey.

"The strange Tarmangani," replied Tarzan.

"Then they must be more powerful than Tarzan," said Manu, "so what good would it do to set you free? If the strange Tarmangani found out that we had done it, they would be angry and come and kill us. Let Tarzan, who for many rains has been Lord of the Jungle, free himself."

Seeing that it was futile to appeal to Manu, Tarzan, as a forlorn hope, voiced the long, plaintive, uncanny help call of the great apes. With slowly increasing crescendo it rose to a piercing shriek that drove far and wide through the silent jungle.

In all directions, beasts, great and small, paused as the weird note broke upon their sensitive eardrums. None was afraid, for the call told them that a great bull was in trouble and, therefore, doubtless harmless; but the jackals interpreted the sound to mean the possibility of flesh and trotted off through the jungle in the direction from which it had come; and Dango, the hyaena, heard and slunk on soft pads, hoping that he would find a helpless animal that would prove easy prey. And far away, and faintly, a little monkey heard the call, recognizing the voice of the caller. Swiftly, then, he flew through the jungle, impelled as he was upon rare occasions by a directness of thought and a tenacity of purpose that brooked no interruption.

Tarzan had sent Tantor to the river to fetch water in his trunk. From a distance he caught the scent of the jackals and the horrid scent of Dango, and he hoped that Tantor would return before they came creeping upon him. He felt no fear, only an instinctive urge toward self-preservation. The jackals he held in contempt, knowing that, though bound hand and foot, he still could keep the timid creatures away; but Dango was different, for once the filthy brute realized his helplessness, Tarzan knew that those powerful jaws would make quick work of him. He knew the merciless savagery of the beast; knew that in all the jungle there was none more terrible than Dango.

The jackals came first, standing at the edge of the little glade watching him. Then they circled slowly, coming nearer; but when he raised himself to a sitting position they ran yelping away. Three times they crept closer, trying to force their courage to the point of actual attack; and then a horrid, slinking form appeared upon the edge of the glade, and the jackals withdrew to a safe distance. Dango, the hyaena, had come.

Tarzan was still sitting up, and the beast stood eyeing him, filled with curiosity and with fear. He growled, and the man-thing facing him growled back; and then from above them came a great chattering, and Tarzan, looking up, saw little Nkima dancing upon the limb of a tree above him.

"Come down, Nkima," he cried, "and untie the thongs that bind my wrists."

"Dango! Dango!" shouted Nkima. "Little Nkima is afraid of Dango."

"If you come now," said Tarzan, "it will be safe; but if you wait too long, Dango will kill Tarzan; and then to whom may little Nkima go for protection?"

"Nkima comes," shouted the little monkey, and dropping quickly through the trees, he leaped to Tarzan's shoulder.

The hyaena bared his fangs and laughed his horrid laugh. Tarzan spoke. "Quick, the thongs, Nkima," urged Tarzan; and the little monkey, his fingers trembling with terror, went to work upon the leather thongs at Tarzan's wrists.

Dango, his ugly head lowered, made a sudden rush; and from the deep lungs of the ape-man came a thunderous roar that might have done credit to Numa himself. With a yelp of terror the cowardly Dango turned and fled to the extremity of the glade, where he stood bristling and growling.

"Hurry, Nkima," said Tarzan. "Dango will come again. Maybe once, maybe twice, maybe many times before he closes on me; but in the end he will realize that I am helpless, and then he will not stop or turn back."

"Little Nkima's fingers are sick," said the Manu. "They are weak and they tremble. They will not untie the knot."

"Nkima has sharp teeth," Tarzan reminded him. "Why

waste your time with sick fingers over knots that they cannot untie? Let your sharp teeth do the work."

Instantly Nkima commenced to gnaw upon the strands. Silent perforce because his mouth was otherwise occupied, Nkima strove diligently and without interruption.

Dango, in the meantime, made two short rushes, each time coming a little closer, but each time turning back before the menace of the ape-man's roars and savage growls, which by now had aroused the jungle.

Above them, in the tree tops, the monkeys chattered, scolded and screamed, and in the distance the voice of Numa rolled like far thunder, while from the river came the squealing and trumpeting of Tantor.

Little Nkima was gnawing frantically at the bonds, when Dango charged again, evidently convinced by this time that the great Tarmangani was helpless, for now, with a growl, he rushed in and closed upon the man.

With a sudden surge of the great muscles of his arms that sent little Nkima sprawling, Tarzan sought to tear his hands free that he might defend himself against the savage death that menaced him in those slavering jaws; and the thongs, almost parted by Nkima's sharp teeth, gave to the terrific strain of the ape-man's efforts.

As Dango leaped for the bronzed throat, Tarzan's hand shot forward and seized the beast by the neck, but the impact of the heavy body carried him backward to the ground. Dango twisted, struggled and clawed in a vain effort to free himself from the death grip of the ape-man, but those steel fingers closed relentlessly upon his throat, until, gasping for breath, the great brute sank helplessly upon the body of its intended victim.

Until death was assured, Tarzan did not relinquish his grasp; but when at last there could be no doubt, he hurled the carcass from him and, sitting up, fell quickly to the thongs that secured his ankles.

During the brief battle, Nkima had taken refuge among the topmost branches of a lofty tree, where he leaped about, screaming frantically at the battling beasts beneath him. Not until he was quite sure that Dango was dead did he descend. Warily he approached the body, lest, perchance, he had been mistaken; but again convinced by closer scrutiny, he leaped upon it and struck it viciously, again and again, and then he stood upon it shrieking his defiance at the world with all the assurance and bravado of one who has overcome a dangerous enemy.

Tantor, startled by the help cry of his friend, had turned back from the river without taking water. Trees bent beneath his mad rush as, ignoring winding trails, he struck straight through the jungle toward the little glade in answer to the call of the ape-man; and now, infuriated by the sounds of battle, he came charging into view, a titanic engine of rage and vengeance.

Tantor's eyesight is none too good, and it seemed that in his mad charge he must trample the ape-man, who lay directly in his path; but when Tarzan spoke to him the great beast came to a sudden stop at his side and, pivoting, wheeled about in his tracks, his ears forward, his trunk raised, trumpeting a savage warning as he searched for the creature that had been meancing his friend.

"Quiet, Tantor; it was Dango. He is dead," said the ape-man. As the eyes of the elephant finally located the carcass of the hyaena he charged and trampled it, as he had trampled Dorsky, to a bloody pulp; as Nkima fled, shrieking, to the trees.

His ankles freed of their bonds, Tarzan was upon his feet; and, when Tantor had vented his rage upon the body of Dango, he called the elephant to him. Tantor came then quietly to his side and stood with his trunk touching the ape-man's body, his rage quieted and his nerves soothed by the reassuring calm of the ape-man.

And now Nkima came, making an agile leap from a swaying bow to the back of Tantor and then to the shoulder of Tarzan, where, with his little arms about the ape-man's neck, he pressed his cheek close against the bronzed cheek of the great Tarmangani, who was his master and his god.

Thus the three friends stood in the silent communion that only beasts know, as the shadows lengthened and the sun set behind the forest.

16

"Turn Back!"

THE privations that Wayne Colt had endured had weakened him far more than he had realized, so that before
his returning strength could bring renewed powers of
resistance, he was stricken with fever.

The high priestess of the Flaming God, versed in the lore of
ancient Opar, was conversant with the medicinal properties
of many roots and herbs and, as well, with the mystic powers
of incantation that drove demons from the bodies of the sick.
By day she gathered and brewed, and at night she sat at the
feet of her patient, intoning weird prayers, the origin of which
reached back through countless ages to vanished temples,
above which now rolled the waters of a mighty sea; and while
she wrought with every artifice at her command to drive out
the demon of sickness that possessed this man of an alien
world, Jad-bal-ja, the golden lion, hunted for all three, and
though at times he made his kill at a distance he never failed
to carry the carcass of his prey back to the hidden lair
where the woman nursed the man.

Days of burning fever, days of delirium, shot with periods
of rationality, dragged their slow length. Often Colt's mind
was confused by a jumble of bizarre impressions, in which La
might be Zora Drinov one moment, a ministering angel from
heaven the next, and then a Red Cross nurse; but in whatever
guise he found her it seemed always a pleasant one, and when
she was absent, as she was sometimes forced to be, he was
depressed and unhappy.

When, upon her knees at his feet, she prayed to the rising
sun, or to the sun at zenith, or to the setting sun, as was her

wont, or when she chanted strange, weird songs in an unknown tongue, accompanying them with the mysterious gestures that were a part of the ritual, he was sure that the
fever was worse and that he had become delirious again.

And so the days dragged on, and while Colt lay helpless,
Zveri marched toward Italian Somaliland; and Tarzan, recovered from the shock of his wound, followed the plain
trail of the expedition, and from his shoulder little Nkima
scolded and chattered through the day.

Behind him Tarzan had left a handful of terrified blacks in
the camp of the conspirators. They had been lolling in the
shade, following their breakfast, a week after the killing of
Dorsky and the escape of his captive. Fear of the ape-man at
liberty, that had so terrified them at first, no longer concerned
them greatly. Psychologically akin to the brutes of the forest,
they happily soon forgot their terrors; nor did they harass
their minds by anticipating those which might assail them in
the future, as it is the silly custom of civilized man to do.

And so it was that this morning a sight burst suddenly upon
their astonished eyes found them entirely unprepared. They
heard no noise, so silently go the beasts of the jungle, however
large or heavy they may be; yet suddenly, in the clearing at
the edge of the camp, appeared a great elephant, and upon
his head sat the recent captive, whom they had been told was
Tarzan of the Apes, and upon the man's shoulder perched a
little monkey. With exclamations of terror, the blacks leaped
to their feet and dashed into the jungle upon the opposite side
of the camp.

Tarzan leaped lightly to the ground and entered Dorsky's
tent. He had returned for a definite purpose; and his effort
was crowned with success, for in the tent of the Russian he
found his rope and his knife, which had been taken away
from him at the time of his capture. For bow and arrows
and a spear he had only to look to the shelters of the blacks;
and, having found what he wanted, he departed as silently as
he had come.

Now the time had arrived when Tarzan must set out rapidly
upon the trail of his enemy, leaving Tantor to the peaceful
paths that he loved best.

"I go, Tantor," he said. "Search out the forest where the
young trees have the tenderest bark and watch well against
the men-things, for they alone in all the world are the enemies
of all living creatures." He was off through the forest then,
with little Nkima clinging tightly to his bronzed neck.

Plain lay the winding trail of Zveri's army before the eyes of the ape-man, but he had no need to follow any trail. Long weeks before, as he had kept vigil above their camp, he had heard the principals discussing their plans; and so he knew their objectives, and he knew, too, how rapidly they could march and, therefore, about where he might hope to overtake them. Unhampered by files of porters sweating under heavy loads, earthbound to no winding trails, Tarzan was able to travel many times faster than the expedition. He saw their trail only when his own chanced to cross it as he laid a straight course for a point far in advance of the sweating column.

When he overtook the expedition night had fallen, and the tired men were in camp. They had eaten and were happy and many of the men were singing. To one who did not know the truth it might have appeared to be a military camp of French Colonial Troops; for there was a military precision about the arrangement of the fires, the temporary shelters, and the officers' tents that would not have been undertaken by a hunting or scientific expedition, and, in addition, there were the uniformed sentries pacing their beats. All this was the work of Miguel Romero, to whose superior knowledge of military matters Zveri had been forced to defer in all matters of this nature, though with no dimunition of the hatred which each felt for the other.

From his tree Tarzan watched the scene below, attempting to estimate as closely as possible the number of armed men that formed the fighting force of the expedition, while Nkima, bent upon some mysterious mission, swung nimbly through the trees toward the east. The ape-man realized that Zveri had recruited a force that might constitute a definite menace to the peace of Africa, since among its numbers were represented many large and warlike tribes, who might easily be persuaded to follow this mad leader were success to crown his initial engagement. It was, however, to prevent this very thing that Tarzan of the Apes had interested himself in the activities of Peter Zveri; and here, before him, was another opportunity to undermine the Russian's dream of empire while it was still only a dream and might be dissipated by trivial means; by the grim and terrible jungle methods of which Tarzan of the Apes was a past-master.

Tarzan fitted an arrow to his bow. Slowly his right hand drew back the feathered end of the shaft until the point rested almost upon his left thumb. His manner was marked by easy, effortless grace. He did not appear to be taking conscious aim; and yet when he released the shaft, it buried itself in the fleshy part of a sentry's leg precisely as Tarzan of the Apes had intended that it should.

With a yell of surprise and pain the black collapsed upon the ground, more frightened, however, than hurt; and as his fellows gathered around him, Tarzan of the Apes melted away into the shadows of the jungle night.

Attracted by the cry of the wounded man, Zveri, Romero, and the other leaders of the expedition hastened from their tents and joined the throng of excited blacks that surrounded the victim of Tarzan's campaign of terrorism.

"Who shot you?" demanded Zveri when he saw the arrow protruding from the sentry's leg.

"I do not know," replied the man.

"Have you an enemy in camp who might want to kill you?" asked Zveri.

"Even if he had," said Romero, "he couldn't have shot him with an arrow because no bows or arrows were brought with the expedition."

"I hadn't thought of that," said Zveri.

"So it must have been someone outside camp," declared Romero.

With difficulty and to the accompaniment of the screams of their victim, Ivitch and Romero cut the arrow from the sentry's leg, while Zveri and Kitembo discussed various conjectures as to the exact portent of the affair.

"We have evidently run into hostile natives," said Zveri.

Kitembo shrugged non-committally. "Let me see the arrow," he said to Romero. "Perhaps that will tell us something."

As the Mexican handed the missile to the black chief, the latter carried it close to a camp fire and examined it closely, while the white men gathered about him waiting for his findings.

At last Kitembo straightened up. The expression upon his face was serious, and when he spoke his voice trembled slightly. "This is bad," he said, shaking his bullet head.

"What do you mean?" demanded Zveri.

"This arrow bears the mark of a warrior who was left behind in our base camp," replied the chief.

"That is impossible," cried Zveri.

Kitembo shrugged. "I know it," he said, "but it is true."

"With an arrow out of the air the Hindu was slain," suggested a black headman, standing near Kitembo.

"Shut up, you fool," snapped Romero, "or you'll have the whole camp in a blue funk."

"That's right," said Zveri. "We must hush this thing up." He turned to the headman. "You and Kitembo," he commanded, "must not repeat this to your men. Let us keep it to ourselves."

Both Kitembo and the headman agreed to guard the secret, but within half an hour every man in camp knew that the sentry had been shot with an arrow that had been left behind in the base camp, and immediately their minds were prepared for other things that lay ahead of them upon the long trail.

The effect of the incident upon the minds of the black soldiers was apparent during the following day's march. They were quieter and more thoughtful, and there was much low voiced conversation among them; but if they had given signs of nervousness during the day, it was nothing as compared with their state of mind after darkness fell upon their camp that night. The sentries evidenced their terror plainly by their listening attitudes and nervous attention to the sounds that came out of the blackness surrounding the camp. Most of them were brave men who would have faced a visible enemy with courage, but to a man they were convinced that they were confronted by the supernatural, against which they knew that neither rifle nor bravery might avail. They felt that ghostly eyes were watching them, and the result was as demoralizing as would an actual attack have been; in fact, far more so.

Yet they need not have concerned themselves so greatly, as the cause of all their superstitious apprehension was moving rapidly through the jungle, miles away from them, and every instant the distance between him and them was increasing.

Another force, that might have caused them even greater anxiety had they been aware of it, lay still further away upon the trail that they must traverse to reach their destination.

Around tiny cooking fires squatted a hundred black warriors, whose white plumes nodded and trembled as they moved. Sentries guarded them; sentries who were unafraid, since these men had little fear of ghosts or demons. They wore their amulets in leather pouches that swung from cords about their necks and they prayed to strange gods, but deep in their hearts lay a growing contempt for both. They had learned from experience and from the advice of a wise leader to look for victory more to themselves and their weapons than to their god.

They were a cheerful, happy company, veterans of many an expedition and, like all veterans, took advantage of every opportunity for rest and relaxation, the value of both of which is enhanced by the maintenance of a cheerful frame of mind; and so there was much laughing and joking among them, and often both the cause and butt of this was a little monkey, now teasing, now caressing, and in return being himself teased or caressed. That there was a bond of deep affection between him and these clean-limbed black giants was constantly apparent. When they pulled his tail they never pulled it very hard, and when he turned upon them in apparent fury, his sharp teeth closing upon their fingers or arms, it was noticeable that he never drew blood. Their play was rough, for they were all rough and primitive creatures; but it was all playing, and it was based upon a foundation of mutual affection.

These men had just finished their evening meal, when a figure, materializing as though out of thin air, dropped silently into their midst from the branches of a tree which overhung their camp.

Instantly a hundred warriors sprang to arms, and then, as quickly, they relaxed, as with shouts of "Bwana! Bwana!" they ran toward the bronzed giant standing silently in their midst.

As to an emperor or a god they went upon their knees before him, and those that were nearest him touched his hands and his feet in reverence; for to the Waziri Tarzan of the Apes, who was their king, was yet something more and of their own volition they worshipped him as their living god.

But if the warriors were glad to see him, little Nkima was frantic with joy. He scrambled quickly over the bodies of the kneeling blacks and leaped to Tarzan's shoulder, where he clung about his neck, jabbering excitedly.

"You have done well, my children," said the ape-man, "and little Nkima has done well. He bore my message to you, and I find you ready where I had planned that you should be."

"We have kept always a day's march ahead of the strangers, Bwana," replied Muviro, "camping well off the trail that they might not discover our fresh camp sites and become suspicious."

"They do not suspect your presence," said Tarzan. "I

listened above their camp last night, and they said nothing that would indicate that they dreamed that another party was preceding them along the trail."

"Where the dirt of the trail was soft a warrior, who marched at the rear of the column, brushed away the freshness of our spoor with a leafy bough," explained Muviro.

"Tomorrow we shall wait here for them," said the ape-man, "and tonight you shall listen to Tarzan while he explains the plans that you will follow."

As Zveri's column took up the march upon the following morning, after a night of rest that had passed without incident, the spirits of all had risen to an appreciable degree. The blacks had not forgotten the grim warning that had sped out of the night surrounding their previous camp, but they were of a race whose spirits soon rebound from depression.

The leaders of the expedition were encouraged by the knowledge that over a third of the distance to their goal had been covered. For various reasons they were anxious to complete this part of the plan. Zveri believed that upon its successful conclusion hinged his whole dream of empire. Ivitch, a natural born trouble-maker, was happy in the thought that the success of the expedition would cause untold annoyance to millions of people and perhaps, also, by the dream of his return to Russia as a hero; perhaps a wealthy hero.

Romero and Mori wanted to have it over for entirely different reasons. They were thoroughly disgusted with the Russian. They had lost all confidence in the sincerity of Zveri, who, filled as he was with his own importance and his delusions of future grandeur, talked too much, with the result that he had convinced Romero that he and all his kind were frauds, bent upon accomplishing their selfish ends with the assistance of their silly dupes and at the expense of the peace and prosperity of the world. It had not been difficult for Romero to convince Mori of the truth of his deductions, and now, thoroughly disillusioned, the two men continued on with the expedition because they believed that they could not successfully accomplish their intended desertion until the party was once more settled in the base camp.

The march had continued uninterruptedly for about an hour after camp had been broken, when one of Kitembo's black scouts, leading the column, halted suddenly in his tracks.

"Look!" he said to Kitembo, who was just behind him.

The chief stepped to the warrior's side; and there, before

him in the trail, sticking upright in the earth, was an arrow.

"It is a warning," said the warrior.

Gingerly, Kitembo plucked the arrow from the earth and examined it. He would have been glad to have kept the knowledge of his discovery to himself, although not a little shaken by what he had seen; but the warrior at his side had seen, too. "It is the same," he said. "It is another of the arrows that were left behind in the base camp."

When Zveri came abreast of them, Kitembo handed him the arrow. "It is the same," he said to the Russian, "and it is a warning for us to turn back."

"Pooh!" exclaimed Zveri contemptuously. "It is only an arrow sticking in the dirt and cannot stop a column of armed men. I did not think that you were a coward, too, Kitembo."

The black scowled. "Nor do men with safety call me a coward," he snapped; "but neither am I a fool, and better than you do I know the danger signals of the forest. We shall go on because we are brave men, but many will never come back. Also, your plans will fail."

At this Zveri flew into one of his frequent rages; and though the men continued the march, they were in a sullen mood, and many were the ugly glances that were cast at Zveri and his lieutenants.

Shortly after noon the expedition halted for the noonday rest. They had been passing through a dense woods, gloomy and depressing; and there was neither song nor laughter, nor a great deal of conversation, as the men squatted together in little knots while they devoured the cold food that constituted their midday meal.

Suddenly, from somewhere far above, a voice floated down to them. Weird and uncanny, it spoke to them in a Bantu dialect that most of them could understand. "Turn back, children of Mulungu," it cried. "Turn back before you die. Desert the white men before it is too late."

That was all. The men crouched fearfully, looking up into the trees. It was Zveri who broke the silence. "What the hell was that?" he demanded. "What did it say?"

"It warned us to turn back," said Kitembo.

"There will be no turning back," snapped Zveri.

"I do not know about that," replied Kitembo.

"I thought you wanted to be a king," cried Zveri. "You'd make a hell of a king."

For the moment Kitembo had forgotten the dazzling prize

that Zveri had held before his eyes for months—to the king of Kenya. That was worth risking much for.

"We will go on," he said.

"You may have to use force," said Zveri, "but stop at nothing. We must go on, no matter what happens," and then he turned to his other lieutenants. "Romero, you and Mori go to the rear of the column and shoot every man who refuses to advance."

The men had not as yet refused to go on, and when the order to march was given, they sullenly took their places in the column. For an hour they marched thus; and then, far ahead, came the weird cry that many of them had heard before at Opar, and a few minutes later a voice out of the distance called to them. "Desert the white men," it said.

The blacks whispered among themselves, and it was evident that trouble was brewing; but Kitembo managed to persuade them to continue the march, a thing that Zveri never could have accomplished.

"I wish we could get that trouble-maker," said Zveri to Zora Drinov, as the two walked together near the head of the column. "If he would only show himself once, so that we could get a shot at him; that's all I want."

"It is some one familiar with the workings of the native mind," said the girl. "Probably a medicine man of some tribe through whose territory we are marching."

"I hope that it is nothing more than that," replied Zveri. "I have no doubt that the man is a native, but I am afraid that he is acting on instructions from either the British or the Italians, who hope thus to disorganize and delay us until they can mobilize a force with which to attack us."

"It has certainly shaken the morale of the men," said Zora, "for I believe that they attribute all of the weird happenings, from the mysterious death of Jafar to the present time, to the same agency, to which their superstitious minds naturally attribute a supernatural origin."

"So much the worse for them, then," said Zveri, "for they are going on whether they wish to or not; and when they find that attempted desertion means death, they will wake up to the fact that it is not safe to trifle with Peter Zveri."

"They are many, Peter," the girl reminded him, "and we are few; in addition they are, thanks to you, well armed. It seems to me that you may have created a Frankenstein that will destroy us all in the end."

"You are as bad as the blacks," growled Zveri, "making a mountain out of a mole hill. Why if I——"

Behind the rear of the column and again apparently from the air above them sounded the warning voice. "Desert the whites." Silence fell again upon the marching column, but the men moved on, exhorted by Kitembo and threatened by the revolvers of their white officers.

Presently the forest broke at the edge of a small plain, across which the trail led through buffalo grass that grew high above the heads of the marching men. They were well into this when, ahead of them, a rifle spoke, and then another and another, seemingly in a long line across their front.

Zveri ordered one of the blacks to rush Zora to the rear of the column into a position of safety, while he followed close behind her, ostensibly searching for Romero and shouting words of encouragement to the men.

As yet no one had been hit; but the column had stopped, and the men were rapidly losing all semblance of formation.

"Quick, Romero," shouted Zveri, "take command up in front. I will cover the rear with Mori and prevent desertions."

The Mexican sprang past him and with the aid of Ivitch and some of the black chiefs he deployed one company in a long skirmish line, with which he advanced slowly; while Kitembo followed with half the rest of the expedition acting as a support, leaving Ivitch, Mori, and Zveri to organize a reserve from the remainder.

After the first widely scattered shots, the firing had ceased, to be followed by a silence even more ominous to the overwrought nerves of the black soldiers. The utter silence of the enemy, the lack of any sign of movement in the grasses ahead of them, coupled with the mysterious warnings which still rang in their ears, convinced the blacks that they faced no mortal foe.

"Turn back!" came mournfully from the grasses ahead. "This is the last warning. Death will follow disobedience."

The line wavered, and to steady it Romero gave the command to fire. In response came a rattle of musketry out of the grasses ahead of them, and this time a dozen men went down, killed or wounded.

"Charge!" cried Romero, but instead the men wheeled about and broke for the rear and safety.

At sight of the advance line bearing down upon them, throwing away their rifles as they ran, the support turned and fled, carrying the reserve with it, and the whites were carried along in the mad rout.

In disgust, Romero fell back alone. He saw no enemy, for none pursued him, and this fact induced within him an uneasiness that the singing bullets had been unable to arouse. As he plodded on alone far in the rear of his companions, he began to share to some extent the feeling of unreasoning terror that had seized his black companions, or at least, if not to share it, to sympathize with them. It is one thing to face a foe that you can see, and quite another to be beset by an invisible enemy, of whose very appearance, even, one is ignorant.

Shortly after Romero re-entered the forest, he saw someone walking along the trail ahead of him; and presently, when he had an unobstructed view, he saw that it was Zora Drinov.

He called to her then, and she turned and waited for him.

"I was afraid that you had been killed, Comrade," she said.

"I was born under a lucky star," he replied smiling. "Men were shot down on either side of me and behind me. Where is Zveri?"

Zora shrugged. "I do not know," she answered.

"Perhaps he is trying to reorganize the reserve," suggested Romero.

"Doubtless," said the girl shortly.

"I hope he is fleet of foot then," said the Mexican, lightly.

"Evidently he is," replied Zora.

"You should not have been left alone like this," said the man.

"I can take care of myself," replied Zora.

"Perhaps," he said, "but if you belonged to me——"

"I belong to no one, Comrade Romero," she replied icily.

"Forgive me, Señorita," he said. "I know that. I merely chose an unfortunate way of trying to say that if the girl I loved were here she would not have been left alone in the forest, especially when I believe, as Zveri must believe, that we are being pursued by an enemy."

"You do not like Comrade Zveri, do you, Romero?"

"Even to you, Señorita," he replied, "I must admit, since you ask me, that I do not."

"I know that he has antagonized many."

"He has antagonized all—except you, Señorita."

"Why should I be excepted?" she asked. "How do you know that he has not antagonized me also?"

"Not deeply, I am sure," he said, "or else you would not have consented to become his wife."

"And how do you know that I have?" she asked.

"Comrade Zveri boasts of it often," replied Romero.

"Oh, he does?" nor did she make any other comment.

17

A Gulf That Was Bridged

THE general rout of Zveri's forces ended only when their last camp had been reached and even then only for part of the command, for as night fell it was discovered that fully twenty-five percent of the men were missing, and among the absentees were Zora and Romero. As the stragglers came in, Zveri questioned each about the girl, but no one had seen her. He tried to organize an expedition to go back in search of her, but no one would accompany him. He threatened and pleaded, only to discover that he had lost all control of his men. Perhaps he would have gone back alone, as he insisted that he intended doing; but he was relieved of this necessity when, well after dark, the two walked into camp together.

At sight of them Zveri was both relieved and angry. "Why didn't you remain with me?" he snapped at Zora.

"Because I cannot run so fast as you," she replied, and Zveri said no more.

From the darkness of the trees above the camp came the now familiar warning. "Desert the whites!" A long silence followed this, broken only by the nervous whisperings of the blacks, and then the voice spoke again. "The trails to your own countries are free from danger, but death walks always with the white men. Throw away your uniforms and leave the white men to the jungle and to me."

A black warrior leaped to his feet and stripped the French uniform from his body, throwing it upon a cooking fire that burned near him. Instantly others followed his example.

"Stop that!" cried Zveri.

"Silence, white man!" growled Kitembo.

"Kill the whites!" shouted a naked Basembo warrior.

Instantly there was a rush toward the whites, who were gathered near Zveri, and then from above them came a warning cry. "The whites are mine!" it cried. "Leave them to me."

For an instant the advancing warriors halted; and then he, who had constituted himself their leader, maddened perhaps by his hatred and his blood lust, advanced again grasping his rifle menacingly.

From above a bow string twanged. The black, dropping his rifle, screamed as he tore at an arrow protruding from his chest; and, as he fell forward upon his face, the other blacks fell back, and the whites were left alone, while the Negroes huddled by themselves in a far corner of the camp. Many of them would have deserted that night, but they feared the darkness of the jungle and the menace of the thing hovering above them.

Zveri strode angrily to and fro, cursing his luck, cursing the blacks, cursing every one. "If I had had any help, if I had had any cooperation," he grumbled, "this would not have happened, but I cannot do everything alone."

"You have done this pretty much alone," said Romero.

"What do you mean?" demanded Zveri.

"I mean that you have made such an overbearing ass of yourself that you have antagonized everyone in the expedition, but even so they might have carried on if they had had any confidence in your courage—no man likes to follow a coward."

"You call me that, you yellow greaser," shouted Zveri, reaching for his revolver.

"Cut that," snapped Romero. "I have you covered. And let me tell you now that if it weren't for Señorita Drinov I would kill you on the spot and rid the world of at least one crazy mad dog that is threatening the entire world with the hydrophobia of hate and suspicion. Señorita Drinov saved my life once. I have not forgotten that; and because, perhaps, she loves you, you are safe, unless I am forced to kill you in self-defense."

"This is utter insanity," cried Zora. "There are five of us here alone with a band of unruly blacks who fear and hate us. Tomorrow, doubtless, we shall be deserted by them. If we hope ever to get out of Africa alive, we must stick together.

Forget your quarrels, both of you, and let us work together in harmony hereafter for our mutual salvation."

"For your sake, Señorita, yes," said Romero.

"Comrade Drinov is right," said Ivitch.

Zveri dropped his hand from his gun and turned sulkily away; and for the rest of the night peace, if not happiness, held sway in the disorganized camp of the conspirators.

When morning came the whites saw that the blacks had all discarded their French uniforms, and from the concealing foliage of a nearby tree other eyes had noted this same fact —gray eyes that were touched by the shadow of a grim smile. There were no black boys now to serve the whites, as even their personal servants had deserted them to foregather with the men of their own blood, and so the five prepared their own breakfast, after Zveri's attempt to command the services of some of their boys had met with surly refusal.

While they were eating, Kitembo approached them, accompanied by the headmen of the different tribes that were represented in the personnel of the expedition. "We are leaving with our people for our own countries," said the Basembo chief. "We leave food for your journey to your own camp. Many of our warriors wish to kill you, and that we cannot prevent if you attempt to accompany us, for they fear the vengeance of the ghosts that have followed you for many moons. Remain here until tomorrow. After that you are free to go where you will."

"But," expostulated Zveri, "you can't leave us like this without porters or askaris."

"No longer can you tell us what we can do, white man," said Kitembo, "for you are few and we are many, and your power over us is broken. In everything you have failed. We do not follow such a leader."

"You can't do it," growled Zveri. "You will all be punished for this, Kitembo."

"Who will punish us?" demanded the black. "The English? The French? The Italians? You do not dare go to them. They would punish you, not us. Perhaps you will go to Ras Tafari. He would have your heart cut out and your body thrown to the dogs, if he knew what you were planning."

"But you can't leave this white woman alone here in the jungle without servants, or porters, or adequate protection," insisted Zveri, realizing that his first argument had made no impression upon the black chief, who now held their fate in his hands.

"I do not intend to leave the white woman," said Kitembo. "She is going with me," and then it was that, for the first time, the whites realized that the headmen had surrounded them and that they were covered by many rifles.

As he had talked, Kitembo had come closer to Zveri, at whose side stood Zora Drinov, and now the black chief reached out quickly and grasped her by the wrist. "Come!" he said, and as he uttered the word something hummed above their heads, and Kitembo, chief of the Basembos, clutched at an arrow in his chest.

"Do not look up," cried a voice from above. "Keep your eyes upon the ground, for whosoever looks up dies. Listen well to what I have to say, black men. Go your way to your own countries, leaving behind you all of the white people. Do not harm them. They belong to me. I have spoken."

Wide-eyed and trembling, the black headmen fell back from the whites, leaving Kitembo writhing upon the ground. They hastened to cross the camp to their fellows, all of whom were now thoroughly terrified; and before the chief of the Basembos ceased his death struggle, the black tribesmen had seized the loads which they had previously divided amongst them and were pushing and elbowing for precedence along the game trail that led out of camp toward the west.

Watching them depart, the whites sat in stupefied silence, which was not broken until after the last black had gone and they were alone.

"What do you suppose that thing meant by saying we belong to him?" asked Ivitch in a slightly thickened voice.

"How could I know?" growled Zveri.

"Perhaps it is a man-eating ghost," suggested Romero with a smile.

"It has done about all the harm it can do now," said Zveri. "It ought to leave us alone for awhile."

"It is not such a malign spirit," said Zora. "It can't be, for it certainly saved me from Kitembo."

"Saved you for itself," said Ivitch.

"Nonsense!" said Romero. "The purpose of that mysterious voice from the air is just as obvious as is the fact that it is the voice of a man. It is the voice of someone who wanted to defeat the purposes of this expedition, and I imagine Zveri guessed close to the truth yesterday when he attributed it to English or Italian sources that were endeavoring to delay us until they could mobilize a sufficient force against us."

"Which proves," declared Zveri, "what I have suspected

for a long time; that there is more than one traitor among us," and he looked meaningly at Romero.

"What it means," said Romero, "is that crazy, harebrained theories always fail when they are put to the test. You thought that all the blacks in Africa would rush to your standard and drive all the foreigners into the ocean. In theory, perhaps, you were right, but in practice one man, with a knowledge of native psychology which you did not have, burst your entire dream like a bubble, and for every other hare-brained theory in the world there is always a stumbling block of fact."

"You talk like a traitor to the cause," said Ivitch threateningly.

"And what are you going to do about it?" demanded the Mexican. "I am fed up with all of you and your whole rotten, selfish plan. There isn't an honest hair in your head nor in Zveri's. I can accord Tony and Señorita Drinov the benefit of a doubt, for I cannot conceive either of them as knaves. As I was deluded, so may they have been deluded, as you and your kind have striven for years to delude countless millions of others."

"You are not the first traitor to the cause," cried Zveri, "nor will you be the first traitor to pay the penalty of his treason."

"That is not a good way to talk now," said Mori. "We are not already too many. If we fight and kill one another, perhaps none of us will come out of Africa alive. But if you kill Miguel, you will have to kill me, too, and perhaps you will not be successful. Perhaps it is you who will be killed."

"Tony is right," said the girl. "Let us call a truce until we reach civilization." And so it was that under something of the nature of an armed truce, the five set forth the following morning on the back trail toward their base camp; while upon another trail, a full day ahead of them, Tarzan and his Waziri warriors took a short cut for Opar.

"La may not be there," Tarzan explained to Muviro, "but I intend to punish Oah and Dooth for their treachery and thus make it possible for the high priestess to return in safety, if she still lives."

"But how about the white enemies in the jungle back of us, Bwana?" asked Muviro.

"They shall not escape us," said Tarzan. "They are weak and inexperienced to the jungle. They move slowly. We may always overtake them when we will. It is La who concerns me most, for she is a friend, while they are only enemies."

Many miles away, the object of his friendly solicitude approached a clearing in the jungle, a man-made clearing that was evidently intended for a camp site for a large body of men, though now only a few rude shelters were occupied by a handful of blacks.

At the woman's side walked Wayne Colt, his strength now fully regained, and at their heels paced Jad-bal-ja, the golden lion.

"We have found it at last," said the man; "thanks to you."

"Yes, but it is deserted," replied La. "They have all left."

"No," said Colt, "I see some blacks over by those shelters at the right."

"It is well," said La, "and now I must leave you." There was a note of regret in her voice.

"I hate to say good-bye," said the man, "but I know where your heart is and that all your kindness to me has only delayed your return to Opar. It is futile for me to attempt to express my gratitude, but I think that you know what is in my heart."

"Yes," said the woman, "and it is enough for me to know that I have made a friend, I who have so few loyal friends."

"I wish that you would let me go with you to Opar," he said. "You are going back to face enemies, and you may need whatever little help I should be able to give you."

She shook her head. "No, that cannot be," she replied. "All the suspicion and hatred of me that was engendered in the hearts of some of my people was caused by my friendship for a man of another world. Were you to return with me and assist me in regaining my throne, it would but arouse their suspicions still further. If Jad-bal-ja and I cannot succeed alone, three of us could accomplish no more."

"Won't you at least be my guest for the rest of the day?" he asked. "I can't offer you much hospitality," he added with a rueful smile.

"No, my friend," she said. "I cannot take the chance of losing Jad-bal-ja; nor could you take the chance of losing your blacks, and I fear that they would not remain together in the same camp. Good-bye, Wayne Colt. But do not say that I go alone, at whose side walks Jad-bal-ja."

From the base camp La knew the trail back to Opar; and as Colt watched her depart, he felt a lump rise in his throat, for the beautiful girl and the great lion seemed personifications of loveliness, and strength, and loneliness.

With a sigh he turned into camp and crossed to where the blacks lay sleeping through the midday heat. He awoke them, and at sight of him they were all very much excited, for they had been members of his own safari from the Coast and recognized him immediately. Having long given him up for lost, they were at first inclined to be a little bit frightened until they had convinced themselves that he was, indeed, flesh and blood.

Since the killing of Dorsky they had had no master, and they confessed to him that they had been seriously considering deserting the camp and returning to their own countries; for they had been unable to rid their minds of the weird and terrifying occurrences that the expedition had witnessed in this strange country, in which they felt very much alone and helpless without the guidance and protection of a white master.

* * *

Across the plain of Opar, toward the ruined city, walked a girl and a lion; and behind them, at the summit of the escarpment which she had just scaled, a man halted, looking out across the plain, and saw them in the distance.

Behind him a hundred warriors swarmed up the rocky cliff. As they gathered about the tall, bronzed, gray-eyed figure that had preceded them, the man pointed. "La!" he said.

"And Numa!" said Muviro. "He is stalking her. It is strange, Bwana, that he does not charge."

"He will not charge," said Tarzan. "Why, I do not know; but I know that he will not because it is Jad-bal-ja."

"The eyes of Tarzan are like the eyes of the eagle," said Muviro. "Muviro sees only a woman and a lion, but Tarzan sees La and Jad-bal-ja."

"I do not need my eyes for those two," said the ape-man. "I have a nose."

"I, too, have a nose," said Muviro, "but it is only a piece of flesh that sticks out from my face. It is good for nothing."

Tarzan smiled. "As a little child you did not have to depend upon your nose for your life and your food," he said, "as I have always done, then and since. Come, my children, La and Jad-bal-ja will be glad to see us."

It was the keen ears of Jad-bal-ja that caught the first faint warning noises from the rear. He halted and turned, his great head raised majestically, his ears forward, the skin of his nose wrinkling to stimulate his sense of smell. Then he voiced a low growl, and La stopped and turned back to discover the cause of his displeasure.

As her eyes noted the approaching column, her heart sank. Even Jad-bal-ja could not protect her against so many. She thought then to attempt to outdistance them to the city; but when she glanced again at the ruined walls at the far side of the valley she knew that that plan was quite hopeless, as she would not have the strength to maintain a fast pace for so great a distance, while among those black warriors there must be many trained runners who could easily outdistance her. And so, resigned to her fate, she stood and waited; while Jad-bal-ja, with flattened head and twitching tail, advanced slowly to meet the oncoming men; and as he advanced, his savage growls rose to the tumult of tremendous roars that shook the earth as he sought to frighten away this menace to his loved mistress.

But the men came on; and then, of a sudden, La saw that one who came in advance of the others was lighter in color, and her heart leaped in her breast; and then she recognized him, and tears came to the eyes of the savage high priestess of Opar.

"It is Tarzan! Jad-bal-ja, it is Tarzan!" she cried, the light of her great love illuminating her beautiful features.

Perhaps at the same instant the lion recognized his master, for the roaring ceased, the eyes no longer glared, no longer was the great head flattened as he trotted forward to meet the ape-man. Like a great dog, he reared up before Tarzan. With a scream of terror little Nkima leaped from the ape-man's shoulder and scampered, screaming, back to Muviro, since bred in the fiber of Nkima was the knowledge that Numa was always Numa. With his great paws on Tarzan's shoulder Jad-bal-ja licked the bronzed cheek, and then Tarzan pushed him aside and walked rapidly toward La; while Nkima, his terrror gone, jumped frantically up and down on Muviro's shoulder calling the lion many jungle names for having frightened him.

"At last!" exclaimed Tarzan, as he stood face to face with La.

"At last," repeated the girl, "you have come back from your hunt."

"I came back immediately," replied the man, "but you had gone."

"You came back?" she asked.

"Yes, La," he replied. "I travelled far before I made a kill, but at last I found meat and brought it to you, and you were gone and the rain had obliterated your spoor and though I searched for days I could not find you."

"Had I thought that you intended to return," she said, "I should have remained there forever."

"You should have known that I would not have left you thus," replied Tarzan.

"La is sorry," she said.

"And you have not been back to Opar since?" he asked.

"Jad-bal-ja and I are on our way to Opar now," she said. "I was lost for a long time. Only recently did I find the trail to Opar, and then, too, there was the white man who was lost and sick with fever. I remained with him until the fever left him and his strength came back, because I thought that he might be a friend of Tarzan's."

"What was his name?" asked the ape-man.

"Wayne Colt," she replied.

The ape-man smiled. "Did he appreciate what you did for him?" he asked.

"Yes, he wanted to come to Opar with me and help me regain my throne."

"You liked him then, La?" he asked.

"I liked him very much," she said, "but not in the same way that I like Tarzan."

He touched her shoulder in a half caress. "La, the immutable!" he murmured, and then, with a sudden toss of his head as though he would clear his mind of sad thoughts, he turned once more toward Opar. "Come," he said, "the Queen is returning to her throne."

The unseen eyes of Opar watched the advancing column. They recognized La, and Tarzan, and the Waziri, and some there were who guessed the identity of Jad-bal-ja; and Oah was frightened, and Dooth trembled, and little Nao, who hated Oah, was almost happy, as happy as one may be who carries a broken heart in one's bosom.

Oah had ruled with a tyrant hand, and Dooth had been a weak fool, whom no one longer trusted; and there were whisperings now among the ruins, whisperings that would have frightened Oah and Dooth had they heard them, and the whisperings spread among the priestesses and the warrior priests, with the result that when Tarzan and Jad-bal-ja led the Waziri into the courtyard of the outer temple there was no one there to resist them; but instead voices called down to them from the dark arches of surrounding corridors pleading for mercy and voicing earnest assurance of their future loyalty to La.

As they made their way into the city, they heard far in the interior of the temple a sudden burst of noise. High voices were punctuated by loud screams, and then came silence; and when they came to the throne room the cause of it was apparent to them, for lying in a welter of blood were the bodies of Oah and Dooth, with those of a half dozen priests and priestesses who had remained loyal to them; and, but for these, the great throne room was empty.

Once again did La, the high priestess of the Flaming God, resume her throne as Queen of Opar.

That night Tarzan, Lord of the Jungle, ate again from the golden platters of Opar, while young girls, soon to become priestesses of the Flaming God, served meats and fruits, and wines so old that no living man knew their vintage, nor in what forgotten vineyard grew the grapes that went into their making.

But in such things Tarzan found little interest, and he was glad when the new day found him at the head of his Waziri crossing the plain of Opar toward the barrier cliffs. Upon his bronzed shoulder sat Nkima, and at the ape-man's side paced the golden lion, while in column behind him marched his hundred Waziri warriors.

*   *   *

It was a tired and disheartened company of whites that approached their base camp after a long, monotonous and uneventful journey. Zveri and Ivitch were in the lead, followed by Zora Drinov, while a considerable distance to the rear Romero and Mori walked side by side, and such had been the order in which they had marched all these long days.

Wayne Colt was sitting in the shade of one of the shelters, and the blacks were lolling in front of another, a short distance away, as Zveri and Ivitch came into sight.

Colt rose and came forward, and it was then that Zveri spied him. "You damned traitor!" he cried. "I'll get you if it's the last thing I do on earth," and as he spoke he drew his revolver and fired point blank at the unarmed American.

His first shot grazed Colt's side without breaking the skin, but Zveri fired no second shot, for almost simultaneously with the report of his own shot another rang out behind him, and Peter Zveri, dropping his pistol and clutching at his back, staggered drunkenly upon his feet.

Ivitch wheeled about. "My God, Zora, what have you done?" he cried.

"What I have been waiting to do for twelve years," replied the girl. "What I have been waiting to do ever since I was little more than a child."

Wayne Colt had run forward and seized Zveri's gun from the ground where it had fallen, and Romero and Mori now came up at a run.

Zveri had sunk to the ground and was glaring savagely about him. "Who shot me?" he screamed. "I know. It was that damned greaser."

"It was I," said Zora Drinov.

"You!" gasped Zveri.

Suddenly she turned to Wayne Colt as though only he mattered. "You might as well know the truth," she said. "I am not a Red and never have been. This man killed my father, and my mother, and an older brother and sister. My father was—well, never mind who he was. He is avenged now." She turned fiercely upon Zveri. "I could have killed you a dozen times in the last few years," she said, "but I waited because I wanted more than your life. I wanted to help kill the hideous schemes with which you and your kind are seeking to wreck the happiness of the world."

Peter Zveri sat on the ground, staring at her, his wide eyes slowly glazing. Suddenly he coughed and a torrent of blood gushed from his mouth. Then he sank back dead.

Romero had moved close to Ivitch. Suddenly he poked the muzzle of a revolver into the Russian's ribs. "Drop your gun," he said. "I'm taking no chances on you either."

Ivitch, paling, did as he was bid. He saw his little world tottering, and he was afraid.

Across the clearing a figure stood at the edge of the jungle. It had not been there an instant before. It had appeared silently as though out of thin air. Zora Drinov was the first to perceive it. She voiced a cry of surprised recognition; and as the others turned to follow the direction of her eyes, they saw a bronzed white man, naked but for a loin cloth of leopard skin, coming toward them. He moved with the easy, majestic grace of a lion and there was much about him that suggested the king of beasts.

"Who is that?" asked Colt.

"I do not know who he is," replied Zora, "other than that he is the man who saved my life when I was lost in the jungle."

The man halted before them.

"Who are you?" demanded Wayne Colt.

"I am Tarzan of the Apes," replied the other. "I have seen and heard all that has occurred here. The plan that was fostered by this man," he nodded at the body of Zveri, "has failed and he is dead. This girl has avowed herself. She is not one of you. My people are camped a short distance away. I shall take her to them and see that she reaches civilization in safety. For the rest of you I have no sympathy. You may get out of the jungle as best you may. I have spoken."

"They are not all what you think them, my friend," said Zora.

"What do you mean?" demanded Tarzan.

"Romero and Mori have learned their lesson. They avowed themselves openly during a quarrel when our blacks deserted us."

"I heard them," said Tarzan.

She looked at him in surprise. "You heard them?" she asked.

"I have heard much that has gone on in many of your camps," replied the ape-man, "but I do not know that I may believe all that I hear."

"I think you may believe what you heard them say," Zora assured him. "I am confident that they are sincere."

"Very well," said Tarzan. "If they wish they may come with me also, but these other two will have to shift for themselves."

"Not the American," said Zora.

"No? And why not?" demanded the ape-man.

"Because he is a special agent in the employ of the United States Government," replied the girl.

The entire party, including Colt, looked at her in astonishment. "How did you learn that?" demanded Colt.

"The message that you sent when you first came to camp and we were here alone was intercepted by one of Zveri's agents. Now do you understand how I know?"

"Yes," said Colt. "It is quite plain."

"That is why Zveri called you a traitor and tried to kill you."

"And how about this other?" demanded Tarzan, indicating Ivitch. "Is he, also, a sheep in wolf's clothing?"

"He is one of those paradoxes who are so numerous," replied Zora. "He is one of those Reds who is all yellow."

Tarzan turned to the blacks who had come forward and were standing, listening questioningly to a conversation they could not understand. "I know your country," he said to them in their own dialect. "It lies near the end of the railroad that runs to the Coast."

"Yes, master," said one of the blacks.

"You will take this white man with you as far as the railroad. See that he has enough to eat and is not harmed and then tell him to get out of the country. Start now." Then he turned back to the whites. "The rest of you will follow me to my camp." And with that he turned and swung away toward the trail by which he had entered the camp. Behind him followed the four who owed to his humanity more than they could ever know, nor had they known could have guessed that his great tolerance, courage, resourcefulness and the protective instinct that had often safeguarded them sprang not from his human progenitors, but from his lifelong association with the natural beasts of the forest and the jungle who have these instinctive qualities far more strongly developed than do the unnatural beasts of civilization, in whom the greed and lust of competition have dimmed the luster of these noble qualities where they have not eradicated them entirely.

Behind the others walked Zora Drinov and Wayne Colt, side by side.

"I thought you were dead," she said.

"And I thought that you were dead," he replied.

"And worse than that," she continued, "I thought that, whether dead or alive, I might never tell you what was in my heart."

"And I thought that a hideous gulf separated us that I could never span to ask you the question that I wanted to ask you," he answered in a low tone.

She turned toward him, her eyes filled with tears, her lips trembling. "And I thought that, alive or dead, I could never say yes to that question, if you did ask me," she replied.

A curve in the trail hid them from the sight of the others as he took her in his arms and drew her lips to his.